AGAINST THE GRAIN

ANNE DIMOCK

AGAINST THE GRAIN

Anne Dimock

Woodhall Press
Norwalk, CT

woodhall press

Woodhall Press, 81 Old Saugatuck Road, Norwalk, CT 06855

WoodhallPress.com

Cover Design: Amy Rosenberg
Layout Artist: Zoey Moyal

Library of Congress Cataloging-in-Publication Data available

ISBN 978-1-954907-02-7 (paper: alk paper)
ISBN 978-1-954907-03-4 (electronic)

First Edition

Distributed by Independent Publishers Group

(800) 888-4741

Printed in the United States of America

This is a work of fiction. Names, characters, business, events, and incidents are the products of the author's imagination. Any resemblance to actual persons, living or dead, or actual events is purely coincidental.

For the Gerlachs and Fieldings

CONTENTS

February 5, 1964

Spring 1964

Summer 1964

Fall 1964

FALL 1962

Helen Ransom

Helen Ransom parked her car in one of the diagonal spaces in front of the bank, a new arrangement that put more parking right in the center of Jamestown. She smoothed her hair, re-applied her lipstick, and went into the bank to get one hundred dollars in cash for the week. That was a lot of money for people in this town; one hundred dollars would have constituted their monthly budget. But she had a different household.

True, it was only Earl and Celia at home with her, but the whole Hamel University campus was part of her household too. At times it was like she had 1,600 children, 120 relatives, and 50 domestic staff. They had their privacy as a family, and she did not have to be the caretaker of all these people, but she took her role on the campus seriously. She was her children's mother first, her husband's helpmate next, but then she was the first lady of the campus, managing social events, dropping in on various colloquia, being an important interface between Town and Gown. Her shopping trips were meant to bring the college community closer to the town that hosts them. Helen was earnest and sincere about this, not like some of the other college presidents' and deans' wives she had met over the years. In their previous posting (for she did see it a little like a joint posting in the Foreign Service), the campus professionals didn't bother to hide their disdain for the miners and farmers in their community. Helen was more self-assured and confident to stoop to that, but her husband Earl had been only an associate dean then and had to play academic politics to launch out of there. The presidency of Hamel University in Jamestown was just the sort of soft landing they had imagined for themselves. Not too complacent, there were rough edges on the campus and in the town, but with its proximity to New York City, the sophisticated student body, and the pleasant town and surroundings, they felt they were in the best position they could possibly be. She made sure to spread that one hundred dollars around each week.

Helen's husband, tall and handsome Earl Ransom, a distinguished man of letters from Brown University before World War II, was Hamel University's president. They had met when Helen was in her final year at Wellesley, and he was finishing his PhD at Harvard. He and Helen married before the war, and the first of their three children was a toddler when he left for Europe. He served in the Air Force and was stationed in England. Afterward there were several years they lived the gypsy-scholar life, but things came together, and two more children with it, when Earl easily attained tenure, then a deanship at a minor college in Pennsylvania. From there they made the leap to Hamel and couldn't be happier with their situation. The two older Ransom children were grown and on their own, but Celia, their youngest, was still at home, a senior this year at Jamestown

High School. Celia benefitted greatly from the aura of the college presidency. The teachers delighted over her, and if the high school had an academic queen instead of a homecoming one, it would have been Celia.

The Hamel University campus fronted the main road through town and extended back through woods and streams until its stone walls met up with more wooded roads lined with prosperous homes. Originally the estate of one of New York's Gilded Age financiers, Hamel, named after a Methodist bishop, underwent a transformation from the country home of the founder of a second-tier investment house given to flamboyant excess, to a second-tier Ivy League school. Both were born in emulation of the originals.

Hamel was still a work in progress and had a lot of catching up to do, a challenge wholeheartedly embraced by the current occupants of the president's home. As a fancy estate, Brideswood, as it was called then, never caught on. It was not close enough to the other estates, not convenient for parties, not big enough for hunting, a little too far away from the train station. It was much better suited as a seat of higher education than higher opulence. After a dozen or so years of intermittent occupancy, its original owners conveyed it to the Methodist Church to develop into a university, and quickly Bishop Hamel proved a more accomplished chatelaine than the original. Hiring local tradesmen, Bishop Hamel renovated the original buildings, built a chapel, and, just before his death, oversaw the design of new classroom buildings—labs, music rehearsal halls, a light-filled library—an expansion that filled out the vast green lawns.

The campus, for all its classical beauty and aura of intellect and liberalism, had a gloomy side to it. The grounds were so dense with trees and tall brick and stone buildings that less sunlight penetrated the air and Hamel existed among shadows and dampness. Late winter and early spring were its most cheerful periods, when the lengthening sunlight could reach the damp, dark corners. To any incoming college student or their parents arriving for the first time at Hamel's ivy-infested front door, the college seemed like a portal into intelligence and high culture. To the local families of the town, it remained mysterious and unapproachable. They didn't necessarily think it was forbidden, they just didn't see many reasons to come onto campus.

But the college did affect Jamestown's social structure and economic well-being. The faculty and their families and the administrative and support staff could send their children to college with tuition waivers. And the sixteen hundred students needed to buy shampoo, nylons, haircuts, and pizza. Some of the foreign students had such heavy accents that the shopkeepers would refer them one more store down the road, because they could not understand them. One of the stores where students showed up on occasion was Tanzer's Jewelry Store. They needed their watches repaired, the charms of their charm bracelets soldered, and their pearls restrung. Toward Christmas, a few couples who would be graduating the next semester would come in for engagement rings. Entertainment on campus was open to the town too, but there was not a lot of crossover. The social hangouts of pizza, soda, and ice cream shops and the movie theater and drive-in were dominated by the high school set. On football Saturdays no one would ever know there was a college nearby.

Helen Ransom did her banking, then walked around the corner to Tanzer's Jewelry Store. She had a strand of pearls that needed to be restrung. She did a modest amount of business with this store—watches and jewelry repair; they were by far the best in town—and she bought some of her special occasion gifts for new babies, showers, and weddings here too. She did not personally admire the jewelry in the store, nor did she believe people should spend so much money on the status symbols of dinner rings and diamond earrings.

Mrs. Tanzer came out to greet Helen Ransom, each of them addressing the other as Mrs. Tanzer and Mrs. Ransom, never Elma or Helen. Mrs. Tanzer personally strung all the pearl necklaces herself and was quite good at it. Helen's husband had given her these pearls for their tenth wedding anniversary. Next year they would have their twenty-sixth. She adored these pearls and took great care of them, having them restrung every three years or so to make sure they never broke.

The two women discussed the length Mrs. Ransom wanted. She was a slender woman and liked the pearls to fit a little closer to her neck. They discussed whether Mrs. Tanzer should remove one or two pearls as well as tightening up the knots between each bead. No, they decided, let's leave all the pearls in but remove the two gold spacers that had been added to the clasp. While standing at the front counter with Mrs. Tanzer, a young Black teenage girl came out of the other room, stood off to one side, and waited to ask Mrs. Tanzer a question.

"Mrs. Betty wants to know if you want us to begin cleaning the display window," the girl politely asked.

"Yes, yes, please get started on that," replied Elma Tanzer and returned her attention to Mrs. Ranson's necklace.

Helen watched the young girl as she returned to the back of the other side of the store. She wondered which family she was from; she looked familiar but Helen couldn't immediately place her. She was different looking from the other Black girls in town. She interrupted Mrs. Tanzer.

"Do you have a new girl here?"

"New? Oh yes, that is Fleur Williams. She works for us now after school and on Saturday. Nice girl."

"I'm sure she is. Does she go to the high school?"

"Yes. Her mother works at the laundry and her father works for the municipality."

Helen Ransom remembered now, she'd seen Fleur in the context of the Catholic church events, not the Bethel AME church or the Jamestown Community Center, which was where she would most likely encounter the town's African Americans. Fleur had already disappeared into the back room. Mrs. Ransom didn't see her again while she was still in the store, but her eyes darted over to the back a few times while she and Mrs. Tanzer finished up their discussion of her pearls. As she prepared to leave, she asked, "How long has the girl worked for you?"

"Just a few weeks. She came when school started up this fall."

"And she is working out well?"

"Yes, just fine." Elma Tanzer was noncommittal in her response. "I can have your pearls done for you by next week. Will that be alright?"

"Just fine, Mrs. Tanzer. Thank you very much."

Helen Ransom left the store. She pondered why she had never seen an African American worker in any of the stores on Main Street. She was certain Fleur couldn't be the only one. But was she? And she saw her only for a fleeting moment before she retreated to the back. Was that where she did all her work for the Tanzer's?

She stopped at the Catherine Ridgeway Dress Shop to try on a dress for the Catholic church's semi-annual fashion show. It was one of those covered-dish suppers and fashion show events meant to raise money for the church and school. Catherine asked Helen to model a couple of outfits in the show, which was coming up soon. She agreed to do this only once each year, thinking it would be too much exposure for the Protestant wife of the local liberal arts college to be seen both spring and fall. She was careful to spread herself around and not become too closely associated with any one church or club. She and Catherine Ridgeway discussed which ensemble to wear for the show. A special winter ensemble, a short-sleeved sheath dress with a matching jacket. Forest green tweed. They discussed accessories she would use from the store—a purse, shoes, bracelet, and earrings—but she knew that her pearls would look best of all.

The rest of Helen's day passed quickly enough, and soon it was time to prepare her family's dinner. They didn't often all sit down together, not with Celia's music schedule, Earl's evening meetings, events on the campus, and her own volunteer work. This evening would be no different. Celia, her youngest but practically a grown-up, didn't need the anchor of family meals as she did as a child—she didn't want them either. There were so many events on the campus that Earl had to attend, however briefly, and Helen liked to be there for some of them, too. So she gave up on traditional sit-down family dinners a few years ago and instead had her household help lay out a cold board of salads and cold cuts that they could help themselves to whenever they were home and hungry. It worked out so much better this way. Honestly, she thought, some of these conventions outlived their place in modern life. She didn't miss them at all and thought women overworked themselves adhering to them.

Tonight would be one of those nights of each arriving home, peckish or not, and having to run out to something else right away. Celia to be with her friends and studying; Earl to the lecture by the visiting religion professor, Simon Schatzen, whose book just came out to a very small audience. And herself, well, she could go to the religion lecture; she could go to a ladies' meeting at the Presbyterian church; she could go play bridge with the few casual friends she had in this town with whom she could relax and let her hair down. But she decided she liked the idea of being at home tonight, and so kicked off her shoes and removed her stockings and girdle and wrapped a housecoat over the rest until it was a more reasonable time to prepare for bed. "Ahhhhh," she sighed, that felt good. She waited for Celia before she took any supper for herself, and soon her vibrant, popular daughter came home and dumped all her books and purse and packages on the kitchen table.

"Mother," she exclaimed, "I can't believe what that old goose of a gym teacher told us today about exercising during our periods. Wait, is this chicken salad? Oh please tell me this is chicken salad."

"It is." Helen smiled at her daughter's unbridled appetite for so many things, food and beyond. She watched Celia eat and talk and gesticulate and page through her notebook—all at the same time. There was no reigning in her energy. Celia would be off in a few minutes to meet up with her friends to study together—the telephone was already ringing to that effect. But she wanted to talk to her for just a little while, and she had a couple of questions. After Celia returned to the table, Helen Ransom said, "Celia, dear, do you know a Fleur Williams at school?"

Celia thought for a moment. "Negro girl?"

"Yes."

"I think she's in the class behind me, maybe even younger. Definitely not in my class."

"Do you know her?"

"She's at least a grade behind me. Why would I know her?"

"Is she in any of your classes?"

"No."

"In any of the clubs you're in?"

"No! That would be unusual."

"Yes, it would."

"Why do you want to know?"

"I saw her today when I was in Tanzer's Jewelry Store to get my pearls restrung. Apparently she has an after-school job there."

"Fleur Williams . . . is she the one with the skinnier nose and lighter eyes? Ohhh, that explains it now."

"Explains what?"

"Well, some of Jamestown's finest daughters are unhappy that she got that job."

"Why?"

"Because they think they should work there instead of waitressing or clerking at the bowling alley."

"Are they unhappy because she's a Negro?"

"Mother, you always see everything in these broad social terms. It's not always like that. Sometimes it's just because they don't like her."

"Why ever not?"

"I don't know. It's not like I hang around with them and know all their secret motives for liking or not liking something. Anyway, they're twerps."

"And Fleur?"

"Why are you so interested in her anyway?"

"I don't really know. I just got this impression that . . ."

"Mom, no offense, but don't get all wrapped up in your impressions; sometimes you overthink things."

Her daughter was right, and she thought how odd that her daughter was giving her advice like this and not the other way around. But still, something wasn't quite right about Fleur's employment with the Tanzers.

"So, some of the senior girls would like to work there instead?"

"Yeah, it can't be that hard to stand around all the gold and diamonds and wait on people."

That was it! Fleur wasn't waiting on people.

Celia continued, "You get to help brides pick out their dinnerware, and pick out their bridesmaids' gifts. It's a lot more desirable than restocking smelly bowling shoes after people get done on league night."

Helen recalled Fleur was in the back room the whole time, emerging for just the briefest of inquiries, then scuttling back. Why wasn't she out front waiting on people? Well, she could just imagine why, and she silently fumed.

"Mom? Mom, are you listening? All the girls think it would be a nice after-school job. They don't understand why she got it."

"Why did she get it?"

"Nobody knows. Nobody even knew they were looking for someone. That's why some of them think it's unfair, 'cause there wasn't any sign posted, no applications accepted."

"How disappointing for them," Helen replied blandly. "Anyway, what sort of girl is Fleur Williams? What is she like at school?"

"She's sort of a loner. Average student, I guess. I don't see her in any of the school clubs. The other Negro girls don't seem to like her very much."

"What?! Why not?"

"I don't know. You should ask them."

"I just might."

"Mother, please. I don't know if they don't like her or not. It just seems like it since they don't seem to be friendly. They just kind of ignore her."

"Why would they do that?"

"Fleur came over from the Catholic school; she didn't grow up with the other Negro families here. Her mother is from Barbados or Monserrat or someplace like that. And her father is a garbage man. They think her mother is stuck up and her father is just a garbage man."

Helen Ransom mulled this over in her head all evening and throughout the next week. She wondered about some of the other stores, on Main Street and off. Did any of them have African Americans working for them? She made a mental note whenever she saw an employed Black person on the job or on their way to it. There were stocking clerks at the Acme store but not at the A&P. There was a delivery man for the bakery, but not for the florist. There were Fleur's mother and two other ladies at the laundry, but none at Catherine Ridgeway's store.

She started looking in her own backyard, literally, and found two local Black men working on the campus grounds crews and two more in maintenance and janitorial service. She knew these were considered good jobs, that working on the university campus, even as a janitor, came with a set of democratically delivered benefits—tuition waivers, whether you were a full professor or a secretary. A few cafeteria workers, one assistant librarian, and the only African American faculty member, Henry Davis Smith, a professor of sociology, rounded out Hamel University's Black experience. They had a few African Americans in the student body, and some foreign students from Mauritania and Liberia, but no students from local families. How could she have missed this? This was the heart of the problem; people like her just didn't see it. It was wrong, dead wrong, and it would have to change. They must all start seeing and having their eyes opened the way she had hers by that Fleur Williams. In time she would learn that there were more African Americans employed in Jamestown, but they were either in domestic service—cleaning ladies and housekeepers—or they worked in the shops and businesses that catered to their community. The shoe repair shop and barber. The Atkins's Funeral Home. The Jamestown Community Center. The barbeque shop and one of the liquor stores. None of these establishments was on Main Street, or even close to it.

"Mom, I'm going over to Susan's to practice our lines for the play."

Celia and her best friend were both in the senior play next semester, Oscar Wilde's *The Importance of Being Earnest*. Such a silly play, Helen thought, a waste of everyone's talent, especially Wilde's. Susan had the part of Cecily in the play, and Celia had the role of Miss Prism, the only sensible character of the whole cast. They had to practice these terribly affected aristocratic British accents that Helen Ransom found irritating and loathsome. The choice of this piece of fluff irritated her; so many other important plays to select from, and this old chestnut of community and campus theater prevailed. What were they doing over at that high school, preparing the students to eat cucumber sandwiches? What were they doing on her campus?

She knew it wasn't the play that was getting her so worked up. She bade Celia to drive carefully and reminded her of her orthodontist appointment in the morning. She picked up the few plates and silverware she and Celia used and washed them herself in the kitchen sink. She could have left them there and presidential manor staff would take care of them in preparing the rooms for the trustee meeting late morning tomorrow. But they would have enough to do without wiping the forks that fed the white missus and daughter. And suddenly Helen Ransom felt she was no better than a plantation chatelaine with staff to launder and cook and serve. She would take care of her own dishes tonight, she should do that at the very least. And tomorrow she would try to do more.

Fleur Williams

Fleur Williams grew increasingly anxious as the school day wore on. She had never interviewed for a job before. What should she do or say? Her mother had gotten her the summer job at the laundry. Would her parents approve of this new arrangement? This seemed like an awfully quick transition from school to work. She replayed the confusing start to her junior year at Jamestown High School. A shortage of typing teachers forced a change in her expected school schedule. She was offered an extra study hall or an early work release for an after-school job.

Finally school was done and Fleur rushed out of the building, clutching a scrap of paper in her hands from her guidance counselor—"Tanzers' store, 3:30 pm." She reached downtown in just ten minutes and decided to walk around the block and try to compose herself. She walked on the opposite side of the street so she could get a good look at the store. "Tanzers' Jewelry Store" it said plainly enough in a simple painted script. She walked by trying to see all she could without staring. She paused and smoothed out her skirt and blouse and patted the sides of her hair, then rounded the corner passing by the first display window of the store. She saw rows of jewelry boxes with pins and rings and pendants, surrounded by more boxes of necklaces and bracelets, surrounded by more watches. She slowed to a stop and stared at all the little things in the window—shiny and delicate, some with brilliant stones, some just plain silver or gold, some carved with initials or names, some enameled with blue and pink roses. "Oh, my," she inhaled and held her breath for a moment as she took the entire display in. Then she glanced up and saw her own reflection in the glass window, a large-eyed Fleur superimposed upon the field of gold and silver, floating above it all. She caught her eyes in her reflection and thought, *Hello Fleur.* It seemed like the right thing to do, to greet herself as she was about to enter the store. She blinked and moistened her lips, and entered.

A bell jangled, but for a few moments she was alone. She looked around and took in all the display shelves—china vessels of all sorts, crystal goblets, and vases. So many candlesticks. Jewelry and watches on one side, pearls and engagements rings on the other. She looked into the adjoining room and saw tables laden with plates and glasses and silverware in such elegance as she'd never seen before. It only took a few seconds to take it all in, this small store with all its shelves and tables and cases, but she swept her eyes front and back and left and right and was completely, utterly dazzled. A middle-aged woman came out from the back and asked, "May I help you?"

A startled Fleur turned around and opened her mouth, but nothing came out. The woman asked, not unkindly, "Can I help you with something?" Again, nothing came out of her mouth. Now another older woman came out from the back, and she and the first exchanged a glance. The older of the two approached a few spaces and said in a German accent, "It's alright, dear, tell us what you're here for." Fleur stammered, "Mr. Tanzer called for a new girl."

The woman's natural smile faded and she looked at the other, who ducked back into the workroom. She returned quickly and said, "Mr. Tanzer will be right out," exchanging another silent communiqué. In a few seconds, Mr. Tanzer appeared, and as he shuffled out and took the jeweler's loupe off of his eyeglasses, his eyes widened and mouth parted and he stammered in heavily accented German, "Hello, hello. I'm Mr. Tanzer. You must be . . ."

"Fleur Williams, sir."

The words "Fleur Williams" floated between the two women. The younger one recognized the name, the face, the family, and the young girl standing before them. She spoke first, "You must be Mathilde's girl."

"Yes, ma'am. I am."

"I'm Joyce Dunn. You may know Tommy and Marie from school."

"Oh, you're Marie's mother? I'm glad to meet you!" Marie had been in Fleur's class at the Catholic elementary school.

Joyce explained, "Fleur's mother is Mathilde Williams in our church. She's very active with the women's group."

"Oh, very nice. And where does your father work?"

"He works for the town, sir." She knew how to not say her father was a garbage man.

"Oh yes, very nice. Well, Fleur, we need an extra girl here now, to help out Mrs. Tanzer, Joyce, and the others and do lots of things we can't get to when the customers are here. Have you ever worked before?"

"All this summer, sir. I worked at the laundry."

"Very good, hard work that, I imagine. Can you stand on your feet all day?

"Oh yes."

"Can you . . . ? Dust?"

"Pardon?"

"Dust. Clean. Sweep a little."

"Oh yes, sir. I can do that."

"Very good, well then. Can you work every day after school?"

"Every day?"

"And Saturdays?"

"Every Saturday?"

"Yes, all day on Saturdays. We start to be very busy in November, and December is the busiest of all."

Joyce smiled an encouraging smile at Fleur. Mrs. Tanzer remained impassive and thin-lipped.

"Yes, I think so."

"You'll make $1.15 an hour. When can you begin?"

"I need to talk with my parents."

"Of course, of course, yes, talk to them. Do you want me to call them?" asked Mr. Tanzer.

"Oh no, I'll talk to them. Does that mean you want me to work here?"

"Well, I don't see why not. Do you, girls?" he turned to his wife and Joyce, who in turn muttered yes, of course, so lovely. Fleur regarded them all and did not detect mockery, did not see smirks or daggers in their eyes. She did not know yet how to discern motives, did not understand about employment law, she was too young and trusting. But most of all, when she looked at their faces, she saw eyes that were wide like her own. She saw they were in some small way a little taken aback, just like her. She sensed a change within herself, and for the first time that day, Fleur smiled.

"Yes, I'd like to work for you, Mr. Tanzer."

"Good, very good. When can you come back? Tomorrow? Can you come tomorrow?"

"Yes. The school will let me go early on Tuesday and Thursday; I can be here by 2:30."

"Wonderful. Well then, Fleur. We will see you tomorrow."

"Thank you, sir. Thank you, ladies. Thank you, thank you. Oh, I'm a little excited!" And she smiled an embarrassed smile, but her heart opened inside, and that somehow showed in her bright face. "Thank you. I will see you all tomorrow."

Fleur turned around and walked right into one of the display cases, rattling the china upon it, dangerously but without any breakage.

"Careful, careful," Mr. Tanzer said as he gently steered her around the case toward the door. He opened the door for her and led her out, closed the door and walked back to where Mrs. Tanzer and Joyce were silently standing.

"Well, what do you think of that?" he asked them.

They looked at Mr. Tanzer and at first said nothing at all. For where should they begin?

Fleur hurried home from her interview at Mr. Tanzer's store. She rushed inside and made sure her younger sister LuLu and brother Charlie were better occupied than usual. She ordered them to pick up their toys and stack up a slipping pile of newspapers. Her father, usually home by 3:30 and taking a nap, was not in the house. She was anxious to gauge his mood, for of her two parents, she thought it more likely that he would object to her new job. Russell Williams believed in work, that working hard could do more for a person than religion, school, or even luck. But Fleur's father was mercurial, prone to a moody darkness of spirit, and she could never really predict how he might react to anything. Fleur's mother would want to know how it would interfere with her chores at home, with going to church and helping out the priests and sisters, with her schooling, and, only last, what sort of duties and how much money. Fleur longed to distance herself from her mother and the church. Working in the laundry all summer with her mother was bad enough, but at least she was relieved of the endless chores of helping to clean the sacristy, pressing vestments, or cooking for the nuns that her mother dragged her to when she was younger. There was rarely a day in any week when she did not appear at the convent or parish hall to perform some act of contrition. Her mother believed that these good acts would help shorten the fires of purgatory for everyone in the family. Mathilde's life was full of joyful penance, and she made her children serve the souls of others with the same commitment as she did. Fleur was tired of it. Cheerful in face when greeting her church elders, Fleur was bored to tears with all the cleaning and cooking her mother pledged to their Catholic community.

Fleur prepared herself for her parents' inquiry into the terms of her job by tidying up the kitchen and setting the dinner table, peeling some potatoes and starting them in their pot on the stove. She found two tomatoes from the backyard plants that were winding down their summer harvest; she sliced them and placed those on the table too. She inhaled the aroma they left on her hands, that sharp tomato smell she loved. Then she retreated upstairs and started her homework.

She heard her father return, then her mother, the kitchen sounds, and her brother and sister making nuisances of themselves. She answered her mother's call to arms when dinnertime was nigh and pitched in without complaint. She saw her parents glance at one another as they tried to decipher Fleur's helpfulness and diligence about her homework. They ate dinner together, the younger children pushing peas off their plates, Russell eating fast and grabbing seconds, Mathilde adding more milk to her mashed potatoes, and Fleur waiting for the right opening to tell them about the new job. Finding none, she just put her silverware down, looked at her plate, and said, "The school found me a job."

Her parents stopped their talk. LuLu and Charlie fell silent and stared at her. Fleur looked up at all of them and said, "They want me to start tomorrow."

"Girl, you better start telling me more," her father said.

She began the long story about the change in her schedule, then the vacant eighth period on Tuesday and Thursday, and by then LuLu and Charlie were rolling their eyes and making faces at each other and were quickly dispatched to do their homework by Mathilde, who didn't miss a single word of Fleur's account. But she still hadn't told them what job and where.

"Where is the job? Who are you going to work for?" Mathilde demanded.

"Mr. Tanzer's store."

"On Main Street?"

"Yes, ma'am."

"That fancy jewelry store?"

"Yes, sir."

Russell and Mathilde looked at one another and a long, uncomfortable silence passed over them. Fleur wondered what was wrong besides not being available for all the Church work.

"Did they tell you what you'll be doing?"

"I'll be the new girl."

Russell burst out laughing. Mathilde tried to hush him, but she too eventually fell to laughing. Fleur's faced heated up in near tears. She jumped up to go to her room when her father straightened up and became serious. "Fleur," he demanded, "you stay right here. The new girl. They tell you what the new girl is supposed to do?"

"Not exactly."

"What do you think?"

"I'll be doing what Mrs. Tanzer and Miz Joyce do."

"Nonsense. You're going to be the cleaning lady."

"Russell, go easy," implored Mathilde.

"No, she's got to know what's what. They're hiring you to do what those white women don't want to do, which is picking up after themselves."

"Daddy, stop, you don't know."

"Oh, I do know, and the sooner you know too, the better prepared you'll be for the rest of this world."

"Russell, let it be."

"I will not. Girl has got to know what this really is about. And it's about time."

"I know Joyce Dunn; she's a good church lady," said Mathilde.

"They aren't like other white people because they bow their heads and kneel? Don't let Fleur think this is like working for the nuns, getting milk and cookies."

"Fleur, what did they tell you at Tanzer's store?"

"Not much really. That I'd have to work each day after school and all the Saturdays."

"What else?"

"I don't know anything else! Why are you spoiling it?" Fleur cried.

"It's for your own good, girl, asking the sort of questions you don't know how to ask yet. Where will you work in this store?"

"I don't know, just in the store. Why are you doing this? It's just an after-school job. Leave me alone!"

Her parents fell silent. Fleur was confused; this was the opposite of what she expected. She didn't really know anything about this job except that she wanted it. How could it be so bad, working around so many pretty things? How could it be worse than the laundry or being a garbage man?

Russell broke the silence. "Fleur, I think you should take this job."

"Russell!" Mathilde called out. "What about . . ."

"Hush! What about what? The nuns, the priests? Let them clean up after themselves for a change. At least with these new white people she would earn some money."

Mathilde picked up the dinner dishes and clanged them about in the sink, angrily washing them and sloshing water on the floor. Fleur smiled to herself. Their family would have to burn off their sins in purgatory just a little longer. She went to join her mother at the sink.

The next morning Fleur got up early to dress herself with great care. She tried on almost everything she had and narrowed it down to two choices: a cotton dress with a belt and short sleeves, and a print blouse and blue skirt, finally settling on the latter. Fleur gathered her books, lunch. and purse, and with posture a little more erect than usual, she walked out the door and into her new life.

She was excited, happy, even a little giddy. She had her father's blessing and her mother's doubts—the opposite of what she had expected—but, no matter, this was the first day of a bright shiny future. She was in love with the image of herself in a smart blue blazer with bright buttons (not that she had one, but she would after she saved enough money), waiting on customers and selling them gold and diamonds. She hurried through the school day, then she left the school grounds at 2:05 and made Main Street by 2:20.

She stopped a half a block away from the store, just the place where yesterday she screwed up her courage to round the corner and enter the store. She smoothed her skirt and hair, pulled up her socks, tried to inject a little sophistication into her walk and posture, then crossed that chasm between high school and worldliness. She paused at the door, whispered a quick invocation to the Blessed Virgin, and walked in.

When Fleur opened the door, it made a little electric jangle in the back rooms. The front rooms with all the jewelry cases and shelves of china had no customers at the moment. Joyce was at the front counter. At the sound of the electric bell, she looked up and met Fleur's eyes. Joyce tried hard not to let her smile unfold into a nervous, grim straight line, but it did, just a little, then up it went again, higher and more extreme. Fleur felt uneasy now. Could this be a mistake? Did she dream the invitation to work here?

She did not.

"Hello, Fleur," purred Joyce. "Did your parents give their approval?"

"Yes, ma'am."

"Then this is your first day. Come with me, I'll show you where to put your things."

She led Fleur into one of the back rooms. The store had originally been two stores. The Tanzers bought the first one, the one where the entry door was, and several years later bought the other side as business began to expand. All the jewelry and watches, the workroom and the safe, the cash register and gift-wrapping station were on one side. The other side contained all the shelving and table and counter displays for china, silver, crystal, and other giftware. Behind this area was a smaller workroom where the women worked. It was a small room with a sink, a counter, and a few cabinets. Fleur immediately saw that it would be cramped with more than three people standing up.

"Here," beckoned Joyce, "put your things over here." She pointed out a corner of the floor. "Do you want a cup of coffee?"

"No, ma'am." Fleur had never had coffee before.

"Alright," Joyce began, "this is where you'll do most of your work. You'll be on your feet a lot, so make sure you wear comfortable shoes. Those look good."

"What do you want me to do, ma'am?"

"It isn't me who wants you to do anything, Fleur. It's the owners, Mr. and Mrs. Tanzer. They hired you, and you do what they tell you to do. Sometimes they'll tell me what they want you to do. Remember: You work for them, we all work for them. They will pay you good money, so you must always do what they ask and you'll be fine."

"Yes, ma'am."

"Let's get started."

Joyce brought Fleur back out into the china showroom and pointed to the top shelf. China sets, crystal glasses, bowls, and figurines—so many beautiful things!

"We're going to wash these today. And the next shelf tomorrow. And then the next one until they are all done. Then we'll do the silver. Then the crystal. Then it will be time to do the china again. Everything gets dusty within two weeks, and the silver dulls and tarnishes. We are always cleaning the merchandise around here. And that's most of what you will do."

Fleur looked at the rows of shelves—five all the way down the entire length of the room. On the other side there were six shelves. In the center of the room stood four cases of sterling silver and two tables set up as if for a fancy dinner party. She felt her face get hot, and she didn't know why. All she knew was that this wasn't what she expected.

Joyce took down one set of china—five pieces in all—and handed two of them, a cup and saucer, to Fleur. "We take these back into the room one place setting at a time." Fleur followed Joyce to the back room, feeling foolish about carrying just a cup and saucer while this short woman, a good thirty years her senior, juggled three plates nestled together.

"Ma'am, let me carry the heavier pieces for you," she offered, stretching out her one hand.

"No!" Joyce sharply rebuked her. "Not yet. These are all very fragile and I don't want you breaking anything on your first day. I have to show you how we handle things here. These are not like the dishes in your own kitchen sink."

Indeed they weren't. These five pieces—a dinner plate, two smaller plates, and a cup and saucer—all had a matching band of fruit and flowers around the perimeter. The largest had a bouquet of the same design in the center, and the cup had one little matching flower in its bottom. Fleur had seen some fancy china before, in the china cabinet of somebody's grandmother and at the church rectory where the priests ate their meals. She had seen sets of fancy teacups by themselves, but never anything like this—five pieces all alike but different sizes.

"All the china here is very delicate. Look." And with one hand Joyce held up the middle-size plate to the window where the sun was coming in. She put her other hand behind it and asked, "How many fingers do you see?"

It was as plain as if that plate had been glass. "Two," she answered. She could see the outline of Joyce's fingers through the plate.

"Now that's good china. This set comes from England."

She learned that this place setting was called "Wild Strawberries" and that it was made by a company called Wedgewood from a town in England of the same name that was famous for its china. She learned that a standard place setting consisted of five pieces: a dinner plate, a salad plate, a dessert plate, and a cup and saucer. Even the term *place setting* was new to her. There was even more to learn about place settings, but that was not for today. Right now, all she needed to know was how to wash these.

"These aren't like your usual dishes at home," Joyce repeated. "They have to be handled with special care."

Joyce began a step-wise demonstration of exactly how Fleur was to wash the dishes. At first Fleur thought this was a little silly. She knew how to wash dishes; didn't she wash dishes every night of her life after dinner? Joyce insisted on washing these dishes in a certain way. First she lay a special mat into the sink and then filled the sink with hot sudsy water. She spoke slow and deliberate, and Fleur was just a little offended but kept silent. This was not like at home, where she rushed through the dishes, setting them into the drying rack as fast as she could with little regard to what they might clank against. The wash soap was special, the dishrag was special— something Joyce called a *shammy*, which much later she would learn was spelled *chamois* and was French for "doe skin." Only one piece of china at a time went into the sink, not a stack of them one on top of another like at home. First the dinner plate, then the salad plate, decreasing in size until the cup at last. And the rinse water had to be hot, hot, hot.

"Your hands will get used to it," said Joyce.

By the time the cup was washed and placed in the dish rack, the dinner plate had mostly air-dried. Still, Fleur was instructed how to take up the drying cloth—another special cloth—and dry the plate some more. Joyce demonstrated with the first two plates and made Fleur finish the rest under her watchful eye. There was even a special way to wipe the dishes.

"Circular, not scrubbing up and down," instructed Joyce. "You don't want to damage the pattern."

Fleur did what she was told, and after each piece of the precious Wild Strawberries place setting was washed and dried, they brought it back to the showroom, wiped the shelf of the offending dust, and reassembled the pieces for display.

Fleur stepped back to look at their work, and while Joyce nodded in approval and gushed about what a difference the washing makes and how bright and sparkly the china was now, it all came upon Fleur in an instant. This would take forever. And when the five shelves on this side were done, and the six shelves on the other side, and the cases and tables in this room, and the other shelves in the next room, it would be time to start all over again. The New Girl was a Cleaning Lady.

Fleur knew that other high school girls had jobs cleaning bathrooms at the motel, waitressing at the diner, ringing up sales at the Five & Dime, or doing the hard, heavy work at the laundry. But she thought this would be different, special, not washing dishes.

As the afternoon progressed, she washed five more place settings of china: Wedgewood Imperial; Lenox Eternity; Minton Summer Garden; Minton Essex; and Damask Rose. Some were the color of heavy cream and some were white. Some had a rim of pure gold or platinum. Some had flowers. One had a band of silver-white etching that was almost invisible, and another had a regal band of cobalt blue—she liked that one. Each was beautiful and unique. These were only five of what must be more than sixty patterns on display. Fleur had never seen anything like this before, all this beautiful china, and she wondered who it was all for.

She would soon come to understand that these were mostly for display, that they usually didn't sell these place settings right off the shelf. They were there for the young women about to be married, and their mothers, to look over and choose their patterns. The store kept a registry for each bride, the date of her wedding, her patterns and other preferences, and a running total of what others had bought for her from the list. People came to the store to buy wedding or shower presents for the couple and usually chose something off the registry. The store would order whatever the customer wanted to buy—an entire place setting or two if he or she was a close family friend, or maybe just a single salad plate if not. It took only a day or two for the pieces of china to arrive at the store. Then the women washed them, wrapped them carefully in a box, and then gift wrapped the box and tied it with a big white ribbon. They even delivered the gift to the bride's home if she was local; otherwise they mailed it well cradled in yet another stiff box.

The store had registry information for a dozen or more soon-to-be brides at any given time. The patterns for upcoming weddings were prominently displayed on one of the showroom floor tables. One table was set with china, crystal, and silverware patterns. A little name card was set upon the top plate with the names of the bride and groom and the date of their wedding. Fleur had never seen anything quite this stunning except maybe in a magazine—a special magazine, not one like the Sears catalog. Currently the place settings for four different brides were on display. In time, Fleur would come to know the names of the bride and groom, the names of all their patterns, and how to line the gift boxes with tissue paper so these fragile items could travel to their new home unscathed. But for now, on her first day, Fleur was simply overwhelmed with the beauty and otherworldliness of these things. And their upkeep.

It was five thirty in the afternoon, and Fleur had washed more dishes more slowly than she ever thought possible. She ached from standing at the sink; her stomach growled from hunger—it had been a long time since her sparse peanut butter sandwich lunch. Mr. and Mrs. Tanzer came out of the workroom and bench to prepare for the store closing at six. They took all the jewelry and other expensive items out of the display windows and counters and placed them in the safe overnight. It was a tedious process performed every day a half hour before closing time; they opened each day with the reverse, bringing them back out and setting them out in pleasing arrangements. Mr. Tanzer saw Fleur putting away the last place setting of china that she had washed, and he came over to speak to her.

"Hello," he said. His voice startled Fleur; she whirled around and bumped the shelf, sending a just-dried teacup to the floor, where it shattered.

"Oh, oh! I'm so sorry, child!" Mr. Tanzer exclaimed. "I didn't mean to startle you. I should have announced myself."

Fleur just stood there looking terrified. Her first day, and she broke an expensive Minton teacup. She thought he would fire her on the spot. But he did not. She did not know what to do or say, so she just stood there frozen. Joyce came over and wordlessly began to pick up the pieces.

Mr. Tanzer looked at the underside of the cup fragment and said, "Hmmmm Minton Essex. Not so popular now. No one has chosen this one in years. We won't miss it." Joyce gathered up the rest of the place setting and carried it off to the back room. Fleur did not know this yet, but the teacup she broke retailed for eighteen dollars and fifty cents, a very expensive cup. And in time she would learn that there was a sort of "graveyard" of odd lots, chipped plates and pieces of old, expired china patterns that nobody chose anymore.

"Child," Mr. Tanzer began, but then cleared his throat. "What is your name again, child?"

"Fleur, sir. Fleur Williams."

"Well, Fleur Williams, your first day of work and you've already had your first accident. Best to get it out of the way as soon as possible."

"Mr. Tanzer, I'm so very sorry. Maybe you don't want me to work for you anymore?"

"Not work for me? After I come up behind you and scare you half to death? Maybe you don't want to work for me."

"I do want to work here, but . . ."

"But what, child?"

"I'm clumsy like this. I might break more."

"Clumsy, eh?" And he gave a little snort that was not quite a laugh. "Well that's not good in a store like this. But we'll try to drum it out of you. How old are you?"

"Sixteen, sir."

"You'll outgrow being clumsy soon."

"I hope so, sir."

"You will. Now help me take the things out of the front window."

For the next ten minutes, Fleur held a large wooden drawer for Mr. Tanzer while he leaned into the bay of the front display window and removed everything of value. He closed and locked the window and took the heavy drawer from Fleur. He walked it over to the counter next to the cash register and set it down on the counter. Then he pulled back a curtain, and behind it was an enormous wall safe. He opened it with a combination unknown to anyone else in the store except Mrs. Tanzer, and then slid the drawer into its slot within the safe. He turned to the cash register, opened it, removed all the dollar bills and checks, and placed them in the safe too. Then he closed it and locked it again.

Fleur had seen a safe like this only in cartoons on TV. The safe was as tall as Mr. Tanzer and held at least a dozen drawers as well as some larger compartments. She had taken for granted that everything in the store was left just where it was where she saw it upon entering the store on that first day. She had never walked by the storefront at night to notice that it was empty. It made more sense after she thought about it, but until then, it hadn't occurred to her that stores in her town might get robbed. She knew it happened in other towns; she read about them in the paper or heard her father talk about them. Newark, Union, East Orange, Patterson. But her town? It hadn't occurred to her that robberies might happen in Jamestown too.

Her first day on the job was over. The Tanzers and Joyce bade her a good night, let her out the front door, and locked it up behind her.

Fleur did not dress in her best outfit the next day. She put on an older skirt and blouse and tucked away the image of the navy blue blazer. She knew what was expected of her, she did not break anything, and she had no lofty expectation of what her role at the jewelry store was going to be.

Joyce directed Fleur to continue washing the china place settings she had started the day before and asked her to try to get the entire shelf completed by the end of the day. Fleur's eyes took in the breadth of the shelf and saw there remained more than double the number she did yesterday.

"Yes, ma'am," said Fleur, "I mean Mrs. Dunn."

After their brief exchange, Joyce returned to the other side of the store. Fleur filled up the sink with hot sudsy water and got to work, daydreaming of beautiful weddings and their beautiful gifts and everything that could happen. Instead, nothing happened except chapped hands.

Soon Mrs. Tanzer taught Fleur how to clean sterling silver. Cleaning silver was even more exacting than washing china. In her usual precise and step-wise fashion, Mrs. Tanzer instructed Fleur to remove any rings or bracelets and watches she might be wearing.

"First, you lightly rinse the silver to wash away any dust that may be on it. Dust scratches, no matter how small the particle. Then you use this pad, and this pad only, with a little dab of silver polish."

Mrs. Tanzer opened up the small jar of silver polish. The polish was a thick pinkish-gray paste with a sharp odor. Fleur wrinkled her nose, and Mrs. Tanzer said she'd get used to the smell. Then she demonstrated by dampening the pad and scooping up a pea-size measure of the paste.

"Make sure the silver piece is still wet. Then start rubbing the polish all over it like you were washing it, *but . . .*" She paused for dramatic effect to underscore the importance of her next words. "You rub the silver along the grain."

Fleur understood the concept of "along the grain" because she'd heard people talk about "going against the grain." She understood *grain* to mean the natural direction of something, and going against it violated expectation and caused problems. She'd seen *grain* in the laundry when some of the ladies talked about the *nap* of fabric and which way the *nap* was. It was something like this with silver—gold too. The metal has a softness that is easily scratched—by a mote of dust, even by polishing with a soft cloth. Mrs. Tanzer taught Fleur how to look for the direction of the grain. At first Fleur couldn't see it, the surface of the silver looked all the same to her, nothing to suggest which way she ought to direct her polishing cloth. But Mrs. Tanzer brought out a retired silver bowl whose grain had been violated by vigorous polishing in the wrong direction—up-and-down in this case rather than straight across the entire circumference. *Ahhh*, Fleur could see it now. There was a slight smudge, an interruption of how the light hit the brilliant surface of the silver, where someone had previously polished in the wrong direction. *Grain was easier to see when someone stepped out of it.*

"It doesn't take much," said Mrs. Tanzer, and she cautioned Fleur to rinse the pad frequently to rid it of any microscopic grit that could damage the surface of the silver. "It would be better for the silver if we didn't wash it so much, but it tarnishes so quickly and we have to keep it bright looking for the customers."

It took only about a week for newly polished silver to lose its brilliance; most people wouldn't know, but all of them in the store did. By two weeks you could see little glints of yellow or brown on the tines of forks and the handles of chafing dishes or a patch of darkening gray on the bowls or platters. If they were caught up in a busy season of selling, they might let the silver polishing go for another couple of days, but by then everybody was pitching in to clean up the silver one piece at a time, fitting it in whenever they got a chance. Mrs. Tanzer and Joyce would wash a silver piece while drinking their coffee on break just to stay on top of the problem.

The little kitchen area would fill with the smell of silver polish. In time Fleur would get used to it, even get used to the gray cast her hands took on from the polish. She learned in her applied chemistry class that the polish did not merely clean the silver, washing off dirt or dust that settled on it, but it actually removed an entire layer of the surface—a minuscule layer, about a couple of molecules thick, that was all. The pasty polish reacted to the silver and wiped away its topmost layer to reveal a shiny new one underneath. That explained why over time silver plate might disappear and its crude base metal poke its nonshiny head through.

At first, polishing the sterling silverware was alright, a chore Fleur neither liked nor disliked with any passion. But over time she came to loathe it. She didn't like the chemical smell that reminded her of home hair relaxers. She didn't like the grey cast that lingered on her hands and under her fingernails. She didn't like the sickly yellow cast of the tarnish that came back all too soon—and it always came back. At first, the ornate silverware was a great novelty and part of the fun of picking out wedding registry patterns. It was one other design element to incorporate into a stylish dinner table, a design that could reveal personality or social status. After years of polishing silver, she would want nothing to do with it anymore; it would have to be gold or platinum or nothing at all. But until then, she dutifully polished silverware, silver plate, silver bowls and candlesticks, silver trays, silver bracelets and earrings, silver watches, and silver bells and whistles. She wiped away the dark, one molecule at a time.

Russell Williams

Russell Williams was impatient and hungry. He'd been up since before dawn. He wanted dinner, a little time with his wife and children, then the balm of sleep. He was still on summer schedule, though it would end next week. By common agreement among the sanitation workers, they advanced their start time an hour and a half in June. He woke at four thirty and was riding his truck in the breaking dawn forty-five minutes later. These days were hard, the need for water and shade already by eight, a lunch break by eleven, persevering through the rotting food stench until two in the afternoon, when he could finish up at the garage and hose down his truck and his body with it. His coverall uniform was stifling, but without that membrane between himself and the people's waste, he was a dead man, no better than the garbage he picked up and flung into the stinking cave of his truck.

He could never get away from the smell in the summer, and he was prideful to not bring too much of it home with him. At other times of the year he waited until he got home to bathe, but summer was different. He didn't even want to get into his car until he had showered at the municipal building. And then he'd still bathe at home with his ritual of half a cigar in his bathtub, that restorative half hour to return to his human self before taking a nap. The things that other families looked forward to during summer—the barbeques, pool parties, picnics—just meant more maggoty garbage for him. Summer was endurance, and Russell closed his nose and pores and marched right through it. This was his twelfth summer in sanitation. A permanent position like he had with the borough was a step up, the steady paycheck, the five paid holidays, the one week's vacation. He knew that the collection men in Sanitation were the lowest of all the borough workforce, that their pay was less, their benefits few, and the town was probably breaking some laws in how they were treated. But it was a damn sight better than what could be had elsewhere. Russell was happy to pick up people's stinking garbage for the respectability he was putting aside.

Irritable and hungry, Russell went back outside to clip some weeds and distract himself. Moving around to the backyard first, he narrowed his eyes to discern any new breach to his vegetable garden. Nothing new since he last checked two hours ago, a small triumph over his enemies, the rabbits. He took the newspaper and sat on his front stoop rereading what he had read two hours ago, raising his eyes occasionally up the street to see if Mathilde was on her way. For all his neighbors knew, here was Russell Williams at his well-deserved leisure, a relaxed man with his newspaper and part of a cigar. Russell kept his own counsel, didn't reveal much to anybody.

Mathilde came into view—finally! Russell went back inside to make sure the children were still alive, then returned to his sentinel post. Only when she reached the sidewalk in front of their house did Russell stir from his studied relaxation. He sauntered to the street and took the bag of groceries from Mathilde. Dinner would be soon now.

Russell was trying to grow a little corn again this year. His garden wasn't really big enough for corn, but he had yanked out the radishes and spinach before they were through and took over some of the flowers so he could try a four-by-four square for corn he'd hand-pollinate if he had to. He'd been nursing this fantasy for months, picking his own sweet corn, husking it on the way back into the house, and plunking it into a pot of already boiling water. He had it all mapped out in his head—when he planted, pollinated, and picked—all timed with the moon, the stars, and the *Farmer's Almanac*. Eating sweet corn on the front porch with his Georgia relations was a cherished childhood memory, perhaps the driving narrative behind his decision to move his young family from Newark to Jamestown. He couldn't see any possible way for a Black man in Newark to grow his own sweet corn. It wasn't going to be easy in Jamestown either, but it was possible.

Earlier attempts yielded stunted ears not filled out with juicy kernels. Russell pined for a few cobs with long rows of plump corn sugar, all the way around, no empty spaces. He worked for this each summer and attached hope, despair, and longing to every effort and outcome. He experimented with composting the kitchen wastes, he bought fertilizers, he folded back the tight sheaths on the ears and examined the tassels looking for borers. It was the doing that mattered almost as much as the taste of sweet corn juices mixed with butter and salt. Pollination gave him the most problem. With barely two dozen corn stalks to rely upon and the breezeless New Jersey summers, each ear was a little island of almost-corn waiting for the happy accident of a fruitful exchange with its neighbors. And just at that time, when the tassels yellowed up and silk began to snake its way forward, something would go wrong—some destructive weather, some gnawing pest, some hazard of blight or heat or wind would set things back so they never got going again, and the ears would have that random pattern of polka dots, sparse kernels for all the effort.

Russell knew it would be easier with a larger plot for the corn; a whole field could shake up enough pollen to do the job. There were still a few farms outside of town, but mostly the corn came from farms you'd have to make a long drive to, nothing like the fantasy of boiling your water first, then getting the corn. What he was trying to do was an experiment. Knowing he was paving the way for all other backyard gardeners with city-size lots helped him get through the disappointment he felt each August when his crop didn't come in. Rabbits were only part of the problem of his garden, but it was the one he most easily focused on. He could hate the rabbits and trap them and kill them, and enough rage would escape to let him go on and try again. He was proud of his tomatoes, his green beans, his lettuce and spinach, his cucumbers. His family ate these things and they didn't have to buy them. These were easier to grow, more accommodating to whatever weather and soil was thrown at them. But Russell was also out to grow some fine sweet corn. Any fool could grow rhubarb.

His eldest child, Fleur, got home and slipped into her place at the dining room table. The family had started eating dinner without her, but there was plenty left. Mathilde made everyone else hold back from seconds until she arrived. She heaped two chicken legs, green beans, and rice onto her plate, she was so hungry tonight. Russell spoke first.

"So, how was it?"

"What?"

"Your new job."

"Oh." She tried to play it cool. "It was alright."

"That good, huh?"

"Uh-huh."

Her mother spoke next. "Did they treat you alright?"

"I guess."

"What do you mean 'you guess'?"

"I mean that I guess they treated me alright, OK?"

Mathilde and Russell glanced at each other; her mother's look warned him from pressing Fleur any further.

The family quickly wrapped up dinner with everyone talking about homework, relatives, teachers, and other people they knew. There was even dessert tonight, ice-cream sandwiches, a midweek treat for no particular reason. Fleur finished her ice-cream sandwich, wadded up the wrapper, and got up to clear her own dishes.

"Can I be excused?" Fleur asked.

"You're going to do the dishes, right?" asked her mother

"Do I have to?"

Her father answered, "Yes, you are going to do the dishes, same as always, that's your job here."

"That's my job there too," Fleur retorted with surprising emotion.

"Then you must already be in the swing of things. Better get started so you don't lose all that good momentum."

"Why do I always have to . . ."

"Enough!" Russell insisted. "You let your mother rest and be with little Charlie. You aren't the only working woman in this family."

Fleur stomped off to the kitchen and began to do the dishes, even before each person brought his or her own plate and silverware to the sink.

Russell could hear her clanking the dishes and glasses with the pots and pans. She wasn't even trying to be careful, almost as if she was trying to break something. He rose and went in.

"Whoa, whoa, whoa, stop right there. What are you doing?"

"Nothing."

"Then why are you trying to bust up the family dishes?"

"They had me wash dishes all day there. I was in a little room washing and drying fancy plates and whatnot the whole afternoon."

"What did you expect?"

"Something different."

"Something better, you mean."

"I guess."

"Look at me, Fleur." Russell raised his daughter's chin and saw that she was blinking back tears. "Look here, look at me now. What was the color of all those folks in the store?"

"They're all white people."

"The customers too, for sure. All our people go somewhere else to buy their rings and watches. Of course they're going to have you wash the dishes. Did you think they were going to let you sell the diamond rings to the fancy folks?"

Fleur didn't say anything. Mathilde came in and glanced between her husband and her daughter. "What's going on?"

Fleur ran out of the kitchen and up the stairs to the bedroom she shared with her sister LuLu, slamming the door behind her.

"What was that all about?" Mathilde asked.

"She doesn't like washing our dishes anymore. Why do you let her go on so, dreaming that the world is just fine for us?"

"It is fine," she replied.

"Dammit, Mathilde, it is not! And you know better yourself, letting those priests and nuns and the laundry give you all their dirty work. The

47

sooner Fleur knows what the world is really like, the better. I think this is a fine job for her to have, give her a real good education."

"Russell, don't start."

"Why, so nobody else in this house knows that we're just barely tolerated out there? Oh, we're a fine bunch, we're the best Negro family around. You wash their clothes, Fleur washes their dishes, and I pick up their garbage. Yes, Mathilde, there's nothing wrong with that at all."

"You the one who wanted to live here."

"You want to go back to Newark?" Russell asked. Mathilde was silent. "Thought not."

Russell left the kitchen and buried himself in the evening newspaper. Some of his irritability drained off; he even caught himself thinking it was a luxury to hate.

When the sun pulled itself down to a reasonable level, he raised himself out of his chair and tended his garden. Some of the anger crept back in as mosquitoes first, then fireflies, returned to the yard. He went from plant to plant, examining each for leaf miners, earwigs, and the blights and wilts common to late summer. He made his youngest, Charlie, march around with him and accept his commands to water this plant, fertilize that one, and bring the wheelbarrow around without tipping the chicken manure in it onto the lawn, where it would be useless and burn a yellow hole into the green. Not that it would matter; he cared little for the lawn, full of crabgrass and dandelions, mowed it only when the bugs got bad. This was the time to teach Charlie how to use the push mower. It would be a better life if he could sit on the back stoop with his wife and a little whiskey and watch someone else run down those weeds.

No, he wanted that chicken manure for the beets, rhubarb, and green beans. He had to steal a couple of minutes off of his garbage rounds to collect the ammonia-laden gold into an old basket. Then he had to talk Floyd Carter, his truck partner, into letting it sit reeking on the passenger-side floor so it wouldn't get tossed in with all the garbage. And he had to pay for that favor by riding the truck on the outside all day while Floyd sat inside driving with the radio on. He had to promise him a rhubarb pie, too, and he wondered how he was going to get that one by Mathilde. He had to tell Floyd all sorts of things about how chicken shit is valuable and can get turned into a rhubarb pie. Floyd laughed at him and said, why sure, he'd love to have a stinking basket of bird doo as his driving partner, and, by the way, when was he going to get that chicken-shit rhubarb pie he promised him?

Elma Tanzer

They had been in business at this location for almost eleven years after owning a store in Livingston for five before that. Jamestown was much better for them. She and Ulrich Tanzer had been married thirty-one years and business partners just as long. They left Germany in 1932 as a newly married couple amidst postwar poverty to seek better opportunities in New York City. It was hard for them, bringing practically nothing but their talent and ambition. Ullie repaired watches and she strung pearls for pennies during Depression-era New York. After one sad stillbirth, Elma had no more pregnancies and poured her prodigious energy into owning their own business. First a stall on Thirty-Fourth Street, later a real store in Livingston, New Jersey. Ullie was content enough in Livingston, but Elma masterminded their move to Jamestown, predicting, correctly, they could grow their business faster and own their own building. She intuited a new prosperity in America and positioned themselves in the suburbs to receive it.

They bought their store on Main Street, then the building next door as they expanded beyond jewelry and watches. The promise of gracious living was everywhere—in the new magazines, the music and cinema, the labor-saving appliances that every housewife wanted, the new cars, and the silk sheath dresses. Ullie questioned whether they should invest so much in china and silver and all the display space it would take up. Elma promised him success, and after just a few bridal registry displays, they got it. Tanzer's became the place for the engagement rings, the shower and wedding gifts, then the engraved baby spoons and anniversary and graduation gifts. Every step up the ladder to a better life was marked by a purchase from their store where everything represented love and esteem.

As they set themselves up in Jamestown, they felt the distrust of some other Jamestown merchants, especially those who fought in WWII. No matter that they left Germany and became US citizens well before the war, they would always be outsiders. They had worked with a lot of Jewish jewelers over the years; they empathized with what they had been through and respected them as business people. But they also took care to not allow themselves to be thought of as Jewish. They were not churchgoers; Sunday was their only day off from the business. They would rather relax, read the paper, and go out for dinner. And they ate pork with a flourish.

Elma Tanzer appeared all business but harbored surprising pockets of sentimentality. One was for the large, heavy cast-iron bow-making machine they crated up and brought over from Germany. Emblematic of everything their business stood for, it spun out bows in any size or color the customer wanted. Ullie questioned why they should bring such a heavy apparatus with them, but Elma prevailed. The cast-iron armature was a prophet for their eventual success and sat on the work counter behind the cash register. She patted it as if it were the head of a cute toddler.

The other reservoir of affection, which she kept well hidden, was for the store's help. Shopgirls and watch repairmen came and went over the years, some better than others. Elma thought it was her duty to counterbalance

Ullie's more generous and open nature. She was a rigorous employer and kept that soft spot well hidden, but she deeply appreciated how the staff helped the store to grow. Ullie may have been the head of the business, but his wife was the neck and could make the head turn any way she wanted. But it was a surprise when he told her he had gone ahead and requested that the high school send over a girl who needed an after-school job.

The store had just opened, and Joyce Dunn, the longest serving of their employees, was removing items from the safe to arrange in the display windows. Elma helped her, but needed to leave for a doctor's appointment. At fifty-three she felt well enough, but arthritis was creeping into her hands from years of stringing pearls. She let her husband and Joyce know she would be gone for a short while. By the time she came back an hour and a half later, the damage had been done. A tearful Joyce explained that she'd been interrupted while restocking the window, forgot to lock it, and now a few things were missing. Mr. Tanzer, absorbed in some complicated watch repair, had not answered her request for help out front when several customers arrived. One of them was a thief. Now he was muttering about getting a new girl.

"Don't blame yourself, Joyce, Mr. Tanzer didn't keep an eye out for customers like he said he would. You know how absent-minded he is."

"But I keep thinking someone was watching all the time, waiting for us to make that one little slipup, then swoop in and steal from us. It's awful, that feeling."

"Yes, but still not your fault. People will steal anyway."

"And Mr. Tanzer said he was going to get another girl."

At just that moment, her husband came into the back room and said, "I have some good news. You girls are going to have some more help. I'm hiring a high school girl to come in after school to give you both a hand. You'll meet her this afternoon; she'll come by after three o'clock."

Although they had discussed whether it was time to bring in another employee, Elma was angry that he went ahead and decided without her. They argued a bit, and Elma, less miffed about the theft, put him in the doghouse for neglecting the storefront and acting without her. Everyone was in a sour mood, but Elma reassured Joyce she still had her job. At least her husband had the sense to call the high school and ask them for a junior or senior girl for after-school work. That they could afford.

So it was a surprise when Fleur Williams showed up. She, Joyce, and Ullie were all taken aback. A *schwarze* girl - Black. Perfectly nice, but . . . unexpected. Flustered and not wanting to give offense, Ullie hired her on the spot.

"Now what are we going to do?" Elma cornered him at his workbench and argued in German so Joyce wouldn't understand, though the tone of her voice was a giveaway. "Some people in this town aren't going to be happy to see this."

There weren't any Black people working in shops like theirs, a nice store on Main Street. Theirs would be the first. Who might become upset, customers or their fellow merchants? They took care not to make any enemies, but that didn't prevent them from their private opinions about other business owners, and some of their customers. There were still many things they did not understand about Americans, but they understood this would not go unnoticed. It's true that Elma Tanzer and her husband were absorbed in their business, focused on riding the postwar boom that contributed to their success. It's also true they exuded a whiff of superiority and desire to prove they could be better Americans than the originals. Elma and Ullie agreed it would be difficult to back out of the offer; they would proceed with training Fleur Williams and see how she worked out. It wasn't long before they started getting the side eye from the other merchants on Main Street.

Father Halligan

"Dominus vobiscum."

    "Et cum spiritu tuo."

    "Sursum corda."

    "Habemus ad Dominum."

    "Gratias agamus Domino Deo nostro."

    "Dignum et justum est."

    "Vere lignum et justum est, nos tipi semper et ubique gratias agere: Domine Sancte, Pater omnipotens . . ."

So went the singsong exchange with the altar boys and laity. Father Halligan continued the Preface, then launched himself solidly through the Canon. He exercised that talent his teachers in seminary noted so long ago—he could say Mass with truth and heart while also thinking about something else. Several minutes ago, as he was wrapping up his sermon on the Gospel, he saw one of his less-distinguished parishioners make his furtive entrance in the back.

Mario Sposeto was one among those clots of Italian men who stationed themselves outside the church doors during Sunday service, rarely moving inside to take their place with their wives and children kneeling in the pews and taking Communion. Mario was one of the guys all the black-clad women were praying for. Standing outside the church doors, smoking, talking with each other, a few jokes about how their sinfulness keeps them unworthy to enter the church and partake of the services. Jokes about how much time in purgatory was at this moment being prayed away for them by their family inside. Father Halligan knew some of his Irish countrymen were guilty of the same behavior, but they had enough sense to stay away from the church doors. These rude Italians had no shame about their hypocrisy. They took their negligible presence on the stone steps as sufficient for their Sunday Mass obligation. They fooled themselves to think they were not racking up any more mortal sins than they already had by dropping the wife and kids off, driving around the block a couple of times, finding a parking spot that would erase a good ten minutes of attendance, then mock the Mass by sauntering up the sidewalk and waiting outside until it was over.

Father Halligan heard their confessions, not often—only a couple times each year, once because the wife nagged and another because they had dark reasons to be guilty. He heard what they did, what they thought, and he forgave them, because that was his job. But these men who hung around the church without participating in the Mass had no favored status with him or Him. They would squeak by because they had all those hand-wringing women to pray over them. God allows all types to pass through to eternal salvation, and, although he had been a priest for twenty-three years and pastor at Holy Trinity for twelve, Father Halligan couldn't begin to understand why.

"Per omnia secula seculorum. Amen."

Onward. The Sanctus, the Consecration, his private prayer to God before taking his own Communion. Then his parishioners, sans Mario Sposeto, processed to the altar for theirs, genuflected, and returned to their pews to consider the holy gift they received. Father Halligan allowed himself a glimpse of his flock with their heads bowed into their praying hands. It was a moment of the Mass he had a particular fondness for, the hush in the church, the satisfaction of the shepherd with his spiritually fed sheep. Time to draw this to a close.

"Benedictat vos omnipotens Deus, Pater, et Filius, et Spiritus Sanctus. Amen."

Mass was over. Father Halligan retreated to the sacristy and removed the heavy vestments. His soul was well taken care of and he could now give his mind over to what was really troubling him. And Him. The ominous signs coming from Cuba and Vietnam. It had been an optimistic year until now. President John Fitzgerald Kennedy's youthful optimism spilled over the country with his great promise to put a man on the moon within the decade. The world prayed for him, and Father Halligan predicted the young Catholic president would bring honor to the Church and the nation, and he asked for prayers to guide him.

The prayers were needed sooner than any of them thought. Just as the president declared the United States would prevail in the space race, Soviet nuclear missiles were being assembled in Cuba. The undeniable evidence was published on the front page of the newspapers, was broadcast into living rooms, frightening all. Everyone in Jamestown was jumpy. Legions of Holy Trinity women answered his call to make a Novena. Elsewhere in town, adults wore grim faces and snapped at their children who played games about 20-megatron bombs.

Then suddenly it was over, ships turned away and went back to wherever they came from. He praised the president and called for more prayers.

Jamestown let out a sigh of relief; grimness pivoted to giddy elation and then a quick return to normalcy.

But Father Halligan intuited these were not normal times. More was coming. Rumblings from South Vietnam as President Diem, a Catholic nationalist, alienated his own largely Buddhist people. And James Meredith finally began his classes at the University of Mississippi. It was 1,028 miles from Jamestown to Selma, Alabama; 1,090 miles to Oxford, Mississippi; 1,309 miles to Havana, Cuba; 8,849 miles to Saigon. Anything could happen.

But unlike the ships that went back to where they came from, Father Halligan's unease remained.

Mario Sposeto

Mario Sposeto opened his barbershop at eight forty-five in the morning, just like every other morning of the week. He was the third Sposeto in this shop; he had worked here for years, as long as he could remember, as a little boy sweeping up for his father. It was his father's father who came over from Palermo, Italy, where he had been a barber. "A starving barber!" he liked to bellow at his grandchildren. "So eat everything that's put on that plate in front of you, because you never know when it will be nothing but rocks." Both gone for many years now, Mario never failed to smile at the memory of them. He believed they were still with him in this shop of his—of theirs.

He had only a few minutes to get everything set up before the parade of old Italian men began anew. The old ones come in the morning, because they don't work anymore and have nothing else to do and want to get out of the house as early as possible before a wife or daughter gives them some errand or chore. They want desperately to escape their domestic cocoon and enjoy the worldliness of other men, even if it is the same bunch of coconuts they've been hanging out with for twelve years, boring each other with their stories and made-up news. Their hair hasn't grown very much since the last haircut a week or two ago. Old men's hair slows down just like everything else. Old Tootie Manzano would be one of the regulars in soon. For the 111th time he'll say, "Any hair grown back on top yet, Mario? No? Maybe you can shave my pecker then," and he'll laugh and laugh at himself, and the other men will egg him on. One or two of these jokers will ask for a shave, just to make sure Mario has a few paying customers to pay the way for the rest of the peanut gallery. Mario will respond with, "Pecker or cheeks?" And another round of guffaws and scatological humor will work its way around the four or five men who are gathered and will stay put until lunchtime. "Cheeks" always got them going again. Mario liked this routine, he liked these men; they were all old family friends who knew him when he was a little boy sweeping up. Everybody currently in the shop had been there for years and would be there every morning until he dies. No one was sad about this.

A couple of working men would come in around eleven thirty to try to fit a haircut into their busy day. This little uptick in business lasted until about one o'clock, and then the shop would more than likely be empty for a little while. The old men were back home taking naps after lunch, and the school kids and their mothers wouldn't be in for a couple of hours. It was the lull of the day, when Mario ate his egg salad sandwich with pickles and radishes and read his newspaper. The *Jamestown Gazette* weekly paper had arrived that morning, and he liked to give it a thorough reading. Not that he didn't know everything that was already in these pages—this was a barbershop after all, so he was always among the first to hear about things. He was more curious about what was left *out* of the paper, or the particular slant the editor gave a certain story. Mario knew everything that was going on—or about to go on—in Jamestown. The *Jamestown Gazette* was more like the funny papers—entertainment.

He leafed through the sixteen pages quickly, first looking to make sure his advertisement was in the right place—the sports section; they had goofed last time—then looked at the high school football scores for the other schools in their conference. Montclair was up, Paterson up—nothing new there—Jamestown Dodgers were at the tail end of a mediocre season. Then he looked at the editorial pages, or what passed for them. This was a small town, and this was a small town paper. He didn't know why some of his friends and regular customers got so exorcised over whatever weak opinions were expressed on these pages. This was a newspaper for Main Street and the rest of the shopkeepers, a way to juice business a little by offering this or that at a little discount, just something to remind people they needed a screwdriver set or were overdue to check on their furnace. Ads didn't cost that much; Mario had one in every other week, a little two-column inch ad to remind people that they were open late on Wednesdays, shopping night in town.

His eyes lighted on the ad for Tanzer's Jewelry Store, also reminding shoppers they were open late on Wednesdays and that Thanksgiving and Christmas were coming up, so why not stop in and buy some expensive thing to show off how well you were doing. He had no time for those Krauts. First, the war; that was obvious. Second, they acted like reconciliation and the Marshall Plan were their ideas. Third, they hired a Black girl to work for them. Mario didn't care about that, but many of the old knuckleheads in the peanut gallery did and wouldn't shut up about it. Maybe they had a point; maybe the Tanzers did too. Mario didn't care who they hired, as long as nobody told him who he could bring into his shop. He didn't care that Catherine Ridgeway and Roy Levine and the Puglio brothers were up in arms about a Black kid working on Main Street and how that might alarm their fancy-pants customers. They were in the business of sucking up the new money moving into town and didn't care about poor families on the north end, where the family size was large and the paychecks small. Families like his, descended from starving barbers and longshoremen from Sicily. He didn't usually patronize the shops on Main Street, and they took their haircuts elsewhere. It was a free world last time he checked—no thanks to the Germans. So the Tanzers gave the Black girl a job and taught her how to work, nothing wrong with that. And if they were going to rub Ridgeway's and Levine's and the Puglio's noses in it, he was going to bring the popcorn and enjoy the show. But if this got any bigger and threatened those who sat in his peanut gallery, that would be too far. Didn't they have enough to worry about with the Russians, the Cubans, and who was going to shake him down next for the orphans and widows fund? Nobody told Mario Sposeto what to do. Except God.

Helen Ransom

"Can we go home now?" Celia whined to her mother, who insisted she join her in some afternoon errands.

"Just this last stop at Tanzer's Jewelers," Helen Ransom told her impatient daughter. "My pearls are ready."

They heard a little bell ring as they entered, and right away Mrs. Tanzer came out to wait on her. Celia wandered to the other side of the store while Helen and Mrs. Tanzer conferred over the pearls, their luster, their provenance, the gold clasp. From the corner of her eye, Helen could see Celia begin talking with Fleur Williams, who was dusting the china shelves. She kept talking with Mrs. Tanzer, trying on the pearls, demurring whether they sat on her neck just right. While she was killing time, she took in the entirety of the store and concluded that there must be a lot of cleaning to be done.

The pearl business finally concluded, she walked over to her daughter. "Who is your friend, Celia?" she asked.

"This is Fleur Williams from school," Celia answered, though Helen already knew.

Mrs. Ransom walked over to Fleur, removed her gloves, and extended her hand. "I'm very pleased to meet you, Fleur. I'm Celia's mother."

The young girl did not know what to do. She glanced over to Mrs. Tanzer's impassive face that told her Fleur should accept the hand offered her. And so Fleur did, quickly stashing her polishing cloth in the cabinet drawer below.

"I'm pleased to meet you," said Fleur Williams.

Helen shook her hand warmly and took in Fleur's features. A little younger and shorter than Celia. Dark skin and dark hair held back by a headband and straightened. Her nose was thinner, and her eyes light brown with flecks of green. She saw a complicated history and understood what Celia meant.

Fleur withdrew her hand first, feeling awkward and shy. A moment of silence passed among them before Celia broke it with an impatient plea for them to return home.

"In a moment, dear, I just remembered something," Helen said. "I need to buy a shower gift. Celia dear, would you and Fleur go pick out something lovely for your cousin Adele?"

"But she's not getting married until May. Do we have to now?"

"Celia. Please."

Mrs. Tanzer interrupted, "I can have Joyce come help you."

"No, don't disturb her. In fact, I'd like a young person's perspective. Adele will be such a young bride, I can't see her wanting the same nut dishes her mother and aunt have."

"Is the young lady registered yet?"

"Not yet. Fleur, please help my daughter pick out a nice engagement present for her cousin."

Fleur and Celia went around to the other side of the store and made polite small talk, but they were awkward with each other. Then Fleur began to suggest certain items in the store, though Celia had no idea what an engagement present ought to be. Helen seized the moment to point out to Mrs. Tanzer how well Fleur was handling herself.

"Fleur does quite well with sales, don't you think?" When Mrs. Tanzer said nothing, Helen added, "You were lucky to get such a poised high school girl. It would be a shame to keep her in the back cleaning."

"She is a new employee," Mrs. Tanzer replied tersely.

"And working out so well! Times are changing, Mrs. Tanzer. Some people might think that limiting Fleur to washing dishes is treating her like a domestic servant. Is Fleur to be a cleaning lady, or is she being prepared for well-rounded employment? Lord knows the high school has few ambitions for girls like Fleur."

Celia decided that Fleur's suggestion of a porcelain swan was probably the best they would come up with, so they returned to Mrs. Tanzer and Celia's mother with one of the small ones in hand.

"Delightful," cooed Helen Ransom. "I'm sure Adele will love it. Did you pick that out, Celia?"

"It was Fleur's suggestion."

"Very good. Would you gift wrap it and mail it for me please, Fleur?"

"Of course, ma'am."

"In fact, would you have two more in the same size?"

"I think there are more in the back."

"I'll buy three of them, but I'll take the other two with me." Helen could feel Celia rolling her eyes behind her back.

Mrs. Tanzer stood silent and watched Fleur handle herself. Helen Ransom wrote out a "Congratulations" card for her niece and jotted down the mailing address.

"What color ribbon would you like for the wrapping for the other two?" asked Fleur.

"Hmmm? Oh yes. Pink will do fine."

Fleur wrapped them up while Helen paid Mrs. Tanzer for three swans, the shipping, and the restringing of her pearls. Helen imagined herself as a catalyst and smiled serenely as she bade Fleur and Mrs. Tanzer goodbye, leaving an uncomfortable silence between them in her wake. It was easy, really.

Back at the Ransom home, Celia stomped around the kitchen, wolfing down some food so she could quickly be out and on her way. Earl Ransom came in from work and asked how the ladies were.

"Mom's doing some sort of social experiment again."

"How's that?" he asked.

"It has to do with race relations among swans. Ask her. 'Bye." And she was off.

"A social experiment?"

"It's not an experiment," Helen replied.

"What is it then?"

"It's not anything at all. I went to Tanzer's Jewelry Store to pick up my pearls. I decided to speak with Elma Tanzer about that girl they have there, the Negro girl. It's not right that they have her do only the cleaning there."

"How do you know that is all she does?"

"Oh, don't worry, I was diplomatic, I wasn't rude about this. I pointed out how well Fleur handled herself with customers and what a shame it would be to confine her only to cleaning. I asked if they had plans to bring Fleur out to work in front with the customers."

"Kind of a leading question then."

"Well, how else is one supposed to bring this up?"

"Maybe it's not your place to bring it up."

"That is so much nonsense, Earl Ransom, and you know it." He did.

"Maybe it's better for their merchant society to deal with this on their own terms."

"That bunch of dinosaurs? You think all those Italians are going to allow anyone else but another Italian succeed in this town?"

"What did Elma Tanzer say?"

"Not very much, but she thanked me for my interest in her business and the girl."

"Very diplomatic of her."

"And just to put a fine point on it, I increased my purchase and bought three china swans instead of one, because Fleur had suggested them to Celia."

"Ah, I was wondering what swans had to do with it. What do you wish to accomplish with this?"

"It's not about me, Earl, what I want to accomplish."

"Nonsense. You know that's part of it, don't pretend it's not."

"I want to see this town become a little more integrated, and I want to see that girl get a little more useful job experience than pushing around a dust rag."

"Nothing wrong with that, darling. I just think we should be prepared to follow this through."

"How so?"

"It won't stop with Tanzer's store suddenly becoming a font of opportunity for the local Negroes. No matter how the Tanzers respond to your throwing down the gauntlet . . ."

"I didn't throw down any gauntlet."

"Of course you did."

"You weren't there, you didn't hear me. This wasn't an ultimatum. I'm not organizing a boycott."

"Don't get sore. All I'm saying is that you used your position of us, of the university, to accelerate social change, and that is a challenge to this community. You aren't wrong to do so. You just need to be prepared for what comes of it."

They talked some more about this, this satisfying back-and-forth that had been part of their marriage and courtship before that. They challenged each other, fumed, raised their voices, but in trust and support. They were a good team. They knew this change was coming to Jamestown—it wasn't all happening in the South—this town would have its own problems in shifting race relations from its present state. They were already addressing it on campus, there was already talk of bringing the academic community deeper into race-relations struggles. And now on the domestic front too. It was a gathering storm. They hoped they would all weather it.

Elma Tanzer

Mrs. Elma Tanzer stood silent and watched Fleur handle herself with Helen Ransom. The child did alright. She thought about what Helen Ransom had just said to her and wondered whether the woman was an earnest busybody, or a decent human being looking out for others. She didn't know what to think about allowing Fleur to wait on customers in the front of the store. Elma Tanzer remained more quiet than usual the rest of that day. There was only a short time left before closing, so she had Fleur and Joyce begin to lock away the jewelry a little earlier than usual. She even dismissed them ten minutes early. She and Mr. Tanzer locked up the store in record time and were themselves on their way home within a minute of their six o'clock closing time. On their way home this October evening, Elma Tanzer unloaded her pique to her husband.

"That woman! Meddlesome! Self-righteous! Who appointed her savior of the Negro cause?"

"What was it she said exactly?" Ullie inquired.

"That we should set an example for all the other businesses and bring Fleur out from her slavery in the back of our store!"

"She said *slavery*?"

"No, but she inferred it. How can she presume the terms we have with our staff? As if we have a different set of rules for Fleur than for the others! That woman infuriates me!"

"Do we have a different set of rules for Fleur?"

"Of course not! And how would I know? You hired her. What did you tell her she would be doing?"

"I told her she'd be the new girl. I don't know what all the fuss is, everyone does cleaning. Did Fleur complain, I wonder?"

"No the girl didn't complain. She can hardly speak up for herself. We are very kind to her, Ullie. I don't know that we did anything wrong."

Elma Tanzer was more hurt than annoyed by Helen Ransom's suggestion to bring Fleur out from the back of the store. How could anyone assume they were like those Southerners who openly hated Black people? Did they mistreat Fleur? No. Did they fail to pay her? Were they ever insulting? Of course not! Her husband, if anything, was overly generous. She had to keep that generous side of him in check if they were ever to succeed in their business. And they liked Fleur, her cheerful nature, her obvious infatuation with everything in the store. Her delight was contagious, and that was good for business.

Elma Tanzer stewed about her encounter with Helen Ransom the rest of the night; she tossed and turned and barely slept. Mr. Tanzer just tried to stay out of her way. She had no more perspective on this the next morning, but she did have a plan.

"Ullie, we are going to let that girl Fleur do everything in the store that Joyce does for us. That is still a great deal of cleaning. What would Helen Ransom know about that? She has help in her own house to keep that big silver service they have clean and shining. That woman can come into the store and buy whatever she feels like, but she will not dictate the terms of employment for any of our staff."

"I still don't see what has you so upset."

"Open your eyes! We have a Negro girl working for us. And when we have her waiting on customers just like everybody else, some people in this town aren't going to like it. You brought her into our store and, yes, we were surprised, but we have grown to like her. She's just as good a worker as any other high school girl who would have come to us, maybe better. But we don't hire any of our employees to be our business partners. They do the work we need them to do."

"As you say, Elma."

Nothing more needed to be said. Without any explanation to anybody, Elma stepped in and began training Fleur in other aspects of the store's work. How to operate the cash register, and how to write up the credit account when somebody charged something. How to talk about jewelry that was gold filled and not 14 karats. Maybe they had assumed that Fleur would always be a minor character in the store's business, but wasn't that because of her youth and part-time schedule? Maybe Joyce had off-loaded more of the cleaning onto Fleur. But isn't that what happens to new girls everywhere? Maybe she and Ullie had not fully realized the delicacy of the times. Although they had been in America for many years, some things about the country still eluded them. They ran their business well, according to how they knew best. They worked hard. But Americans were still funny people, and some of the people in Jamestown were nervous and jumpy about a lot of nonsense—Cubans, communists, African Americans. Some of the other business owners were the worst among them: the greengrocer Puglio brothers; Roy Levinson, the florist; even Catherine Ridgeway. Mrs. Tanzer thought they would be the first ones to notice that Fleur now waited upon customers in the front of the store and have something to say about it.

Whether those merchants were the first or not, it didn't take long before she and Mr. Tanzer were getting sidelong glances from others on Main Street. She and Mr. Tanzer had never been tight with the chamber of commerce leadership, nor the cadre of Main Street merchants. They were Germans and would always be outsiders. Well, let them stew in their own juices, thought Elma Tanzer. At least now Helen Ransom will have one less place for her urge to get mixed up in other people's business. If she says anything more to her about Fleur's employment, she will politely suggest she turn her attention to the other merchants on Main Street.

Elma Tanzer noted that Helen Ransom returned to the store often to make a few more purchases. "Early Christmas shopping," the college president's wife said. More like checking to see if Fleur was now waiting on customers, which she was. This time, though, Helen Ransom extended an olive branch.

"Mrs. Tanzer, I want to thank you for giving that girl a chance."

"No need to thank me," Elma Tanzer replied, all business. "She is a good worker at all her chores. Ah, here she is with our ribbons. Fleur, please make a bow for this gift box. Red or green, Mrs. Ransom?"

"Green, please."

"Green it is. I'll ring this up for you while Fleur wraps it."

Helen watched Fleur place a spool of green satin ribbon in the works of an old-looking cast-iron machine and adjust its two arms to a shorter length. She watched intently as the girl threaded the ribbon into a groove and then began turning a crank, looping the ribbon onto the adjustable arms.

"Why, how clever! I don't think I've ever seen anything like that before."

Mrs. Tanzer handed Helen her receipt and said, "It's an old machine we brought over from Germany. It makes any size bow you want. Sturdy. Heavy. You won't find a machine like this anywhere else."

Fleur stopped the crank after about ten turns, snipped it from the spool, deftly lifted the wad of ribbon by her thumb and forefinger, and inserted it in a spline that held it tight while she pressed a cutting wedge that notched both sides in the middle. She tied a string tightly there, removed it, and began pulling the loops out one by one in opposite directions to create a perfect half dome. Mrs. Tanzer smiled as they watched Fleur work the machine as if she had been born to it.

"Astonishing!" said Helen, "How wonderful! I've never seen a bow made before. Well done!"

Fleur smiled broadly. "Mrs. Tanzer taught me. There were a few bows that didn't turn out so well at first."

Elma Tanzer looked fondly at Fleur and said that she picked it up very quickly. "When it gets busy here, we have to make bows of many sizes ahead of time. Fleur, you will make a great many bows before the year is out. You will have callouses on your hands from making them!" Fleur laughed and returned to some other work in the store.

Helen admired the wrapped present and said, "Such a clever machine. When did you bring it over from Germany?"

"We brought it with us when we first arrived. That was in 1932. We had to leave so much behind. But not our bow machine."

"I'm so sorry," Helen said.

"Pish! We were fortunate. We saw what was happening. We were not Jewish but worked with them. The economy—very bad. And they blamed the Jews. But so long ago now. We have much to be thankful for."

"Yes we do. Thank you for your story. When did you come to Jamestown?"

"We bought our store here ten years ago. Before that, we were in Livingston. Much better here."

Helen broached the sensitive topic. "Have you had any, ah, comments about your new employee?"

"Not much. It does not matter. The other businesses don't like us much anyway. Their people fought the Germans in the war, and, well, you know. They already whisper behind our backs. What's one more thing to whisper about? They are just whispers."

"I hope that's all they are," said Helen.

"Time will tell. Anyway, Fleur is a good worker all around, and that's what Mr. Tanzer and I focus on."

Olive branch accepted.

1962 – 1963

Fall to Winter 1962

Winter to Spring 1963

Fleur Williams

Fleur wasn't sure what had happened that made Mrs. Tanzer pensive and a little irritated, but she let her go home a little early and she wasn't going to argue with that. The next day Mrs. Tanzer said, "Fleur, we need you to wait upon customers with the rest of us. We are about to enter the busy season. Would you like to do this?"

"I'll do whatever you want me to do, Mrs. Tanzer."

"Then that is how it will be. I'll tell the others. But I'll still need you to help with all the cleaning here."

"Of course, Mrs. Tanzer, I'll still be cleaning. Everything gets dusty or tarnished pretty fast."

"Come with me. First you will learn how to write up a sale."

Fleur smiled, happy that there would be more to her life at the store. Now, instead of looking for another shelf of china to wash, she could linger in the front of the store polishing bracelets. She also organized the window displays and registry tables, showing a knack for design that the other ladies did not have. She helped Mr. Tanzer unpack the large drums of china coddled in shredded newspaper. She ran errands to the bank and the stationery store. And she sold jewelry. Her first sale, a plain silver disk for a mother's charm bracelet, was to be engraved with the name and birthdate of a newborn. She meticulously wrote the name "James" and the date "11-5-1962" and intuited it should be in block letters, but checked with the customer just the same. Now she could see where all the cleaning led to. Customers delighted in the variety of gifts they could choose from to express an occasion or tender feeling. Everyone was happy when everything sparkled with possibility. Fleur threw herself into all the work now that all that cleaning had a reason.

She busied herself with the crystal shelves. She added some extra ammonia with the dish soap for washing crystal that earned them an extra day or two before they would need to be washed again. Everything bright, everything sparkling.

Tanzer's display windows protruded out into the world like a merchant's rug laden with treasures from the East. It beckoned to enter the store; it suggested new ways to adorn oneself or the family table. Nobody truly needed anything they had to sell. But desire? Yes, the window's job was to ignite the desire for gracious living. Fleur turned her eye toward making the displays as exciting as the fantasies she spun about the lives these gifts were about to enter.

The smaller window by the front door held jewelry and smaller items like silver candy dishes. There were fashionable scarab stone bracelets, dinner rings with large aquamarine stones, engravable gold and silver pendants—a display of items featuring the birthstone of the month. There was a section for teenage fashion, the emblems of youth—charm bracelets and ID bracelets. A section for men—cuff links, tie bars, money clips— gold, silver, decorated with black onyx or tiger's eye. But there was no story, nothing that connected this random assembly, nothing that suggested the steps taken to end up with a gift of love. She started there. Soon the teenage ID bracelets were nestling up to each other in pairings she imagined among her classmates. The baby cups segued to mothers' charm bracelets. The birthstone displays migrated through the months like a sun dial. For October there were iridescent opals from Australia, some pale with veins of pink and blue, others fiery with flashes of orange, yellow, and green. Topaz. Lapis. Garnet. Amethyst. Faceted or cabochon cut, they gleamed in settings of gold and silver, promising the wearer that those who love them most would remember the day they were born.

Working in the laundry had been hard, but Fleur experienced nothing there like the Christmas shopping season at Tanzer's Jewelry Store. And she liked it. December came and went like a snowball gathering momentum, picking up money with every pass, growing bigger with presents for everyone. From the day after Thanksgiving until six in the evening on December 24th, when Mrs. Tanzer, with a weary but satisfied sigh, closed and locked the store's door, Fleur worked every non-school hour. She was on her feet every day, running from back room to front room with gift boxes, newly washed silver and china, spools of ribbon, and drawers of jewelry that had to be put to away every night. The store was open extra evenings and still closed on Sundays, but Mr. Tanzer came in then to catch up on the engraving orders. Mrs. Tanzer asked Fleur to come in too to help wash the inventory and wrap and pack up fragile gifts to be mailed.

These Sunday afternoons were quiet without customers, and Mrs. Tanzer and Fleur talked more. Fleur learned about how they came over from Germany and what Christmas was like there. Mrs. Tanzer brought in some slices of stollen with their lunch and gave one to Fleur. She didn't like it so much but ate it to be polite. Other days she got to sample a slice of a new sausage, which she did like, and some peppery ginger cookies that she dunked in coffee. Mrs. Tanzer was more talkative on these days while they tackled the yellowing silver together. And this year business was good. People were happy, the economy hummed, the threat of nuclear war dissipated as fast as it arose. They made most of their money during the month of December, and they made it on love.

Fleur was amazed at all the merchandise that went out their door wrapped up in green or red bows. More charms and charm bracelets, but also expensive jewelry sets of matched necklaces and earrings, strands of pearls, special serving dishes, carving sets, engraved cuff links, and pewter tankards. She saw people she knew from church and school come in to buy an extravagant piece of jewelry for a wife, and she saw little kids with their dad, each with a dollar or two to chip in on a charm for their mother's bracelet. Boyfriends and girlfriends bought ID bracelets for each other. So many things to be engraved—monograms, names, dates—Mr. Tanzer spent hours in the back room in silent concentration moving the engraving tool along dies of scrolling script letters. Monograms, initials, names, dates. Block letters and script flourishes. "All my love, Jim - 12-25-1962." "MBJ." "I Love You."

They sold lots of china place settings, silverware, and crystal for a flurry of December brides. Mr. Tanzer sold diamond engagement rings to the young men who would declare their troth to their beloveds on Christmas or New Year's Eve. And Fleur cleaned every gift, nestled it in cotton in a cozy box, and wrapped it in festive paper and bows. She got very good at it, and the Tanzers appreciated how quick and tidy her gift wrapping had become. Fleur made many bows of different sizes to have some ready during the busiest times. Saturdays were blurs of carved ivory rose pendants and scarab bracelets. Pink coral circle pins and gold earrings. The special winter patterns of china with holly sold well—platters and covered dishes, soup tureens and matching bowls. She put together a special display table for the holiday ware. She had an eye for these things, though it surely came from her imagination, not any family experience. The Lenox "Noel" china place settings paired with holly leaf salt and pepper shakers. The gold-rimmed goblets—two sizes—for red and white wine. Red and green napkins gathered into china rings. It was all so very beautiful, and customers liked to admire it. Nobody really *needed* anything in Tanzer's store—but they *wanted* plenty. Everything in the store was a dream about love. The dream of getting engaged at Christmas and married in June. The boyfriends and girlfriends buying love tokens for each other. Children scraping together a few dollars to buy their mother a Christmas tree charm for her bracelet.

While all this merchandise was leaving their store in wrapped and bowed boxes, more inventory was coming in from delivery trucks. The Tanzers would never be caught without something beautiful and alluring when people were anxious to buy. Fleur washed and wrapped, but she also sold. The Tanzers handled the customers for the most expensive items, but Betty, Joyce, and now Fleur could sell anything else—etched crystal vases, silver baby cups, and delicate birthstone rings. Fleur learned something new every day. She learned the difference between 17- and 21-jewel wristwatches, that pewter was softer than silver, and that topaz was the birthstone for November. She learned how to make a sale on a charge account, how to operate the cash register, how to give complimentary ring cleanings in the ultrasonic jewelry cleanser, and how to pack delicate crystal wine glasses for a wedding in Colorado. It was a magical time with everyone wishing each other Merry Christmas and buying the most beautiful things for someone they loved. Although still shy, Fleur's confidence grew as she happily assisted customers and the Tanzers. Her work mattered, and they were pleased with how she was working out. By the time Mrs. Tanzer closed the store on Christmas Eve, the year's profit was secured, and everyone's feet hurt.

"Thank you, all" said Mrs. Tanzer. "We will celebrate next week. Go home to your families and have a Merry Christmas!"

"Merry Christmas!" they all called to each other as they put on their coats to depart. Mrs. Tanzer handed an envelope each to Betty, Joyce, and Fleur as they departed. It wasn't the day they got paid, that was Saturday. Fleur walked home feeling tired and happy, eager to get home to her family's Christmas festivities, but her curiosity about the envelope made her stop and open it. A twenty dollar bill in a Christmas money holder. She decided not to tell her parents about this windfall; she'd keep it a secret and save it for something special she'd want next year. Then she thought of something else—her New Year's resolution. She would begin to save some money every time she got paid. The new year, 1963, was almost here. Surely there would be something wonderful ahead for her.

But one dark thought intruded—all the customers were white. Fleur had never seen another Black person come into the store.

Fleur read a note Mrs. Tanzer left for her above the sink. "Box up the green ribbons and put them in storage; keep the red ribbons out." Mid-January, a slow time for the store. But Valentine's Day was coming up, and Mrs. Tamzer expected the store would need more red bows.

Only Mr. Tanzer got to conduct the sales of diamond rings, but occasionally Joyce or Betty would be called over to model several rings if the young man was going to surprise his hoped-for fiancée. Today they were cleaning the engagement rings and wedding bands, and Mrs. Tanzer called Fleur over to have a look.

"I never had an engagement ring," said Mrs. Tanzer. "We were just starting out, and I told him to just put it into the business, that he could give me one later on. I still don't have one!" She laughed.

"Which one would you want?" asked Fleur.

"I don't want a diamond ring now. I see them all the time here, it's nothing special."

"I didn't get an engagement ring either," said Betty holding out her hands. "I never got engaged, we just eloped!" And she laughed.

"Which would you choose if you could?" Mrs. Tanzer asked.

Betty looked over the tray of rings and chose a large marquise-cut diamond with two baguettes on each side. "This one," she said trying it on. They admired this handsome ring, easily the most expensive of all of them. Fleur was dazzled. What wouldn't she do for the man who would give her that ring.

"Fleur, which one would you choose?" Mrs. Tanzer asked.

"Me? Oh my, I have no idea."

"Here, try them on, see which one you like." Mrs. Tanzer nodded in encouragement, so Fleur picked out the smallest diamond and tried it on.

"It's small, but this one is a very brilliant stone, a very good diamond." She showed Fleur the price tag, $485.

"Oh my goodness!" she exclaimed, and the other women laughed at her surprise. They bid Fleur to try on the other rings, and she did, one by one, working her way from left to right across the small tray. They commented on which ones looked best on her long, young fingers; which cut brought out the most sparkle in the stone; whether white gold or yellow gold looked better. The white gold caught the bright sparkle of the diamond and carried it all round the finger, but the yellow gold offered a beautiful contrast between Fleur's brown skin and white-hot sparkle of the gem. The ring she liked best was the large, round, brilliant-cut diamond set very simply into the yellow band. The other ladies agreed it was perfect.

"Now all you have to do is find the young man to buy it for you," Mrs. Tanzer chided. "Any boyfriends out there for you, Fleur?"

"Me? Oh, no. Boys aren't interested in me. I don't have any boyfriend." Fleur answered a little too quickly. But she immediately thought of the one she would like to have—Johnnie Abercrombie. Tall and skinny, on the basketball team, and in her algebra class.

"You are still young and have plenty of time. Oh, I want you to plan a new window display for Valentine's Day. The garnets have had their time. I think we could use a young person's perspective. Try to have it up by next week."

Fleur began her romantic Valentine's Day reveries. She hadn't even had a first kiss yet, but she wanted to be ready when it happened. She wanted to know when to turn her neck, how much, whether to open her mouth and invite something more to come in. Her pillow gave her only so much information, so she imagined how it would happen. In the back seat of a car? In the back row of the movie theater? In the back of a classroom after everybody had else had left? Or maybe it would be under the bleachers in the school gym, or under a blanket in a park, or under the boardwalk at the shore. And a hand might reach under her blouse and touch her. Would she brush that hand away? Maybe. Maybe not. It would depend. She had imagined all this many times before and let her pillow hold her daydreams. But now Mrs. Tanzer opened the door to a vast room of longing with her overture to try on engagement rings. Now her fantasies could have a legitimate goal—marriage.

Fleur was caught up in a moist, warm daze the rest of the afternoon. It was like a flood had rushed over her and now she was buoyed up by her own steam, floating down a river to the inevitable. Love! She was practically dizzy with the possibilities for her life with Love just around the corner. Valentine's Day was four weeks away. Could she get with Johnnie Abercrombie by then?

By the time Fleur got home, she had already attracted, dated, romanced, and French kissed Johnnie Abercrombie three times over. By the time she fell asleep that night, he had proposed and gotten her the engagement ring she tried on that afternoon. By the next week, Fleur picked out all her patterns for her wedding registry (Lenox "Eternity," Towle "Grande Baroque," and Westford "Mirabelle"—this week anyway). She floated on a cloud of pretend Love. She shimmered, vibrated, and moved as if she were slow oil. She looked at herself in the bathroom mirror with half-closed goat eyes, imagining Johnnie Abercrombie looking back. He was there, looking deep into her, knowing the thoughts that tumbled in her head like furtive limbs. Hands first, then arms, then . . .

The new display was up. January's garnets segued to February's amethysts, while Fleur's deep-purple longing throbbed in the Tanzer's store windows. Sets of His and Hers ID bracelets. Filigreed hearts on chains. Gold earrings of Xs and Os. Gone were the fussy nut dishes, the Wedgewood jasperware, and the divided serving dish. Instead there was a grand tableau of romance and love. Red and white satin drapery framed an engagement scene of champagne flutes, dessert plates with chocolates, and delicate silver forks. A silver candelabra with red tapers stood sentinel, guarding the pillow boxes of rings, pearls, and bracelets. A silver picture frame held an engraved announcement: "Mr. and Mrs. T of Jamestown, New Jersey, announce the engagement of their daughter Hillary to James R H . . ." China and crystal vases held red roses, and they looked real. If a young lady wasn't already engaged walking past this store, she was certainly thinking about it now.

Wednesday at work brought a glimpse into the world of grown-up women who had already made their bargains with men and sex. There were whispers about the impending Marianne Balto and Sal Giordano nuptials, arranged hurriedly but still with an engagement ring and bridal registry. The first of the three banns of marriage were published in the Holy Trinity Church bulletin just three days ago. And the store was doing a brisk business of shower gifts (a single silver spoon of Towle "Eternal"), followed by larger wedding gifts (an entire place setting) for a ceremony that was only four weeks away. People bought both at the same time.

"Not even a June bride," said Joyce, shaking her head.

The Balto/Giordano display went up on the table overnight on Monday. The bride-to-be and her mother were in the store several times, the last time just an hour ago to pick out the bridesmaid gifts—silver lockets monogramed with each bridesmaid's initials. The groomsmen's gifts could wait another week, but they had to get Mr. Tanzer started on the engraving job to get it all done in time. Fleur observed them closely and thought both daughter and mother were very business-like.

"You should have thought of that before," Mrs. Balto rebuked her daughter after Marianne mused aloud about the minor tragedy of not being able to secure the country club for the reception. Fleur felt the weight and chill of the mother's disappointment in her daughter when they left the store.

"They don't seem to be very excited about the wedding," said Fleur to no one in particular.

"Not all weddings are silly pageants," replied Mrs. Tanzer in her own businesslike way.

The older women knew and Fleur suspected that Miss Marianne Balto was pregnant. The usual timeframe of months to prepare for a wedding—

engaged at Thanksgiving, married in June—contracted into five weeks. Marianne Balto was going to just squeak by without harsh judgment; she was going to get the church wedding, if not the wedding of her dreams. Fleur noted how disillusion and silence could be part of a bridal trousseau as surely as silks and laces. She tested these new waters at home that evening.

After dishes were done, Fleur announced, "The banns were published last Sunday for the Balto/Giordano couple."

"Praise them," mumbled her father.

"They are buying everything in a hurry in our store," she replied.

Mathilde and Russell gave each other a look.

"It's not your store, Fleur," said her father plainly. "Don't say so. Someone won't like that." And he turned the page of his newspaper.

Fleur thought a lot about baseball. She had her first kiss with Johnnie Abercrombie in the baseball dugout at school after sharing her homework with him. His kiss was like a reward for her help, and she floated on air. Every time Fleur let him copy her homework, there was another secret kiss. And then Johnnie wanted something else. Fleur said no, and Johnnie dropped her like a hot potato. It was all so confusing. All the baseball girls really had to keep track of was first, second, and third base—boys kept trying to get there and the girls had to make all the decisions about how far they would let the boys advance. And the game changed with each boy. Nobody wanted to kiss Ralph Artigliano with his moss mouth and bad breath. But Tyler Swoots or Johnnie Abercrombie? A girl could get talked into things. And not just talked into, a girl could feel some urges of her own and explore and experiment.

The baseball analogy didn't explain everything. Sometimes who was good and who was bad surprised Fleur. She heard a rumor that Tom

O'Connor lost his virginity with Andrea Cartwright, a smart girl who got good grades, was elected to the student council, and was a soloist in the choir at every student assembly. Her? She wasn't a white trash girl, didn't smoke or wear teased-up hair or lots of makeup. She didn't stroll the hallways in perpetual heat like the widely acknowledged loose girls did. Andrea Cartwright? It was supposed to have happened at a party where somebody's parents were gone. These chances didn't come up very often, and everyone made the most of them. Tom and Andrea were seen making out in a dark corner, then they weren't seen. The next school day the boys were all talking about it like common gossips, racing to be the first to tell the next guy. Tom had hit a home run. His first time out with Andrea Cartwright, and he had gone all the way.

Everyone expected Tom to preen and brag and shun Andrea. Everyone expected Andrea to now wear tight pencil skirts and mascara and challenge every boy and girl with her daring eyes, or to drop out of school for all the embarrassment and shame. But neither happened. The week wore on with everyone going to classes, and after the first two days of inflating the tantalizing episode with new gossip, there was less and less to say without some sort of action from the two main players. Tom and Andrea were silent, they weren't seen looking at each other in the hallways with daggers or bedroom eyes, they did not fall in side-by-side in a chance hallway migration. No one was leaning on anyone's locker in the hallway. Each in their own way acted as if—as if!—nothing had happened. By the end of the week, a new rumble rippled through the hallways. "It never happened." "He lied." "She lied." "A sick prank." "She's still a slut."

During the second week, Tom and Andrea emerged from the silence as a couple, quiet and shy, as if they had simply tried holding hands during a movie. The first time they were seen talking together in the "C" corridor, the antennae of every junior and senior lit up with new, confusing information. None of this followed the usual patterns of harlotry, conquest, or shame.

As the weeks and months went on, Tom and Andrea were in each other's company a lot. The gossip evaporated, and everyone treated them as a couple going steady. Most important, Tom did not scorn Andrea; he did not dump her, he did not talk about her with his friends, he continued to play his sports, hang out with his friends, go to school, and deal with his parents, but he inserted Andrea into his life with a naturalness envied by the rest of the student body.

Tom and Andrea went to the junior prom together, each radiating a confidence that wasn't there the prior semester. They remained a couple all through high school, giving the answer to the song "But Will You Love Me Tomorrow?" They were like any other new high school couple, except they exploded into sex first and then tried out courtship and dating. Fleur watched them. She wondered how neither of them went to hell, how Tom softened with respect, how Andrea never tarnished. She watched and learned.

Winter was gone, Valentine's Day now past. The sap rose through the town's maple trees and engorged every cell with new life. Soon the town was green again with the glimmer of the first blades of grass, the chartreuse of new buds of forsythia, and the rain of helicopter seed wings from the maples.

Fleur had her romance with sweet Johnnie Abercrombie. He may have been sweet, but he was also a rogue, untrustworthy, a bad boy who all the other Black girls had experience with. No one warned her. She let him copy her algebra homework. She let him kiss her and a little bit more. It ended as quickly as it began. He tried to seduce her, but she got away. It wasn't at all like Tom and Andrea. No junior prom, not even a real date.

Fleur was humbled and angry that she ever gave him the time of day. That warm current of runny caramel carved a valley within her and wore down her attention and focus. It disturbed her sleep and raised up little sand fleas that bit her and made her want to scratch herself. She dreamed of being on a three-masted whaling ship, no land in sight, but she explored the depth of the sea and its fishes and the breadth of the air and its birds. She awoke exhausted and damp.

At school, she walked from class to class with new eyes. Who was already doing it? Who had gone to third base? Which girl wasn't a virgin anymore, and did she look evil, marked, or damned? Could you go further and not go all the way? The risks were high—would the boy respect you? Would your parents find out? Would you get a bad reputation? Would you get pregnant? Who could tell her what she needed to know? And why hadn't anyone done so yet?

The last period of the day, the last day of the school year, the last time Fleur would hear that class-changing bell until September. Junior year was a disappointment—no new friends, no new romantic possibility after the Johnnie Abercrombie fiasco. Little had changed, except for her job at Tanzer's. She had a torpid, unexciting New Jersey summer to get through, but at least she would not swelter in the laundry, she'd be in air-conditioned splendor in the jewelry store.

The first and most eagerly anticipated benchmark arrived: Fleur turned seventeen on June 11 and was now eligible to get her license to drive. Everybody knew that made you much more of a grown-up. Those juniors with birthdays early in the year had already lorded their new sophistication over anyone not yet seventeen. Fleur quietly turned seventeen out of the glare of the school year. The driver's license changed nothing. The family car worked only half the time. Russell would not allow Fleur to use it much. All her reasoning of how helpful it would be for her to drive, how she could take the younger children to the places they need to go, how she could pick up things for her mother, how she could drive him to work and pick him up—all of this was tamped down by Russell, who knew that they didn't have the money for the car insurance, let alone new tires.

June was busy at the store with graduations, Father's Day, and weddings. It seemed to Fleur that June 11 was just a day like any other, even if it began with a birthday card at her place for breakfast and ended with a cake and a candle. Her parents gave her a transistor radio with an ear plug, and she was pleased and grateful. She noted this was her first birthday with an adult's sensibilities, not a child's desire for attention and presents.

But it wasn't just any other day, as it turned out. Late that night in another time zone and a thousand miles away from Jamestown, an African American man named Medgar Evers was killed in his own driveway in Jackson, Mississippi. He was a race man, a civil rights worker, and he was murdered for it. Her father was up early the next morning on his early summer schedule, and he listened to grim reports on the kitchen radio. Her mother rose to see what Russell was about, clanging around in the kitchen. Fleur heard her parents argue and then the door slam as her father left for work. Soon Fleur began her own preparations to get ready to go to work. She found her mother sitting by the window sipping a second cup of coffee.

"Good morning, Mom."

"The Lord's blessings, child."

"What was Daddy mad about?"

"One of his race men was killed last night in the South."

"Aren't they your race men too? Why do you say they are Daddy's?"

"It's just one of the ways your father and I are different."

"The man who got killed? How did it happen? What does it mean?"

"I'm afraid it will mean very little. As for the rest, you can listen to that new radio of yours to learn the news." And she washed her cup, placed it in the dish rack, and left for work.

Fleur saw Celia Ransom when she came into the store to get the wristband on her new, perfect student watch—a graduation present—adjusted smaller. Mr. Tanzer took care of it while she waited, and Celia spoke to Fleur with excitement and anticipation. She was going to Brown, her father's alma mater. Celia hoped her college roommate assignment wouldn't be someone too studious who wouldn't want to have a little fun or have music on in their dorm room.

"When will you go?" asked Fleur.

"At the end of August. Mommy and Daddy will drive me up there and get me settled. School doesn't begin until after Labor Day, but there's all sorts of freshmen orientation things to do before. I wish they'd just put me on a train and wave good-bye at the station."

"Really? I'd be scared."

"Oh, no, I've been waiting for this. I don't know if I'll even come back at Thanksgiving. Do you ever think you'd like to go to college?" Celia asked.

"Me? Oh, no. I don't think about it."

"Well, my mother is going to ask you that question, so you better think of an answer," laughed Celia. "But you really should think about it . . . for yourself," Celia added as she left the store with her European timepiece stretched just right upon her wrist.

Russell Williams

It was the day after Medgar Evers's murder and four thirty in the morning when his daughter Fleur came downstairs in her bathrobe and sat at the kitchen table, where he was beginning his breakfast of oatmeal.

"Morning, Daddy."

"You're up early," Russell said.

"Can't sleep anymore."

"Something bothering you?"

"That man who died down south. Why was he killed?"

"People thought he was getting out of line."

"Mom says he was a race man."

"He surely was."

"But she said he was your race man, not hers."

Russell snorted. "So you heard us arguing?"

"Yes."

"Your mother and I have different thoughts. Hers are more in heaven, mine here on Earth."

"Who do you think killed him?" Fleur asked.

"Medgar Evers was a threat to people in Mississippi—beyond too. But it probably was someone close by that shot him."

"What did he stand for?"

"The uplift of our people, our right to vote, to work, to go into places like anybody else."

"Are you a threat where you work?"

Russell laughed, "No, I don't think I am. Don't be worried, I don't think anybody's going to pick off your tired old daddy."

Fleur hesitated, then asked, "Am I a threat where I work?"

Russell furrowed his brow, "You been hearing anything? Someone give you a hard time?"

"No, but . . . " Fleur hesitated, "some girls don't like that I got the job and they didn't."

"Sure they don't. They think they should have it, not a Negro girl. You're the first colored person working on Main Street in our town, waiting on customers, selling them things. But they treat you right at the store?"

"Yes, they do."

"Don't give them any excuse not to. You earn that job every day by doing your best."

"Daddy, I learned something there when they taught me how to polish the silver. There's a thing called 'grain,' and you aren't supposed to go against it. If you dry or polish the silver against the grain, it leaves streaks that make it look bad."

"Because the metal is soft. Humph," Russell snorted. "That's as good a description as any for what's happening. You polish the silver the way they taught you."

"Did Medgar Evers go against the grain?"

"Yes. So did others. More will too. Even me and you in our small ways."

"How do you do it?"

"Not so much at work. I have to keep that job so we can stay here. But I went against family wishes to bring us to Jamestown."

It had been his idea to move to Jamestown, a long simmering idea born of childhood memories of his grandparents' and great-grandparents' in rural Georgia. Russell's childhood visits down south in the summertime were arranged by his Southern relatives so the children would learn proper manners and not be destroyed by Northern coarseness. He wanted to have a backyard garden and a wife who would make pickles from what he grew. He got both, but was the price worth it? With all the damn rabbits and corn that wouldn't fill out?

There were backyards in Newark, Jersey City, Union, and Queens, but they eluded him. Where others embraced or tolerated urban living among buildings and streets and concrete parks with fences, Russell chafed and longed for a postage stamp size of green to mow and plant and walk barefoot in. There was a time in his life for enjoying city pleasures, like when he was in the Navy and when he met Mathilde after the war, but that time was over. He was restless by nature, and after Fleur was born, when he had a few extra dollars, he'd take Mathilde and the baby on a Sunday train ride to explore the different spurs that ran out of Newark or Elizabeth. That's how he found Jamestown.

In his methodical, planning way, Russell kept Jamestown, along with a couple of other towns, in mind. The big Catholic church was a plus, because that was how Mathilde was going to be persuaded—not that she wasn't anxious to put more distance between her and Russell's womenfolk, but it was a big step and she thought it should be for wanting to move toward something, not running away from something. Their chance came when Russell found out about a job, a good job, in Jamestown. A friend of his friend Curtis Rainfield told him that the town was hiring some new sanitation workers. Garbagemen. They worked for the town, so the job was steady and the pay OK. More people were moving in, which meant more trash, so Jamestown bought some new trucks and needed a few more men. Russell got on a train right away and went to the Jamestown municipal building and filled out his application. His was the fourth application out of two dozen.

The woman behind the counter took Russell's completed application and retreated to a side office. In a minute, a man came out and spoke to Russell.

"Russell Williams?"

"Yes, sir."

"You want one of our sanitation jobs?"

"Yes, sir."

"Can you drive a truck?"

"I have a commercial B license."

"How much can you lift?"

"A piano, if I have to." He smiled broadly and friendly, but quickly turned it down when he saw his little joke missed its mark.

"People aren't going to throw out their pianos. That's moving company work. Ever work for a moving company?"

"Matter of fact, yes, sir."

The man looked Russell over, then said, "We got some rules here working for the borough. Drinking and smoking on the job are not tolerated. The garbage gets picked up rain or shine or snow. This isn't a private moving company, we serve the citizens of the town and are accountable to the mayor and his officers. People are always looking and complaining and we don't want to give them anything to complain about. Do you understand?"

"Yes, sir."

"It's government," he enunciated.

"Yes, sir."

"In exchange you get a fair wage and steady work."

"I can surely handle that, sir."

"We got another rule. If you work for the borough, you got to live in the borough. Says here you live in Newark. Aiming to leave?"

"That's the whole plan, sir."

"You got a place here yet?"

"Not yet, sir, soon as I get a job though, I'll be moving the family here."

"Can't do that. Got to be living here first before you get the job."

Russell hadn't expected this and didn't know if this was an actual requirement of if this man was playing with him like a fish on a hook.

"Sir, I do want this job, and I will move here to take it. Just tell me what I gotta do."

The man looked Russell over again, looked at everything on his application and took in the other applicants in the waiting room.

"If you can get back here before the end of the day with some proof that you've got a residence here in Jamestown, I'll see what I can do." He left Russell and went back into his office.

Russell thought fast. He walked into the town and found the Black barbershop. He got settled into a chair, and, though he was a stranger, the other men and the barber made friendly conversation while he got his haircut. By the time he left, Russell had a couple of names and phone numbers of people with places to let. He rushed from a phone booth to an address a couple of times before he had to get on his train back to Newark so he could turn around and come back to Jamestown before the end of the day. In the end, with fifty dollars—half he had to borrow—he made it back to Jamestown and to the address of his new landlord and apartment to get a signed receipt and back to the Sanitation office, all by three forty-five.

"Guess you want this job, Williams."

"Yes sir."

"OK. You got to start next Monday. Six in the morning. Show up at the base yard."

Of course there was commotion about this when Russell got back home from his second trip of the day to Jamestown. It had been an expensive day—two train fares, phone calls, apartment deposit, and a haircut he didn't need. But he was pleased, and the first thing he did was go find Curtis Rainfield and take him out for a drink.

"How come you don't want this job for yourself? It's a good paying job," Russell asked.

"Yeah, but you stink to high heaven every day."

"Won't bother me so long as I can smell that steady paycheck."

"You smell so bad anyways, no one will know the difference."

They joked and had another drink and complained about the women in their lives and the poor showing of the Yankees that year. Russell would miss this, and he wondered how things were set up in Jamestown for Black men to blow off some steam together.

"Got to hand it to you, man," said Curtis, "moving away and moving up."

"You could do it too."

"Nah, I'll stay here forever. It'll get better. Just got to get some more jobs and homes for folks, then everything work out for us. You got the moving type feet. I got the staying type feet."

Russell went home to break the news to his family. They had five days to pack up and move their things to Jamestown. He thought everybody would be happier about his news, but Mathilde seemed worried and insecure about fitting into a new church, and the rest of his relations frankly couldn't believe that he would leave them and Newark and go somewhere as foreign to Blacks as Jamestown. Some said they'd be back in six months, run out of town or just lonely for his own kind. But Russell knew he was at a threshold in his life and he had the chance to take his family over it. The corn and pickles beckoned. He rented a truck and they left.

Their first apartment was a horror and they stayed there for just one month. The next one was better, a three-room walk-up over a corner store on Cook and Central. Mathilde mostly stayed indoors with baby LuLu, leaving only to walk little Fleur to a kindergarten class at the Catholic school and to go to Holy Trinity Church. Mathilde made the trip with LuLu in a stroller, keeping her too-broad teeth beneath locked lips and her too-green eyes lowered. She didn't like the way the other Black women looked at her. A few invited her in, invited her and the family to their church services, but Mathilde conveyed her regrets with mumbled "no" and "no thank'm" and left them with the impression of being stuck-up and unfriendly.

Russell knew it had been a hard year for his wife with a new baby; she had fallen into a dark mood. It took a year for Mathilde to emerge from what he thought was a willful sullenness. By then the opinion of the Black women in town was fixed: Mathilde Williams thought she was better than them because of the French white in her. Well, she could go back to Guadeloupe or wherever she came from, or let the Catholic folks do for her and her family.

Mathilde's social missteps isolated them from a genuine welcome by the town's Black families. So too did her eventual embrace of the Holy Trinity Catholic Church—they were the only Black members of the parish. Mathilde's adherence to faith over race was misinterpreted, but as a stranger in a new town, the familiarity of saints, nuns, and priests made perfect sense to her. She established a routine of devotions, bringing herself and her children to Mass every Sunday and sometimes in between.

Russell went with her and the children once, but he refused to worship at a Catholic altar—not that he took up at another one, he didn't, but Catholic Mass was out of the question. Mathilde was used to their mixed marriage, and although the church counseled against it, had special rules about it, it happened often after the war, when people were marrying all sorts of other folks they never would have gotten together with before.

One of those rules was that Russell had to pledge to raise all the children of this union as Catholics and attend to their Catholic education and practice. It was like a loyalty oath, administered in the sacristy of St. Josefina's by Father Alphonse D`Aubrey in Queens, where he and Mathilde married, next to the papal flag of the Vatican. Now it was a new representative of God on Earth, a Father Halligan, who reminded him of his promise. His oldest child, Fleur, started school at Holy Trinity Elementary School, wore its uniform, carried its books, and so did LuLu and Charlie in their turn. It was a promise he came to regret. Eight years later, after some trouble with the nuns, Russell permitted Fleur to go on to the public high school. Father Halligan paid him a visit to remind him of his promise, but Russell stood up to him.

"Can you promise me that my child will not be singled out for discipline and bodily punished by one of your nuns?"

"Discipline is always at the discretion of the teacher," Father Halligan intoned.

"Then I am sending Fleur to the public high school."

Russell was sorry if this put Mathilde on the wrong side with the nuns whom she doted upon and made part of her weekly ministrations in service of the Lord, but he would not subject Fleur to what he thought was unfair and harsh treatment by the nuns.

"So that's another way I went against the grain," Russell said, taking his dishes to the sink. "But I don't think anybody's going to shoot me for it."

Changing the subject, Fleur asked, "Daddy, did you date a lot of girls before you met Mom?"

Russell snorted back a laugh, then answered simply, "Yeah."

"What kind of girls did you like?"

"The kind of girl I hope you'll never be."

"Daddy, how do I get a boy to notice me?"

Russell sat silent for a few moments. How should he answer his daughter, how should he reveal the terrible creatures men are? He was pretty sure his daughter was still a good girl, but she was seventeen now; other branches in his family tree had blossomed and fruited by that age.

Fleur was a good child, she had outgrown a silly infatuation with that worthless Johnnie Abercrombie. He knew the type of boy he was; he had been Johnnie Abercrombie when he was seventeen. Fleur dodged a bullet with that one, and he was very thankful but knew she wasn't out of the woods at all. Now she wants him to tell her how to get boys to like her.

"Fleur, just be yourself."

"That's what everybody says."

"Everybody's right."

"That doesn't help. I don't have any boyfriends, I don't have hardly any friends at all. People don't like me as myself."

"That's not true. You are at a hard age."

"I'm seventeen!"

"It's still a hard age, and you are still young. More important, everyone else in your world is still young. They're still figuring out who they are and what they want. They aren't sure of themselves no matter how tough or cool they think they are."

Russell went to the refrigerator to get the lunch Mathilde had made the night before for him. He stopped for a moment at the opened refrigerator door and looked at the sandwich wrapped in waxed paper with the piece of cake and jar of applesauce set next to it. An unexpected wave of tenderness flowed over him. He had a good wife. And he had a good daughter who asked him for advice he was incapable of giving. He knew in his heart he didn't deserve the goodness in these women, none of the men he knew did. What did they do to repay the love so freely given them? *We are monsters,* he thought. *We don't deserve you.*

He silently picked out his lunch and placed it in his lunch box as he did every day. He never took any comfort in the routine before, in the knowledge that his sandwich was always there for him, until today. He thought about what else he should say to Fleur. Finally, it came to him. "Fleur, I don't need to spell it out for you, do I? You know what boys want in a girl. What you want to know is how to hold on until those boys become better men. I don't know what to tell you to do. Some of those boys aren't ever going to become better men, good enough to deserve women like your mother and you. I can only tell you what not to do. And you already know that. It's never going to be easy for boys to become good men."

Fleur hung her head in disappointment. She didn't know yet that her father was giving her the most practical advice anybody could. She wouldn't understand the wisdom of his words for many years.

"But you're a good man."

"But it took me so long, such a very long, hard time."

He picked up his lunch box, hat, and jacket and left out the back kitchen door.

Helen Ransom

Helen Ransom was in the store to buy another shower present. She knew so many young brides and mothers. "This is the end of junior year for you, isn't it, Fleur?" she asked.

"Yes, ma'am."

"And did your classes go well?"

"Alright, I guess. I had a pretty easy year." Fleur related her schedule with little enthusiasm, the usual English, history, and math, with applied chemistry and business machines.

"What do they teach you in business machines?" Helen asked as she looked at the pink and blue enameled silver baby cups. That should come later after the baby was born; maybe she would purchase a baby spoon.

"How to run the mimeo machine, use a cash register—things I already know how to do."

"Isn't there something else more advanced?" She held a long-handled silver baby spoon. She could have it engraved. But what name?

"Not for me. Guess they're saving that for senior year."

"And what did they have you read in English?" Was there nothing appropriate for a baby shower when the sex and name of the baby can't yet be known?

"*Bleak House* by Dickens. It's bleak."

"Yes, I understand. There could have been a better choice for Dickens." Well, the spoon would have to do. She could have it engraved with simply "Baby" in a nice script. Maybe she should order eight of them the same way. She'd be prepared for a year of baby showers. But then she'd lose the chance to come here and visit with Fleur.

"Who is your guidance counselor, dear?" Helen asked.

"Mrs. Stacy Simpson. Would you like this engraved, or should I gift wrap it for you now?" Fleur was precise and attentive. One would think she had been working in the store for several years.

"You should speak with Mrs. Simpson about your classes. These are your two most important years in high school. Colleges like to see you taking challenging courses." She gave Fleur the engraving instructions and the mailing address for the gift.

"Those classes are for the other students."

Helen Ransom snapped her head up from peering into a jewelry case of bracelets. Did she hear her right? "What do you mean?" she asked.

"The students who are going on to college."

What should she say? "Is it so certain that you are not?" Helen ventured.

"I take the business courses," Fleur explained. "And that's how I got placed in this after-school job. Most of the girls have had typing by now, but not me. They don't have enough typing teachers, and because I hadn't had typing yet, I got this job. Most of the other girls in business track go on to the insurance companies."

"And they let you out of school early?"

"Yes, I get here most days by two o'clock, sometimes earlier. The total charges for the spoon, engraving, and mailing are $18.35. Should I put this on your account?"

Helen had an account there now. "Yes, please," she replied. "Do you find this enough for you?"

"You mean school? I love that I get out of school early, it's so boring. And I have this job in a nice store. I think the other students are a little jealous."

"What are your friends doing?"

"I don't have too many friends, ma'am. I came over from the Catholic school. Most of them went on to St. Agnes High School."

"Do you wish to learn other things? What classes have you enjoyed?"

"Well, I want to get my typing and steno classes in, but then maybe some history. I wish they would make it more interesting, though. It just seems like dates of wars and men on horses."

Helen laughed at Fleur's description and agreed that there could be much improvement in history instruction. "That sounds like the *Bleak House* of history. You know that 'history' is 'his story'? That's why it about wars and men on horses." And now Fleur laughed. Helen noticed her wide smile, her high cheekbones, her crinkled up eyes that closed around her light-colored irises when she laughed. A charming girl. She should have more opportunities.

"Would you like me to speak with your guidance counselor for you?" Helen asked. She immediately saw Fleur's face fall and knew she had overstepped.

"Oh, no. Thank you, ma'am. I can talk to her."

"Of course. But I would like to see you reading something more than *Bleak House* and men on horses." Again she overreached. Best to leave quickly now, before she scares off the girl. She made light of their little history joke and then took her package and left the store, the little bell ringing on her way out.

Outside she stopped to look in the display window again. The charm bracelet section begat an array of trinkets: tiny sewing machines, thimbles, and scissors. Tennis rackets, bowling pins, dogs. Little Christmas trees and pumpkins. She wondered, uncharitably, whether there were charms for mimeo machines and steno pads. As least the horse charms didn't have sabered men riding atop them. The history of girls and women told in charm bracelets. What were they teaching at that high school?

Aquamarine, diamond, emerald, and pearl. Winter to spring to summer. Gratitude for mothers and fathers. Congratulations to the graduates and brides. The second-busiest season at Tanzer's store stretched over these months. The country stretched too, stood up and flexed arms, rolled shoulders, turned necks, and walked and sat down. In Selma, Alabama. Across the Perfume River in Vietnam. In the hearts and minds of women yearning for something more than the June bridal pageantry. In the South, the country walked, rode busses, sat down at luncheonette counters, and endured taunts and worse. Buddhist monks in Hue set themselves on fire. The May 1963 *Playboy* magazine featured a cartoon woman removing bunny cuff links from a man's outstretched arm, she nestled in his hand. It also featured an interview with Malcolm X. Betty Friedan published *The Feminine Mystique*. And Helen Ransom asked herself what all this meant to her.

On campus she entertained the deans' wives at bi-monthly teas with art history speakers. She accompanied Earl on numerous visits. A conference in Philadelphia. Trips into the city to woo alumni donors. The at-home dinners for visiting lecturers. For the first and last, she brought out the president's home silver service and china and thought of Fleur.

On Main Street, the Beautification Committee fanned the whiffs of spring and mandated flower boxes on every block. Holy Trinity Church welcomed a new priest who immediately began preaching against the birth control pill from the pulpit. Jamestown High School asked her to visit for Career Day. She was dismayed to see not one black or brown face in her audience of junior high school girls contemplating college. She asked the guidance counselor Mrs. Stacy Simpson why.

"The students choose which Career Day talks to go to. They are free to pick anything they like," Mrs. Simpson replied with a bit of defensiveness. Helen knew she prided herself in getting any underperforming college prep student into a second-rate college somewhere.

Helen pushed her advantage. "May I see who the other speakers are here today?"

Stacy Simpson shared her clipboard. Chubb Insurance. New Jersey Manufacturers. Secretarial and trade schools. Rutgers. Valley Forge Military Academy. Helen handed it back without reading further.

"I'll give you some suggestions of who else to include for next year."

Helen was ever more alone at home as the crescendo of the school year end surged. Celia will be valedictorian at her high school graduation and on to Brown. She was already halfway out the door, rarely at home. Helen missed her, began to feel the loss of her last child at home. Earl was always busy on campus, and she wanted more to do. Not more entertaining. Maybe she could be an advisor to a student club? Start a campus book group? Earl was surprised when she mentioned it. "It's unprecedented," he replied. Should she dust off her art history degree? She wished she had gone into social work.

May and June arrived with a cacophony of events, and suddenly there wasn't a spare day. Commencement at the campus. Celia's graduation at the high school. Weddings; Mother's Day; Father's Day; more and more weddings—at least four every weekend. More than half the weddings were at Holy Trinity Church, where the banns of marriage were announced weekly in the Sunday Bulletin, three times before exiting the stage and being replaced by the next. The florist, Tanzer's Jewelry Store, Catherine Ridgeway Dress Shop, the stationery store, the banquet halls were all involved in the busy choreography of the weddings. Keeping the customers, the dates, the bride's preferences, and the brides' mothers' preferences straight. It was not unheard of for the employees at one store to offer help to another when they both had pressing demands from the same family and deliveries to go to the same house. The brides were eighteen, nineteen, twenty, and twenty-one—twenty-five on the far end. The burst of weddings came right after high school graduation, or college graduations. A BA in late May, an MRS in June. Everybody was happy.

At Tanzer's Jewelry Store, Fleur cycled the brides' chosen place settings into displays on the showroom floor. Crates of china, crystal, and sterling arrived weekly to keep up. She wrapped shower gifts and bridesmaids' and groomsmen's presents before getting to the big ones. It was a deluge of ribbon when Helen entered one afternoon in the midst of all the matrimonial furnishment.

"Hello, Mrs. Ransom. What can I help you with today?" Fleur's smile was heartfelt, genuine. *How confident the girl has become!* thought Helen, taking a little credit for her transformation.

"Would you help me pick out something else for Celia? I know we just bought her a watch for her graduation, but I was thinking of something else, something more personal. Just from me, mother to daughter."

Fleur furrowed her brow in thought and cleared away the wrapping papers from the counter she was working on. "I see you are very busy," said Helen. "Maybe I should come back later?"

"Oh no, these can wait, I'm happy to help you now. Does she have a birthstone ring?"

"Her birth month is August—the peridot—not an inspiring gem. She doesn't like it much."

"I remember that she has a charm bracelet."

"It's a bit jangly and heavy now with all those trinkets. Something different."

"Does she wear earrings yet?"

"Her ears aren't pierced. I'm afraid she'll lose them."

"Perhaps a strand of pearls?"

Helen mulled that over and let Fleur show her some. But they seemed too extravagant, too adult; her sporty daughter wouldn't grow into a strand of pearls for a while. She demurred.

"Let me show you these," said Fleur as she unlocked a jewelry case and removed a cushion with several gold signet rings planted in blue velvet slits. "These are getting popular now with young women."

Helen looked them over, unaware that signet rings had made the transfer over from men to women. Earl had a nice one of his own and had his father's too. How would the smaller surface area for a woman's ring hold up to the engraving? Fleur showed her some examples.

"The larger ones can really take the full monogram, but if she'd like something more delicate, we might engrave it with just a *C*. Or an *R*. There's even an oblong one that can hold a short name. *Celia* would fit onto this one."

Helen fingered the rings, trying them on herself. The brushed gold looked like fur, it would show off the engraving well. "Which would you choose?" she asked.

Fleur thought for a moment, then picked out a larger oval ring. "This one. With her full monogram. That way *she will always know who she is.*"

Helen agreed, stunned at the simple perfection and Fleur's insight. Fleur showed her several engraving fonts that would work well with Celia's initials *C K R*. They agreed an upright script lent modernity to feminine lines. Mr. Tanzer would engrave it over the weekend, and she could pick it up next week. "Will that be alright?" asked Fleur.

Helen pondered the larger significance of this choice: She will always know who she is. Oh, that someone might have given her a ring that conveyed that self-assuredness!

"Yes, Fleur, that will be just fine."

Amid June's joyous celebrations of love and accomplishment, there occurred another, a minor note in the orchestral suite of bridal and commencement marches. Fleur Williams turned seventeen on June 11. There were cupcakes in the back workroom at Tanzer's store, and Helen learned of their small celebration when she came in to pick up Celia's engraved ring.

"I hear it is your birthday," said Helen brightly as Fleur emerged from the back room.

"Yes, ma'am" Fleur smiled. Helen thought she looked so young. She wondered how things turned out with that boy earlier this year.

"How will you celebrate?" she asked.

"Not too much, ma'am. I expect we'll have cake at home tonight. But tomorrow I get to go for my driver's license!"

"That means you are seventeen. I remember the excitement of each of my children when they reached that threshold. Feeling so grown up. Will you get to drive soon?'

"Not a lot. My father is teaching me. My mother doesn't drive, so maybe it will be helpful that I can."

"You are on the cusp of many new experiences. How exciting! But girls must be careful too." Helen paused to see if this evoked any reaction.

There, a quick glance down, it must be that boy. She pivoted. "Did you do alright in school?"

"I haven't gotten my grades yet for the year, but I think I did alright." *Back to her cheerful self,* Helen noted.

"Lovely. And the whole summer to look forward to. Any holidays for you? A trip to the shore?"

"Oh no, ma'am. We'll all be working this summer. The ladies here will take some time off and I'll fill in. I'll be full-time until school starts up again."

"You seem to be doing so well here."

"Oh, I like it a lot! All the pretty things. Last summer I worked in the laundry with my mother. This is like a dream."

"Yes, this store is filled with young girls' dreams. Older ones too." And they shared a laugh.

Helen knew the Catholic Church's only guidance to women was to save themselves for marriage and then to serve their husbands. The high school didn't offer much more than the sophomore health class with a chapter on human reproduction. She tried another path.

"You know, there is more to love than what people buy to celebrate weddings. All of this is beautiful, sentimental, a sort of dowry for the woman. But you must always remember that not everyone accepts the responsibilities that go along with love. You're seventeen now, Fleur."

Fleur met her eyes and then lowered them. "Yes, ma'am" she said, and left the counter to retrieve Celia Ransom's new signet ring, the one that would always tell her just who she was. Fleur was only beginning to look beyond her own initials to know who she was. Helen wondered if this was a useful exercise for her too.

That night, President John F. Kennedy addressed the nation to explain his decision to send the Alabama National Guard to Tuscaloosa to allow two Black students to register for school. The Ransoms were at home watching Kennedy's speech on CBS Television.

The events in Birmingham and elsewhere have so increased the cries for equality that no city or state or legislative body can prudently choose to ignore them . . . The fires of frustration and discord are burning in every city, North and South, where legal remedies are not at hand . . . We face, therefore, a moral crisis as a country and as a people. It cannot be met by repressive police action. It cannot be left to increased demonstrations in the streets. It cannot be quieted by token moves or talk. It is time to act in the Congress, in your state and local legislative body and, above all, in all of our daily lives . . . I am asking for your help in making it easier for us to move ahead and to provide the kind of equality of treatment which we would want ourselves; to give a chance for every child to be educated to the limit of his talents.

"It's about time he said something," Earl said, getting up to turn off the TV set. "Too many campuses needed to erupt before he called upon Congress to send him a bill."

"Will we start seeing actions on campuses in the North?' asked Celia.

"Not like in the South, but yes. This will be the impetus for our civil rights student club to advance their plans. I plan to check in with them tomorrow."

Helen thought about the Black students in Jamestown and on the Hamel campus, but most of all about Fleur. "Can I stop in with you?" she asked Earl.

"I'd rather you didn't. I don't want a heavy-handed administrative presence. These groups are student-led and are sensitive to interference."

"I'm not interfering," Helen protested.

"I know you aren't, darling, but it won't be seen that way. Be my eyes and ears on Main Street. That would be helpful. And Celia, don't get any ideas," he winked at his daughter. "You aren't at Brown yet."

Annoyed by her husband's response, Helen fumed while setting the kitchen aright before turning in for bed. "Eyes and ears on Main Street," she muttered to herself. Yet she knew the town that hosted them would have its own problems with the president's request of Congress. It had been hard enough for the Chamber of Commerce types to absorb Fleur Williams waiting on customers. Helen now went to Tanzer's store exclusively for all her gift purchases and repairs, but she knew that some customers had retreated from them. But the promise of a civil rights bill on the horizon buoyed her. The ramifications would be wonderful for students like Fleur. She imagined that Fleur's family welcomed the president's speech. She looked forward to seeing her soon. She must have another reason to drop in at the store. She imagined a lot. She wanted to broach the subject of college with Fleur.

But what she didn't imagine was Medgar Ever's assassination the following day.

A week later, Helen Ransom came to Tanzer's Jewelry Store, this time with a ring she wanted to get sized.

"It's an old family ring," she said, "I haven't worn it in years."

A gold filigree band with a pearl solitaire; she placed it on the soft mat Fleur had placed on the counter.

"Let me get Mr. Tanzer for you. He should look at this first."

"Wait. Before you get him, I'd like to ask you something, Fleur. It's not about the ring, but it will take just a moment."

Fleur looked up at Mrs. Ransom, a little timid.

"Fleur, do you ever think about going to college?"

"Why no, ma'am, I don't."

"What do you think you will do after you graduate from high school?"

"I expect I'll be working."

"And . . . ?"

"Well, I'd like to get married someday."

"Of course you would; a good marriage is wonderful. But do you know you can go on in your education and still work and raise a family too? And higher education is not only good for you, it will help your future children."

"I'm sure you are right, ma'am, but I never thought of myself going to college."

Mrs. Ransom paused, then asked, "Would you like to think about it?"

"I don't know, ma'am."

"It doesn't hurt to think about it." But that wasn't quite true, as recent events demonstrated. Helen Ransom continued. "Just because no one in your family has attended college—yet—doesn't mean it can't start."

"I know, ma'am, it's just that . . ." Fleur halted midsentence and tried to think of something to say, but instead dropped her eyes.

Helen Ransom cocked her head and said, "Fleur, I want to invite you to come over to the campus. There is a special presentation on Wednesday the twenty-sixth, most of the day. It's for high school seniors from some of the other cities nearby. It's to talk to them about what college is like and to answer their questions."

"I don't think my family wants me to go to college," she said, averting her eyes.

"They may not have thought it was possible, Fleur. What do you think they would say about you coming over to the campus to just see what it was like?"

"Oh, I don't know, ma'am, I don't think so."

"Fleur, your parents love you and they want to do their best for you. They may not have thought this was possible. Just think about it, Fleur. The day is an information program, nothing more. It wouldn't hurt to find out more about going to college."

"Yes, ma'am, I'll think about it."

"It's coming up soon. I'll ask you when I come back in for my ring."

"Yes, ma'am."

Helen returned on Friday to pick up the ring. "Have you thought about my invitation to attend the college information session?" she asked Fleur.

"I have to work on Wednesday," Fleur replied without really saying "No."

"Of course, your work schedule is important. You are so conscientious, Fleur, the Tanzers are fortunate to have you. It's one of the things that makes me think you might do well in college. Not all young people take the opportunity seriously."

Fleur didn't have an answer to that; she just looked down at her hands holding the wiping cloth she used for the glass countertops.

"Wednesday is shopping night. Maybe you could arrange your schedule to work the afternoon and the evening? I think you could still get quite a bit out of the morning sessions."

Mrs. Ransom left that possibility open as she finished paying for the ring sizing. She slid the antique ring out of its brown paper envelope and put it on her right ring finger.

"I think I'll just wear it home. It belonged to an aunt or a great-aunt, I'm not sure. Pearl is your birthstone, isn't it, Fleur? You're seventeen now. You only have senior year left." And she left the store.

The next day, Mrs. Ransom returned.

"Good afternoon, Mrs. Ransom," said Fleur, surprised to see her again so soon. "Is there something wrong with your ring?"

"The ring is lovely, it fits well. I have a charm that needs to be attached and soldered. Long buried in an old jewelry box. It has sentimental value, as it belonged to my grandmother. Where do your grandmothers live, Fleur?"

"Queens on my mother's side, Newark for my dad's."

"Do you see them often? Are you close to them?"

"I'd like to see both my nanas more often."

"Of course, you would. Family is so important."

"The charm?" inquired Fleur.

"Oh, here it is. Fleur, have you spoken more with your parents about coming to the college?"

"Not yet, ma'am."

"Do you want to?"

"I don't know how they'd feel about it."

"You must find out."

"Yes, ma'am," Fleur said, a little too quickly.

Helen paused, decided to risk it, then asked, "How would it be if I came to your home after dinner sometime to speak with you and your parents together about college? I could answer their questions. What do you think?"

Helen saw Fleur's hesitation and tried another tack. "Let's take this one step at a time. I'll just talk to them about you coming to the orientation session first. That's all. The program to introduce Negro high school students to the idea of college."

"Alright, I guess that would be alright. I'll ask them when you should come over."

"Excellent, Fleur. You can tell me when I come back to pick up my bracelet."

Helen left the store feeling jubilant.

SUMMER 1963

Russell Williams

Russell Williams and his wife Mathilde sat equally erect in separate chairs in their living room, while their guest, Helen Ransom, sat on their sofa. Fleur perched herself on a side chair brought in from the dining room. Russell relegated the younger children to their bedrooms during the visit. Only a few toys suggested their existence. He asked Fleur to serve their guest coffee and a plate of store-bought cookies. After some polite small talk about the city and its plans for a shopping development, Helen Ransom asked, "Has Fleur mentioned that I invited her to attend an information session at Hamel?"

Russell spoke for them. "She has told us."

Helen continued. "We plan several of these each year and invite students who come from families in which college has not traditionally been part of their educational life. What do you think of this for Fleur?"

Russell was ready and met Helen's direct and too personal question. "No offense to my daughter, but her grades at school have been alright, but nothing to brag about. Why Fleur?"

"Our children's gifts unfold at different times," replied Helen, sipping from her coffee. Russell noticed a tiny wince. "She may yet surprise you. But she has shown remarkable initiative in taking on her after-school job. By all accounts, she is doing well at Tanzer's store."

"Then there's business school," countered Russell. "She doesn't need to go to college."

"I could say that about many a young person already on the Hamel campus. The main point here is that Hamel believes it's important to bring the opportunity of college to nontraditional students. President Kennedy set the pace for higher levels of education among all our citizens. So many young women now go to college. It's excellent preparation for motherhood, and many even pursue a career."

Russell straightened his shoulders. "The women in my family didn't prepare for motherhood by going to college."

"And I'm sure they did an admirable job. Fleur has told me about her grandmothers."

Russell gave Fleur the "We'll talk later" look.

"What I mean to say," continued Mrs. Ransom, "is that higher education is now possible for many who had never thought of it before."

A quiet pause while all eyes turned to Russell.

"This is just an information session. To find out more," Helen Ransom offered.

Russell finally broke the silence. "Fleur, are you interested in this?"

"I don't know much about college. Would it be alright to find out more?"

"Don't your teachers talk with you about this?" Russell asked, knowing full well they didn't. Fleur shook her head. Then her dad said, "You may go to the information session."

Helen Ransom smiled, a little too brightly, Russell noted, and his daughter looked relieved. Mathilde kept a poker face. Russell had already considered where this might lead, was genuinely interested but wary of Helen Ransom. Of course he knew there were Black people in Jamestown and elsewhere who went to college, did this college president's wife think he didn't know that? The Atkins and Bullock families regularly sent their children on for more education, they prepared them for it, and that was the difference. There was nothing in his or Mathilde's family, or the Jamestown schools, that prepared a garbage hauler's daughter to go to college.

Russell saw that Helen Ransom was trying awfully hard to put him at ease in his own home. "It appears your family is involved in sports," Helen said brightly, indicating the trophies on the bookcase. Russell let her flounder a bit more, then assumed some better manners. He explained the trophies were his, relics of his high school days in Newark as a wrestler and a source of pride.

"I wish my children were involved in more sports," he said. "It's good conditioning for life. I'd like to see my children's trophies up there next to mine."

"Yes, I agree," offered Helen. "It's a shame Holy Trinity doesn't offer more than recess."

Russell grunted and sent a sideways look at Mathilde. A sore point between them.

"But I understand that's changing," she continued, "due to President Kennedy's Physical Fitness Council." Russell was glad that Holy Trinity was about to hire their first physical education teacher, but he knew it was only because the first Catholic US president advised it.

"The war that you and others fought have given us so many new opportunities," enthused Helen. "I do think we are living in a time of remarkable change. I'm so pleased you will allow Fleur to explore some of these opportunities."

She landed her pitch nicely, thought Russell, got to give her credit for that.

"When should Fleur arrive for the information session?" he asked.

Russell didn't expect to have an argument with his wife about this. Behind the closed doors of their bedroom, she criticized him for his bad manners, and his lack of faith in the wisdom of the priests and nuns.

"If Fleur was meant to go on in school, I'm sure the nuns would have told us," Mathilde argued.

Confused, Russell thought the endorsement of a Catholic president would be all Mathilde needed in persuasion. But he knew his wife was insecure about her own lack of schooling.

"No sense in letting the girl get her hopes up," she added. "College is not for people like us."

"Coloreds can go to college now," Russell countered.

"And get themselves and others killed for it."

"That's not happening here."

"Not yet."

Russell softened his response "It's just an information session. Likely the girl isn't gonna want to go once she learns what it takes."

"You didn't think that when she came home begging us to let her take that job in the white people's store."

"I was wrong. Happy now?"

"No. Lord, that woman is irritating." Mathilde mimicked Helen Ransom's elocution, "'Excellent preparation for motherhood.' Going to college to learn how to be a mother?"

Russell laughed and embraced his wife. Now he understood. "You're a hard-working woman, Tilly. That Ransom woman doesn't know the measure of you. Now don't be hard-headed like your old man."

Russell went downstairs to get himself a glass of water. Fleur was pretending to do her homework at the kitchen table and probably heard them arguing. He turned on the radio.

"President Kennedy outlined his Civil Rights Bill for Congress today…" Russell quickly turned it off.

"Fleur," he began, "you may go to the Hamel information session. In fact you will go. I will write a note to your job asking that you be excused that day."

"I won't need it for work, it will be over in time."

"Don't argue with me."

"I'm not arguing, Daddy. Why are you being so mean about this?"

"I'm not being mean. Look at me. Do you see meanness? Do you?"

"No."

"Well then, you have your answer. But I want you to understand you are just going to find out more. This has nothing to do with your future yet, so don't get your hopes up. Just as likely you're gonna see that you'd have to study harder than you want, that you won't want to go, that you're gonna feel even more an outsider than you do now."

"Maybe that's why I think I can do it."

"You already planning that far ahead? Listen, it's dangerous to count on white people. Even President Kennedy."

Russell washed his glass carefully in the sink, took up the dishtowel, dried the glass, and put it back in the cupboard.

"Good night, Fleur."

"Good night, Daddy. Thank you."

Helen Ransom

Helen was very pleased with herself. She lingered on the front sidewalk of the Williams' home that June night to reiterate, for any neighbors who wanted to hear, that she and the rest of the Hamel community looked forward to welcoming Fleur for a campus visit. She congratulated herself on her tact, her restraint, her seizing upon the sports pivot to gain Russell's interest. She thought it was trust.

She retold the story of her visit to Earl that night, giving all the details her keen eyes took in and her mental calculus at every obstacle. The uncomfortable furniture, the lingering kitchen smells, the modest coffee service, the coiled rag rug dark with age. No wonder Fleur loved working in the Tanzer's store—nothing in her house could have come from there. Earl listened with interest, then some impatience as the story went on a little too long. He had work to do. Helen wrapped it up with a flourish, announcing that Fleur Williams would come to the next information session in two weeks.

"You might be Hamel's best recruitment scout," Earl teased. "Shall I tell the Athletics director that you'll scout for him too?"

That stung. "Don't belittle this!" exclaimed Helen.

"I'm not. I just think invoking President Kennedy's penchant for touch football might have been laying it on a little thick."

"You weren't there."

"No I wasn't. And you should ask yourself whether you should have been there. Celia's right. You are getting over-involved in this girl's life. How do you think this makes her parents feel? The campus first lady swooping in to give something to their daughter that they can't."

"You surprise me. I thought you would be proud of how I handled this."

"I am proud of you, but I think you should exercise more of that restraint you are proud of."

She hadn't expected an argument with Earl. "How is this different from the outreach work of the Admissions staff?"

"They don't invite themselves to have coffee with the parents of salesclerks."

"What's that supposed to mean?"

"Salesclerks that they know, that they do business with. You are too personally involved."

"Isn't that where it starts?" She looked deep into Earl's eyes. How could he not understand this, that the heart's motivation is always personal?

"I just think you should back off a little, give this young girl and her family the courtesy of information and leave it at that." Earl took his leave to his office, leaving Helen to wonder for the first time how well they really understood each other.

In one of the last scheduled events of the academic year before the mass exodus of staff for July vacations, Hamel University hosted an information session for New Jersey high school juniors whose families had never attended college. Hamel was part of a consortium of private liberal arts colleges that notified high school guidance counselors, provided the buses, and paid for the lunches and tote bags for about one hundred students. By nine in the morning, the last of the buses making a circuit of northern New Jersey towns arrived at Hamel's Old Main Administration Building. Helen stood with her husband and greeted each student with a warm, firm handshake. Normally this was a visit they both looked forward to, but with their friction over Helen's interest in Fleur Williams, some part of them was just going through the motions. Anyone looking at them would see a well-dressed, smiling, handsome white couple—the representatives of a city on a hill—making their visitors comfortable in a house they never visited before. That the visitors were entirely Black and Brown teenagers gave the picture a different feeling.

Just as the last bus discharged its wards, Helen saw Fleur Williams arrive on foot—she was not alone but accompanied by her father. Helen introduced both of them to Earl, who beamed broadly at both, shook their hands, and passed a quizzical look to his wife as they followed them into the great hall.

"Why is the father here?" he whispered.

"I don't know," Helen said, as surprised as he was. "But I'll handle it. With restraint."

She caught up to Fleur and her father while Earl made his way to the front of the hall. She took Fleur's elbow and suggested she sit with the other students.

"I'm so glad you were able to make it. Fleur, I think you will get the most out of your visit if you sit with the other students. Would that be alright with you?" she deferred to Russell.

"Where are all the other parents? Only one of us could come with Fleur, otherwise Mathilde would be here too," he said with embarrassment rising in his face.

"Like you and your wife, they are working or home with other children. Most of our visitors are from farther away, and there's only so much room on the buses. I'm glad you are here too. Come sit with me here in the back, and I'll take you on our own tour while the students have theirs." She thought Fleur looked relieved as she took her father in hand. "Please join the others," she encouraged Fleur. "We'll catch up with you later."

The students listened to Earl Ransom's welcome before dividing into four different groups led by the Admissions staff. There were about one hundred students in all, the majority boys, but Fleur had made herself at home with a small group of Black girls. The students departed on their respective tours. Russell Williams shifted uncomfortably next to Helen and watched as his daughter left the hall. Helen knew the routine: They would visit one of the science labs, hear a truncated version of a Sociology 101 lecture, and see the dormitories, chapel, bookstore, and cafeteria. Helen turned to Russell and said simply, "Come with me."

Helen walked Russell around the campus and carried on a mostly one-sided conversation about the history of the campus ("once a Gilded Age estate"), the breadth of the faculty ("including Professor Samuel Watkins, who teaches an Afro-American Studies class"), and the demographics of the student body ("the ratio of female to male students has increased to two to three"). They paused in the shade of one of the large oak trees, and Russell recognized two of the men on the grounds crew as men from Jamestown.

"What do you and others from the town think about us here on the campus?" Helen asked.

"Well, I know the sanitation crew that comes over to pick up the garbage," he chuckled. "There's a lot of food waste from your cafeteria."

"Oh dear," said Helen, amused and glad for the levity. "I do hear complaints about the food from the students. I guess it's not like home cooking."

"I know some of your cooks. They are good ladies and fine cooks at home."

"Earl and I sometimes eat with the students, and I know it's not always up to par. It's quite different feeding a thousand students."

"I'm sure it's better than what they fed us in the service. The young folks don't know that life. They should eat what's put in front of them."

"Our children do not have the same context of privation as we do," Helen replied, immediately regretting including herself in the comparison. "I mean, children now do not intimately know the Depression or the war. On the contrary, they have so many new opportunities. I feel very hopeful for our young people. Do you too?"

"A parent should always be hopeful for their children's world."

"Of course, I mean it seems like a new era for them. The race to space, their joyous music, and more education. We didn't have all that."

"No ma'am, we didn't."

"Did you ever think of more education for yourself? Surely you are eligible through the GI Bill."

"I might be eligible, but that doesn't mean I get them."

"What do you mean?"

"I'm still waiting to get that mortgage they promised me. I think about that more than education. A roof over my family's head, one that we own, that's what's important. Can't do much else if you don't have a home."

"But that's part of the GI Bill, isn't it?"

"It is. It's why we came here to Jamestown in the first place. Thought it would be easier here. But it isn't. When I applied for the sanitation job with the borough, I had to show proof that I lived here. I had to go out and get a haircut I didn't need to get some leads on a rental. One of them worked out, and I got the job. I got to rent one place after another, but I'm still waiting on that GI Bill mortgage."

Helen did not know what to say, so said nothing. They continued walking and she pointed out a few buildings of historic interest and the oldest trees, but the air had gone out of their conversation. It leavened again when she showed him the athletic buildings, track, and football fields, but Hamel was a Division III school and it showed. Helen was struggling for a way to bring up the subject of women's education and how college could help Fleur, could help so many other Blacks, and how Hamel desperately wanted to be part of the change that was coming, that must come. But she didn't have to.

Russell stopped walking, surveyed the green lawns and towering oaks, and spoke again.

"There was a time I wish I had more schooling. When I was in the shipyards fixing up some of the destroyers that got hit, we had problems with some of the solders. Some of them fell apart soon after we applied the weld. I wasn't doing the welding, I was hauling and holding the beams and sheets for the fellows who did, and we had to do it over again many times. Don't know why that solder didn't work well, but I thought if I knew more about it, if I knew what it was made of, maybe I could make a better one. I tried to find out more but the other guys were grunts like me and nobody knew why it wasn't working. It wasn't until the war was over that I got a chance to go to a library and find out. It's a mix of metals, mostly lead, but this one needed something else, some bismuth, antimony, or rosin. I never heard of those words before. I thought it would be a great thing to know the chemical nature of the materials we worked with and how to improve them. How useful and important that would be."

Helen saw that he knew the importance of higher education and wouldn't need her to tell him. But the benefits of women's education were something else. She tried. She invoked President Kennedy and the space race, offered that women's education could be a solder that strengthens the bonds of a family or a community. She detected impatience in him and knew she was trying too hard to win him over, but what else could she do? They wound up their tour and made their way to the Student Union to join the others. As they rejoined the student group, an older Hamel student talked about all the fun and inspiring activities in campus life. They stopped at the office of the Hamel Democratic Society, which was one of the few that had any activity going on over the summer. There were a couple of students there preparing a bus trip to attend a march in Washington D.C. later in August.

"And we've invited Rev. Dr. Martin Luther King Jr. to the campus to speak. He said he would come next year!" one of the Hamel students excitedly declaimed.

There were music ensembles, sports teams, political and social clubs— it seemed like there was something for everyone. The tour moved on to the cafeteria.

Russell held back. "I think I should go now and report in to work. Fleur can walk to work when she's done here."

"Can you see your daughter in a place like Hamel?" Helen asked.

"How many students come here?"

"The student body is about sixteen hundred."

"How many colored?'

"I don't know precisely," Helen stammered. "We have several foreign students from Africa, and others from the tri-state area. The purpose of these information sessions is to recruit more. Hamel has been on the forefront of this effort, organizing these tours."

"Doesn't look like it's working yet."

"It takes time to change things. Do you have other concerns?"

"What religion do you practice here?"

"Hamel is affiliated with the Methodist Church, but we are nondenominational in practice. Our students come from many religions. The chapel hosts Methodist services and there are occasionally other visiting ministers."

"I made a promise to raise my children in the Catholic Church. Are there Catholic schools like yours?"

"Yes." Helen was somewhat bewildered by this concern. "Mr. Williams, I can assure you that we have Catholic students here that worship at Holy Trinity. Our coursework is mostly secular, except for the Divinity and Theology departments. Fleur is already attending a public high school, isn't she? Think of it that way."

"I have to explain it to her mother. She's got to be comfortable with that."

"Assuming we can assure your daughter's continued practice of her faith, what other barriers do you see to her attending college?"

"Well, that's just the beginning. Families like ours can't afford college. Thank you for inviting us to the campus today, Mrs. Ransom." Russell left to return to work.

Helen watched Russell Williams walk away, then went to look for Fleur. She found her in the cafeteria with the rest of the touring students, sitting with a small group of Black girls, chatting amiably. She thought how Fleur looked so natural there. Yes, this was the right path for her, she was sure of it.

The graduations were over and the weddings wound down to just one or two a weekend. The birthstone display in Tanzer's window changed from pearl to ruby to peridot. Jamestown entered a sleepy torpor that matched the weather. July and August were just one glass of iced tea after another.

Helen, Earl, and Celia went for their usual July idyll on Cape Cod, and while driving back through Rhode Island, Celia quipped that they should just drop her off now at the Brown campus.

"Nonsense," said Helen. "We've got shopping to do when we get back."

"For what? I'm ready now. I've got everything I need." Helen had to admit that was true. "I bet I could get into an empty dorm room early, find a job for a few weeks, and save you the extra drive up here." Celia loved teasing her mother.

"You know that isn't how it works," her father said. "Just because you've had the vagabond campus life doesn't mean Brown is going to open up a dorm for you as a professional courtesy."

"And you'll not deprive me of helping you set up your dorm room," Helen added.

"Oh, Mom, can't you just put me on the train with a couple of suitcases? I can take care of myself."

"No, I can't," Helen replied, looking straight ahead as the miles slipped away below them.

Exactly twenty-four days later, at almost the same time of day and mile marker, Helen burst into tears. She and Earl had begun quarreling soon after Celia waved them away from in front of Chaplin Hall. Helen started it, picking apart Celia's decision to follow her father's footsteps and attend Brown. Earl reminded her that the choice was Celia's alone and what Helen was feeling was a natural part of children growing up and moving away. She would have none of that.

"How would you know? You never carried a child in your womb, wiped her nose, and allowed her to grow up and leave you!"

"That's not quite fair, Helen . . ."

"And this war that's brewing!"

"We aren't involved yet."

"All the boys who will die when we do! What are mothers to do when their children leave them? What am I to do?" That was when she burst into tears. Earl pulled the car over and stopped the engine, helpless, confused.

"I . . . I thought you might welcome some of the freedoms that come with no children in the house. You could spend more time doing things you like."

"Playing bridge? Being in church fashion shows?"

"So you don't like those. Find something else that you do."

"I liked being a mother!"

"You are still a mother! And moreover, you are my helpmate. You can help me then!"

"You've made it clear you don't want my help."

"That's not true. I asked you not to get involved in the student clubs, the same as I would ask any faculty. The clubs are to be self-governed."

"Can't I be a faculty advisor?"

"You aren't on the faculty," Earl countered.

"And whose fault is that?" Helen lobbed back. That one stung, for Helen might have continued her studies in art history had she not quickly married Earl Ransom right out of school.

Some silence passed between them. Earl started up the car and pulled out onto the highway. It wasn't until the next mile marker that he broke the silence.

"This is going to be a difficult academic year for me. You know what I'm up against."

She did. Re-accreditation, a new trustee chair, some difficult tenure decisions were ahead.

"Maybe we can take some time together over the Christmas holidays," he continued.

"I wouldn't want to miss Celia's visit home."

A few more miles passed.

"Look," Earl finally said, "I don't know what you want. I don't think you know what you want. But find something, for God's sake, to bring you out of this slump. Children grow up and leave home. That's how it's supposed to happen. This day was always going to come."

"Yes," she agreed, "and it came today."

They drove the rest of the way home in silence.

In mid-August, James Meredith, the first African American student at the University of Mississippi, graduated with a degree in political science. Later in the month, while Helen and Earl were arguing on their way back from driving Celia to her new college life at Brown University, a group of Hamel students drove to Washington D.C. for the March on Washington for Freedom and Jobs and heard the Rev. Martin Luther King Jr. give his speech. The newspapers and TV were full of the news. The students returned and were interviewed by the local paper.

"A historic and life-changing experience—for me and the country," one of them said.

"You could feel the collective will and effort in the air. We are bringing that will back with us," reported another.

Change was coming to Jamestown, however slow it seemed to those accustomed to asserting their will. Helen Ransom prepared herself for the start of another academic year. Bored with ceremonial aspects of her campus role, she wafted through the year-to-year sameness of faculty teas and lunches for the deans' wives. She kept up on the activism going on in the South, wishing she was closer to something important. The news was not always good. For every James Meredith that went to college, there were dozens who never could. So slow the growth, so subtle the movement, she hardly discerned the change happening within.

Mario Sposeto

It was the early afternoon lull, and Mario Sposeto turned his "Open" sign to "Closed" and sat down to eat his salami sandwich. He picked up his bills and Jamestown Gazette that the postman had left earlier. As much as he enjoyed his work, loved his customers, the old men, the little boys with their mothers, he appreciated this restorative pause. It was when he allowed everything to settle—the gossip of the morning, his mental "to do" list, the flow of stories he heard. He figured he was almost like a priest the way people unburdened themselves to him. Mario had thought about becoming a priest—what young Holy Trinity schoolboy didn't?—but his father urged him to join him in the barbershop. "The money's better," he had told Mario. "And you can get laid! Otherwise, there's little difference." He agreed with his father, God rest his soul these past four years, barbering was a holy thing. He hoped his son Andrew would join him in the shop when his turn came.

He opened his bills and set them aside in a chronology of due dates. All manageable this time, thank you St. Martin, patron saint of barbers. He crossed himself and made a mental note to light a candle at church in gratitude. St. Martin's feast day wasn't until November, but he wanted to stay on good terms with his representative before God who would intercede for him on matters of business and otherwise.

Mario finished up his sandwich then opened the *Gazette* to amuse himself with what passed for news. Nothing much he didn't already know, but a guest opinion from Earl Ransom, the president of Hamel University, caught his eye. The paper gave this bozo another mouthpiece every couple of months, as if he needed it. He ran the damn college in town, wasn't that enough to corrupt young minds without putting him in the paper too? The headline read, "Town Invited to Hear Rev. Dr. Martin Luther King Jr.—February 5, 1963." Mario had heard that King was to come to speak at the campus. Hell, he'd heard about everything; there wasn't much that escaped the Italian barber grapevine in this town, but here was a tidy little invitation to the whole town to come listen to what this outsider had to say about race relations. He wondered if many in Jamestown would take Earl Ransom up on his invitation. He doubted few beyond the pointy-headed types serving on the school board and the interfaith committees would be interested. This was still a working-man's town, in spite of the growth of newcomers who commuted to the city for their jobs. Mario lived here all of his thirty-nine years, grew up in this barbershop. There were fewer Blacks back then, hardly any really. They started to come to Jamestown after the war, and now there was a whole neighborhood of them, with their own church, barbershop, luncheonette, and liquor store. There was a little bit of social mixing, like at the bowling alley and movie theater. The town couldn't support more than one of those each, but people were careful and everything worked out most of the time. The Blacks bowled in their lanes; they sat in their own section with each other in the movie theater; they bought their groceries at the Acme and not usually at the A&P; and Mario never saw any in Puglio Brothers. Mostly it all worked out. Mario didn't begrudge their existence in his town; people in Jamestown weren't these Neanderthal types like they had in the South who drew a big black line down the center of a store or restaurant and wouldn't let Blacks come over the line. Jamestown didn't need lines; people knew their place pretty well and didn't try to undo centuries of civilization. But now Earl Ransom was inviting the whole damn town to a Black and white kumbaya party on campus. He snorted a small laugh; he doubted many people would RSVP their attendance for Earl Ransom's little get-together for Dr. King. He turned the page and read the menu for next week's school lunch.

But a sour thought brought him back to the open invitation. It wasn't too long ago that families like his found Jamestown less than cordial to Italians. No one invited anyone from the Knights of Columbus to speak at Hamel University about the discrimination Italians faced. There were still hard feelings about how the Italians were mostly relegated to the north side. Sure, it made for some great neighborhoods and the Italian kids all went to school together, but nobody likes being pigeonholed. The Italians were the cops in town, the barbers, the greengrocers, but not the mayor or aldermen. Even the Archdiocese bestowed its highest offices on its Irish brethren.

Mario looked at Earl Ransom's smiling portrait in the newspaper; his good looks and patrician pedigree irritated him. "Smug bastard," he muttered to himself. "Let him have his college crowd." Although Hamel students and faculty were his steady customers. "And *vaffanculo* to you too!" Then he threw the *Gazette* into the trash.

Father Halligan

Father Halligan escorted the crying woman from his office and bade his housekeeper to serve her some coffee and cookies in the kitchen while she composed herself. He pressed a twenty-dollar bill into the palm of the weeping woman, one of his newer parishioners.

"Go in peace," he intoned and made the sign of the cross.

The housekeeper soon returned with his own cup of coffee—cream and one sugar—and he settled back into his chair and closed his door. These women who sought his counsel for a husband who drank too much, philandered, struck her or the children, "May the Lord bless them." Women were willing to talk to him about anything, to unleash any burden upon their souls to their priest. He knew these women would do that, and some even much more, if he gave it any importance at all. But he did not. Father Halligan reduced any soul-aching problem of a parish woman to female weakness. He doled out recipes of more volunteer work or novenas, or a longer penance of rosaries or stations of the cross, to bear up the faults of their men. All they needed to do was focus on their roles as wives and mothers through more prayer and good works. That was how they could transcend any earthly problem, that was all they needed from him. He thought he understood women well.

He picked up the correspondence and newspapers placed on his desk and leafed through them. The front page of the *Jamestown Gazette* caught his eye. He didn't need to read the weekly paper to know what was happening in Jamestown. As the religious leader of all the town's Catholics, information flowed uphill to his rectory. He knew which business leaders were having financial difficulties, he knew which police officers were on the take, he knew much more than he cared to about the failings of love among married couples. The confessional was a minor conduit for his detailed intelligence about affairs, embezzlement, and Mafia family rivalries.

Father Halligan had known about Rev. Dr. Martin Luther King Jr.'s visit for months. He was consulted, invited, and entreated for his blessing, which of course he gave—how could he not? But his political antennae told him this was not the right way, not the right time, to address race relations. He gave lip service to all the interfaith and ecumenical overtures the town cooked up, but, really, he cared little for them and thought them a waste of time. *Let people go to their own church with their own people*, he thought. He saw precious little benefit to promoting a 'dialog' with any other religious group. Why waste one's time on mutual understanding and action? The whole point to having different religions was so you didn't have to compromise your beliefs and community. As far as race problems were concerned, that was more a matter for Reverend J. P. Giddens of AME Bethel and his deacons; what could he do? Besides, he thought the race problem was being overblown and exploited by outsiders with political agendas. He knew that Black and white people didn't really want to mix with each other, and forcing them to was going to blow up in somebody's face. He looked at Earl Ransom's open invitation with one thought only: how to make sure that nothing would blow up in anybody's face in Jamestown. These battles should be fought in the South, not here in New Jersey where Blacks live and work and go to their church just fine. No, the only thing wrong about the race relations in Jamestown was a bunch of outsiders like the Ransoms, the Hamel students, even Dr. King himself. The Jamestown local people knew how take care of their own problems. Why, Holy Trinity parish had a Black family in its midst—Mathilde Williams and her children. Weren't they relatively well-off and happy? She had a husband, and although he never converted nor attended a church as far as he knew, he held a steady job and provided for his family. That was a lot more than some other families had, and Father Halligan took full credit for that on behalf of Roman Catholicism. Hadn't his church welcomed Mathilde and her family? Wasn't she a constant and cheerful volunteer for the church? Didn't he see her every week involved in something that promoted the life and health of his parish? If the Black people wanted to mix more with white society, they could hardly find a better example than Mathilde Williams.

But as he reflected further, he saw cracks in his viewpoint. He knew that the brave cheerfulness of her deep faith masked a deep loneliness. He knew the other women thought Mathilde foreign and odd, and no amount of church volunteer work was ever going to be enough to invite Mathilde into their kitchens to commiserate about their men and children. And the husband, he pledged to raise his children in the Church but then let his oldest, Fleur, go to the public high school. "That," he muttered to himself, "was their first mistake. Their second was letting their girl work in Tanzer's store on Main Street." He had heard about that within minutes of the first Holy Trinity parishioner who witnessed Fleur's expanded role.

In his fourteen years as the pastor of Holy Trinity and twenty-three in the priesthood, Father Halligan never had to directly confront any racial strife. Could it really happen here in Jamestown? He saw an annoying college president who, along with his "college community" and his busybody wife, wanted to upset the equilibrium of quiet, decent people to advance an ideology that was blind to human nature. He was already thinking about the celebration of his silver year anniversary in the priesthood and further advancement he thought he deserved. He would have to learn how to contain whatever exuberance that flowed over from Dr. King's visit. He had no more words of support for Margaret McCardle, who had just left his office and whose husband walked away two months ago. No protection for Shirley Reid, whose husband drank and hit her. No thoughts for Marguerite Sodano about how to help her parents accept her out-of-wedlock child whom he himself had just baptized. Instead he finished reading the paper, and, after allowing this problem of Jamestown race relations to settle a bit, he picked up the telephone and placed a call to one of his colleagues in Newark. Monsignor Morranz would have some advice for him.

FALL 1963

Elma Tanzer

Elma Tanzer looked over the front window display. Sapphires, the birthstone of September—blue as cornflower when pale, a bottomless azur when deep—sat in the center of Fleur's careful arrangement. Rings, pendants, earrings nestled among anything else in the store that had a hint of blue in it. Lapis and sodalite scarab bracelets and pins. Royal Doulton figurines of dancing ladies in blue gowns. Wedgewood jasperware in matte periwinkle. A place setting of Lenox "Liberty." Bows made out of royal blue, baby boy blue, navy blue, and lapis blue punctuated the thought that September was just the right time to buy a gift for someone. *The girl has a gift for design*, Elma nodded to herself. And not only that, she had the knack of finding just the right gesture to ease her husband's workload.

Elma Tanzer and her husband were getting older. With no children, she always thought there would be some young man, an associate, they would bring into the business at some future date, someone who would begin to take over some tasks. She herself was still energetic, but she noticed her husband's stoop did not quickly resolve after getting up from the engraving table. In time she would have an old man to care for as well as a store. It surprised her that this light-eyed young African American girl effortlessly found the right solution to ease his workload without sacrificing his pride. Fleur ran his errands, shoveled the sidewalk, climbed a ladder into the attic to retrieve supplies, and wrestled with large drums stuffed with shredded paper that cradled china and crystal. It was Fleur who loosened the first strand of Mr. Tanzer's long bow of work. *The world was full of surprises,* Elma marveled. Fleur was strong, willing, and personable with customers. Whatever doubt she had about bringing a Black girl into their store was long resolved. They were lucky to have her.

But that Ransom woman! In the store at least once a week, often more, with some repair or another—all an excuse for her to speak with Fleur. She brought in one old charm bracelet after another, rings to be sized, brooches repaired. Every last heirloom from her family. It was good material, 14-karat gold mostly, but the gemstones were nothing special. Still, Helen Ransom was a reliable source of income for the store, and Elma thought she should be more grateful, but instead mocked her to her husband and referred to the Helen Ransom jobs as the retirement fund.

It wasn't so much that Helen Ransom occupied Fleur's time in conversation. Her meddlesome reputation and magnanimous air among the town's shopkeepers was well-known on Main Street, but Elma Tanzer had another reason for her distrust. She was trying to get to Fleur, like a project or cause. The girl should be allowed her own thoughts and path, but Helen Ransom had an agenda for her. After one particularly intrusive exchange between the two, Mrs. Tanzer spoke to Fleur in the back room.

"Shall I wait on Mrs. Ransom when she comes back?"

"Ma'am?"

145

"Fleur, you and I both see she has taken a keen interest in your opportunities. But your future is yours, Fleur, not somebody's project." She saw Fleur's cheeks redden.

"I would like to find out more about college."

"Do they never discuss college at your school?"

"No ma'am, not with me."

"Why ever not?" Though Elma Tanzer could imagine why. America was full of such contradictions.

"I'm in the business track, not college prep."

"You should find out all you want, then."

"Did you go to college?" Fleur asked Mrs. Tanzer.

"No, it wasn't possible," Elma Tanzer replied. "The times between the wars were very difficult in Germany. The country was poor. Not many went on to university. A shame because the country was vulnerable to ignorance."

"Did you want to go to college?"

"I'm afraid nobody talked about it with me either." They shared a laugh. Mrs. Tanzer continued, "You can have a good life going to college. You can also have a good life not going to college. There are many things to do in this world. That is the promise of America. Of course it is harder when you have to make the decision and not have someone decide for you. You have a lot to think about. It's not easy being a young person when there is so much opportunity."

"Thank you, Mrs. Tanzer. I can still wait on Mrs. Ransom when she comes in."

"You know she will ask for you anyway. I think we should have a little sign between us. If she becomes too much, you say that you are in the middle of helping Mr. Tanzer count the gears in a watch repair. There is no such thing, but it will sound reasonable. That will be good for staying in the back for a good five minutes. Enough time for one of us to wait on the Retirement Fund."

Fleur Williams

How can the world be like this? Fleur asked herself. Two weeks ago, someone in Birmingham, Alabama, placed a bomb in a church and it blew apart. Four little girls perished. It was a Black church, the Sixteenth Street Baptist Church, and the girls were Black and fourteen and eleven years old. Now they were dead. Addie, Cynthia, Carole, and Carol Denise. Close to her sister LuLu's age. They were in the basement of the church putting on their choir robes when the bomb went off.

Fleur was in the store thinking through the change in the display window, September to October, sapphires to opals, and contemplating the murder—yes, murder!—of these little girls. *How could anyone do that? Why do they hate us?*

It had been a hard two weeks. The bombing felt personal, not abstract or far away. Holy Trinity mourned with a special Mass. The parishioners looked woefully at Fleur and her family. Even her father attended. But that was last week, and she didn't know what to do with her sadness now, so she put it into work. The blue theme of September had felt right, and she rotated all the blue merchandise they had into the front window display. She placed some jewelry in groups of four, a subtle memorial to the four girls. Four charm bracelets they would not wear. Four ID bracelets they would not exchange with boyfriends. Four pins that wouldn't rest on the lapels of their Christmas or Easter coats. Four pendants that would not decorate their necks in graduation pictures. She thought about them all the time. Which charm would Addie like? Was Carol a pearl girl or a birthstone girl? What were their birth months? But no more birthdays for them.

She had asked her parents why, how this could happen.

"We remind them of their sin," her father answered.

"We must pray for their souls too," her mother said.

"What are we supposed to do?" cried Fleur. "Will this happen here?" She was afraid.

Now it was the end of September, and the trees began to show their color. The air cooled and people moved on to the rituals of fall and a new school year. The town came alive with football games. Fleur began her senior year in high school. She read the newspaper every night, searching for answers to questions she had only just begun to ask. School was even more boring than last year. Still no typing class—a continuing shortage of teachers—and she was released for work even earlier. She noticed a split in her senior class. One group was talking and planning excitedly for college next year—their choices, applications, campus visits. The other group was already living their after-graduation lives—working at office parks and body shops. Which group was she in—both, neither?

No one had ever talked to her about college before—not her parents, grandparents, guidance counselors, teachers, nuns—until Mrs. Ransom. The college president's wife came into the store a lot. *She brings in all sorts of old jewelry to be repaired. It seems like an excuse to come into the store to talk to me,* Fleur thought to herself. Helen Ransom had become a bit of a joke in the store. Mrs. Tanzer referred to her as the "Retirement Fund" and even marked the envelopes that hold her repair jobs with "RF." Some in Jamestown thought Mrs. Ransom was an arrogant know-it-all, always meddling in things that shouldn't concern her.

But she didn't see it that way. Mrs. Ransom was maybe a little pushy, but so far no one else seemed interested in her future. *She talks to me sort of like I'm her daughter, Fleur noted to herself. I've got my own mother, and she has her own children, but it's nice to have this attention. Daddy says I shouldn't put any trust into white people, what they give us they can easily snatch away. She's not my kin, but no one talks to me about the things she does. She knows things beyond what typing will allow me to do.*

Fleur thought about how her school had run out of things to teach her and pushed her into study halls and work release. Why didn't she take the same science and math classes as the others instead of the easy ones? Was it too late? Could she even get into college? It seems like only a certain class of people in Jamestown went on to college.

That's why most of the Black girls and a lot of the Italian girls take all the business classes and leave school at noon to go work for the insurance companies. I never got typing so that's how I ended up at Tanzer's. Can't say I'm sorry about that, but I wish I had the chance to explore other possibilities.

But Addie, Carole, Cynthia, and Carol Denise didn't even get to go to high school. Fleur felt guilty about wanting more in her life. She couldn't get the thought of their deaths, nor a dream of college, out of her mind. She returned to her work focusing on the front window display. Opals. She went to collect all the jewelry with opals in them. Some were a pale and milky iridescence, others had fiery streaks of orange and aqua. Fleur thought the latter better expressed her own resolve to think more expansively about her life. There were four girls who wouldn't get to. She took four of the most vibrant opal pendants and made them the center of her display.

Helen Ransom

"Hello, Fleur. You made another lovely assemblage out front," exclaimed Helen Ransom on yet another errand to Tanzer's Jewelry Store. Had jewelry ever played an important role in her life before now? Never. She was filling a gap left by the departure of her youngest child.

"Thank you, ma'am," smiled Fleur. "What can I help you with today?"

"Another relic from the jewelry box. Quite old-fashioned, I don't wear it, but it was passed down from a great aunt and I can't very well neglect it." She produced an oval cameo pin with a broken clasp.

"It's a pretty cameo," said Fleur, admiring the well-carved profile of a woman with curly hair. "A keepsake for your family. Of course it should be repaired. I'll write it up for Mr. Tanzer. Would you like an estimate first?"

"Not necessary. I'm committed to being its custodian. Has school begun well for you?"

"It's the second year this has happened," Fleur complained. "They don't have enough typing teachers, and it's my senior year. They put me in a French class with the freshmen."

"That sounds a lot more interesting than typing."

"But how can I go on in business without typing?"

"Typing is useful, but you can always take a typing class. Don't they offer one at the Community House?"

Fleur was silent. Helen knew there was something she didn't want to say. She decided to delicately probe.

"Typing is easy to pick up and practice. I'm sure you could get a lot out of even just a week there."

"I can't go there," Fleur quietly stated.

"Why ever not?

"It's a Protestant place. I can't go because it's not Catholic."

Helen opened her mouth but then stopped. She needed to choose her words carefully. Privately appalled at the sway Holy Trinity Church had over purely secular concerns, she still must be diplomatic. She had heard of Catholic families who would not join the YMCA branch in Jamestown for the same reason. The Community House too?

"I see. Well, I think there must be some other places. I'll be on the lookout for you. You have time enough to learn typing."

"I'm not sure. People at school say I need it to have something to fall back on."

"Nonsense," Helen exclaimed, getting a little mad now at those guidance counselors. "Typing is a useful skill, but it's not the only pathway for employment. Look at everything you've learned here. Do the Tanzers need you to type?"

"No."

"Well then. You don't need anything to fall back on. That's just an excuse people use because they can't think beyond their own prejudices."

Fleur remained silent. Helen regretted letting her anger show. "I'm sorry, Fleur. It's not for me to say. I am frustrated that your school does not offer you the full spectrum of education and gives you only that which will get you a job at an insurance company."

"Thank you for your concern, ma'am."

"Now what's that about a French course?"

Fleur described how French 1 was the only class they could find that would fit her schedule, and how she'd be starting with all the freshmen.

"Don't think badly about that. You will have the advantage of maturity and wisdom over the younger ones. I'm sure they will look up to you. You are mature and responsible—your teacher will notice that. I would not be surprised if she engaged you to help the younger students. And you've had some French already, haven't you?"

"Not the same. My mom—she speaks a kind of French from where she grew up. My nana and papa too."

"It's certainly a type of French, every bit as valid as *'la belle francaise.'* It will surely help you."

"But what would I do with French if I can't even type in English?"

"Quite a bit. A foreign language can open doors for you that mere typing cannot. It is one of the primary languages of diplomacy and arts and culture. Food, fashion, cinema. French is spoken in different parts of the world. There are unfortunate and tragic clashes of people and history, but in each case the French language reflected new and different aspects of all the peoples who came to speak this tongue. Africa, the Caribbean, Indochina, Oceania. And you are already part of that history. Embrace it, Fleur. I think you will do well."

Fleur nodded, was silent and thoughtful. "No one has ever explained it like that to me before."

"That is a shame. There is no reason—none whatsoever—why you shouldn't pursue something beyond occupational training. That's what the typing class is. And the others that they fill your day with."

"Business machines," offered Fleur.

"Exactly! Is that really one of your classes?"

"I had it last year."

"They should teach you and everyone else French so you can read the Enlightenment philosophers in French and English. That's a real education."

Fleur turned thoughtful. "I didn't learn much about chemistry or math."

"Would you like to?" asked Helen.

"I . . . I don't know. There are some things here that would be good for me to know." Fleur gestured to the back workroom of the store. "Things about the metals and stones. It seems kind of interesting."

"It's all interesting. And it can be yours too. Please don't worry about a typing class. Promise me?"

Fleur smiled, "Yes, I promise."

"Good. I'll come back next week for my pin."

When Helen Ransom returned for her pin, she found a happy and excited Fleur, who reported that she was doing well in her French class. Her French teacher called upon her often, and the other students looked up to her, asked her questions about her mother's island, and asked her to help them pronounce some word, parse some verb.

Helen delighted in Fleur's enthusiasm. "Fleur," she asked, "would you like to see a new film of the French cinema? We are having a screening on the campus on Friday night. *Les Parapluies de Cherbourg.* It won the Palme D'Or at Cannes this year."

She was interested, and, fortunately, her parents approved. Helen and Earl picked up Fleur at home and brought her to one of the campus auditoriums. It was full of students and the atmosphere, anticipating this award-winning film, was very fun and festive. They were greeted by students and the French faculty and took care to introduce Fleur to everyone. Many were speaking French, and Fleur tried to keep up, but Helen saw that Fleur caught only some of it. They seated themselves among the students; Fleur sat next to a second-year student named Marlene, who was very cordial toward Fleur. A representative of the French Club introduced the film, said that subtitles would be on, and was sure everyone would enjoy it.

Fleur did seem to enjoy it, although Helen wondered if the subject matter—sex, pregnancy, love—was the right choice. She asked Fleur and Marlene what they thought of the film.

"The music made it seem like a silly story," Marlene offered. "But I like how everyone accepted their choices and moved on in their lives."

"Well said, Marlene." Mrs. Ransom breathed a sigh of relief. "What did you think, Fleur?"

Fleur thought for a moment, then said, "That beautiful blond woman who played Genevieve, she becomes a jeweler's wife, she's rich, and a loving mother. That's a pretty good ending, but sort of like a fairy tale."

"How so?"

"Jewelers work hard and aren't rich like in the movie. Where I work, the people aren't like that. Mrs. Tanzer doesn't even have a diamond ring."

"Do you work in that store?" Marlene wanted to know more.

Helen Ransom left the young women to talk and circulated among the others, pleased that the evening was going so well. She found Earl disengaging himself from Professor Waithe of the Art Department, who was overlong in his criticism of the Palm d'Or jury that chose tonight's film as its winner.

"Thanks for rescuing me! Don't stray too far, I want to leave soon." he said.

"Anytime, dear. Look at Fleur. Don't you think she'd fit right in here at Hamel?"

"I find that it's more a matter of a student's curiosity rather than any innate intelligence or background."

"That's exactly what I mean. I'm trying to get her interested in going to college. What about our college? I think she'd do well here."

"You think that of every student who first walks through the gates of Old Main."

The excitement of a new academic year was bracing for both of them, their quarrels of last month almost forgotten. Helen was almost like a mother for some of the students far from home.

Helen mused aloud, "I don't think we've had any local Negro students from Jamestown in quite a while. Not since from before we arrived. We could change that."

"Let's get some figures first," Earl cautioned, wanting to slow his wife down.

"It would be good for Hamel, don't you think? It's the right time. It would be good for everyone."

Helen wasted no time. She went to Tanzer's the next day, and, as they were busy in the store, she offered to come back at closing time and give Fleur a ride home. There was no reason for Helen to be home at dinner time. Dinner for who? The house was lonely with Celia away.

Fleur gladly accepted the ride home. After the French cinema evening, Helen thought Fleur was opening up a little more.

"Thank you for the ride, Mrs. Ransom. I've got a lot of homework tonight and this helps."

"Fleur, I'd like to ask you something, and I don't want you to answer yet. It's important and you'll need to think about it and talk with your parents."

She glanced over at Fleur who now looked reserved and apprehensive. "It's alright, dear. It's good. What would you think about starting at college next September? At Hamel?"

Fleur's eyes widened; she opened her mouth but said nothing. Helen beamed at her. "Yes, you heard me correctly. Can you imagine yourself one year from this very day on the Hamel campus as a first-year, fully matriculated college student?"

Fleur finally found her voice. "Is this possible? Why me?"

"Why not you, Fleur?" asked Helen, her smile projecting her excitement.

"I don't know what to say."

"I don't want your answer now. I want you to think about it and talk with your parents."

"What should I tell them?"

"First, you must ask yourself if you want this."

"I do want this, I do. I just never thought . . ."

"Then you must tell your parents. I can help you."

"But nobody's gone to college in my family. There isn't money for that."

"That's a problem we can overcome." Helen was almost giddy by this time. She loved how she caught Fleur completely by surprise.

"But how?" asked Fleur.

"I'm the wife of the college president. I can figure that part out," she said triumphantly.

"But . . . but . . ." Fleur stammered, looking a little more frightened than she should. "But what about the protests? The bombs?"

"What do you mean, dear?" Helen was truly puzzled.

"James Meredith. Medgar Evers. The four schoolgirls. People don't want us to go to college."

"No, no, you needn't be afraid. Don't think that. It's not like that here. This is Hamel University in Jamestown, New Jersey; it's not the South. It's not like that up here. No one is going to threaten you if you come to Hamel. Please don't be afraid of that."

"I am afraid of that."

Helen pulled onto Fleur's street. They were both silent the rest of the way to her house. She stopped in front of Fleur's home and turned off the car ignition. Fleur looked at her expectantly. What could she say about fear?

"There are few guarantees in life. Conflict and violence can happen anywhere, and do. And there will always be something to be afraid of." She paused to conclude that thought. "But I can guarantee that education is good on every level—for the person and for their family, their community, and society at large."

Fleur remained silent for a moment, then nodded her head in understanding. "Thank you," she said. "I will think about all this. I'll talk to my parents."

"It's for you to decide, Fleur, whether you want this for yourself."

Fleur thanked her for the ride and bade her a good night. Helen drove home and ate a cold salad alone in her kitchen, thinking about Celia away from home, about Fleur, about planning the next steps.

Helen read Earl's announcement about the Rev. Dr. Martin Luther King Jr.'s visit to the campus in the *Jamestown Gazette*. Now that it was public information, she could speak about it to others. She had bristled under Earl's embargo of this news, had wanted to share it with others, especially Fleur. Now that she could, she thought through how to best tie this to her campaign to get Fleur into college. The girl seemed interested enough, her father too. But she didn't know about her oddly spiritual and very Catholic mother. Fleur going to the public high school was a breach in the commitment to a Catholic education. Her mother would not want that to continue. Perhaps she could get one of the priests to endorse this, or one of the senior nuns. Helen inwardly groaned at the idea of approaching Father Halligan, the pastor of Holy Trinity, who would clearly be the best choice to influence the Williams family. But she already knew where he stood on race relations and women's roles.

Father Halligan had his own mouthpiece in Jamestown, his pulpit and occasional published articles. He spoke little of Vatican II, the world council that was supposed to drag the Catholic Church into modernity, hoping it would bypass his well-cultivated parish. As far as race problems were concerned, he thought the race problem was overblown and exploited by outsiders with political agendas, with Hamel being the worst example. There was no love lost between her husband and Father Halligan, but Earl had to make him aware of Martin Luther King Jr.'s visit and invite him to be part of the proceedings. No, she didn't think he would advocate for higher education for Fleur Williams.

There was no consensus of opinion on Dr. King's campus visit as Helen strolled Main Street from store to store before ending up at Tanzer's Jewelry Store. Quite a few were unaware of the news or nonplussed about such a dignitary visiting their town. Helen read between the vague or diplomatic responses—whatever enthusiasm there was for Dr. King's visit was matched by disinterest—or worse. People would not tell her to her face that they resented the university for bringing a race-relations dialog to their town. It was a new edge to the usual town and gown conflicts that she tried so hard to assuage. She could count on Mrs. Tanzer for blunt honesty.

"People don't want to think about these things. They are focused on their businesses and their families. They resist outside efforts to make them better people," Elma Tanzer replied when asked.

"And how do you and Mr. Tanzer feel?"

Elma Tanzer was quiet and thoughtful before responding. "The college has a special position—like being a teacher and a conscience. We need that, but we may not like it."

"Thank you."

"It is right for you to do this, invite this Negro preacher among us. Some don't like it, think you are interfering. But they don't like Fleur working here either. But we manage, our business grows, and Fleur is a good worker. Change takes time."

Helen decided to keep Elma Tanzer's pragmatic view in mind when she reported back to Earl what the town response likely would be. And she would suggest the student group organizing the visit seek out a local voice to help guide their plans. She knew Fleur would be the perfect bridge.

When Helen Ransom suggested a visit to another campus student gathering, Fleur was willing, almost eager.

"You might like to see some of the other student activities on campus," Helen suggested. "This one is more serious, but it still has its social aspects. These groups are how lots of students meet each other."

She was referring to the Hamel Civil Rights Action Committee, popularly known as CRAC. Their next meeting was coming up, and they had a lot of exciting plans, mostly the upcoming visit by the Rev. Dr. Martin Luther King Jr. Would Fleur like to come with her? She would be welcomed as a member of the local community. Fleur said she would like to attend.

Mrs. Ransom picked Fleur up and brought her to the club's meeting room in the student union. Initially more talkative, Fleur became quiet as they entered the room and she recognized it from her campus visit during the summer. Earl Ransom was already there, actively engaged with the group of eighteen or so students. Whites and Blacks together, everybody was smoking and looked very intense. Fleur was the youngest one there and the only person not part of the university. This was the host committee for Dr. King's visit, and the meeting was already underway. Earl Ransom introduced Fleur as a local community high school student. The others politely nodded. He stayed for a while, spoke some, listened more, then left for another meeting. Helen remained with Fleur, and they silently listened to the rest of the meeting, which went on a long time. They discussed the logistics, made contingency plans for different attendance numbers, and assigned outreach and press responsibilities. They talked about a dinner beforehand and who should attend. Should there be a reception after his speech? No, Dr. King's schedulers had already made that clear. They wrapped up many details and moved on to another agenda item.

Fleur seemed to grow nervous and shy. The room was warm and stuffy. She fidgeted with her hands and looked down at her lap. Then there was a pause in the conversation. Someone had asked Fleur what she thought, but she hadn't been listening. Helen Ransom nudged her and whispered, "Fleur, they are asking you for your opinion." Fleur was clearly caught off guard and the moment left her. The lively conversation stopped as soon as the question was asked—all eyes upon her, all waiting to hear what the local girl thought of their idea. A young Black man seated across from her repeated his question: "Fleur, what do you think?" And the others waited to hear from her.

Fleur parted her lips, opened her mouth, then stalled. Several seconds passed, and she still hadn't uttered a sound. Her audience looked at one another then glanced away, and someone started talking: "Well, if we continue to plan a local demonstration, we must . . . . . ." Fleur looked at her hands and didn't look up again until Helen tapped her shoulder and said, "It's time to go, Fleur," both grateful for an exit.

In the car ride home, Helen Ransom was as quiet as Fleur and worried that she had put Fleur in a position that she was not ready for. Had she briefed Fleur enough? Shared her thoughts about how she could be an important bridge between the town and the campus? What exactly was Fleur supposed to do and be at this meeting?

After they turned onto Prospect Street and were halted by a traffic light, Helen Ransom turned off the radio and spoke.

"Fleur, I'm sorry if you were uncomfortable."

"I'm alright, ma'am."

"Please don't think badly about this."

"Oh no, ma'am, thank you for inviting me."

Quickly they were in front of Fleur's house, and Fleur already had her hand on the door handle. She got out of the car, said nothing more, and walked briskly to her front door.

Helen felt terrible. She imagined Fleur as a younger Celia, full of confidence and daring. She wanted that to be true, but now regretted that she put Fleur into a difficult position. She should have prepared her more and kept her engaged in the conversation. Fleur was intimidated, and Helen felt responsible.

Back at the Ransom home, Earl asked how the rest of the meeting went.

"Alright as to the preparations for Dr. King's visit," Helen answered. "But not well for my plan for Fleur. She was caught out daydreaming when asked to contribute her opinion about something. I feel badly, I should have prepared her better."

"The girl is old enough to be responsible for herself."

"She hasn't had the advantages our children had."

"And are you responsible for closing the gap?"

"In some way, yes, I think I am," mused Helen.

"Helen, dear," Earl intoned. She hated when he called her "dear." "I think you are over-involved in this girl's life. You cannot make up for all the ways society has overlooked people like Fleur."

"How is this different from Hamel endorsing and nurturing the young campus activists? Oh, and do you know they are planning a local demonstration against segregation in the spring?"

"Yes, I know about it, and this is different. We're the academy."

Helen rolled her eyes. "That is so pompous!"

"I'm teasing you, dear, to show you that paving the way for Fleur's blossoming future is no less presumptuous."

He had a point, but Helen wasn't about to concede all.

"Isn't what I'm doing in the same spirit as nurturing student groups to experiment, to even fail?"

"Yes it is, but in the case of the campus group, they have given their consent to the arrangement, and, in fact, would like no faculty involvement at all. Fleur is still young. And I'm not sure you or Fleur have her parents' endorsement. Besides, the girl is a senior in high school. If she is to step up to the challenges of higher education, she can learn to pay attention."

Helen fell silent. Earl missed her point about feeling responsible for leading Fleur into an awkward situation unprepared. She was a mother, not a school principal. And yet, Earl reminded her that she was not Fleur's mother.

"Don't be glum about this," Earl said. "I don't want us quarreling."

"No. I don't either." But Helen couldn't shake her disappointment—in Earl, not Fleur. How could he know about a mother who should not be acting like someone else's mother? Or how girls of any age fail to get the extra encouragement and instruction they need? And all the reasons why they need it in the first place?

Fleur Williams

"Fleur, what do you think?"

The lively conversation stopped as soon as the question was asked, all eyes upon her, all waiting to hear what the local girl thought of their idea. It was worse than any time when she had been caught inattentive by a teacher, for this moment did not pass quickly. What should she say? She did not know what they had been discussing; she had not a single clue about their plan, the ripe idea they were so eager to try out. What could she say to not reveal what a jackass she was? She glanced quickly from face to face—white, white, Black, foreign Black, white, Black, white, foreign, white, white, Black. What must they be thinking about her? That she is hopelessly young and naïve? That she is a mere high school student with no talent for acting older or wiser? That she is dim-witted or inattentive?

She imagined opening her mouth; she could almost see words coming out of it, though she didn't know which words. It was all there ready to happen, her life could then unfold into a carpet of adventures and mysteries in the company of new, exciting friends who didn't ignore her. If only she had been listening!

Her lips parted, then stalled. Several seconds passed and she still hadn't uttered a sound. Her audience looked at one another then glanced away, and someone spoke: "Well, if we continue to plan a local demonstration, we must . . ." And the conversation, which had stopped and paused for her to get on, found its own steam again and left her behind as it wound its way among the students. Fleur flushed with embarrassment, closed her ears and never did learn the topic they were eager to know her opinion on. And her chance was gone. She felt Mrs. Ransom tap her shoulder and say, "It's time to go, Fleur." She was grateful for an exit.

On the car ride home, Mrs. Ransom was as quiet as Fleur. Fleur worried that she had let Mrs. Ransom down, though she hardly knew in what way. What was Fleur supposed to do, to be, at this meeting? Mrs. Ransom turned off the car and spoke.

"Fleur, I'm sorry if you were uncomfortable."

"I'm alright, ma'am."

"Please don't think badly about this."

"Oh no, ma'am, thank you for inviting me."

Fleur quickly got out of the car, said nothing more, and walked briskly to her front door. Inside, Fleur felt the hot eyes of her parents upon her. She ran upstairs and shut her door and wouldn't talk to them. Mathilde tried to get Fleur to open up about her distress. What could she say to her mother when she did not know why she felt so ill of herself? She said little, only that she thought the college students didn't know she was there, which was only part of the truth. Fleur didn't know she was there until it was too late.

If Fleur had not allowed her thoughts to wander, she would have learned their plan was to create a demonstration in town to bring awareness of segregation out in the open. They would do this one customer at a time, and they would start with an African American customer at one of the Italian barbershops in town. They knew what would happen; it had been tried elsewhere, and they welcomed the challenge. They weren't ready to do it yet, but their plans were underway. Soon. In the spring. They would have learned what they needed to know by then.

And Fleur would learn what she needed to know by then too. She would forever rue her inattentiveness, and it became the cautionary tale of her youth. From now on she would never not have something to say.

Several days later Fleur was still chastising herself. She walked to the post office with several packages that Mr. Tanzer wanted mailed, carrying on an internal monologue.

I'm so dumb and stupid! I listened and tried to follow everything they were saying. It was warm and close in that room, and everybody was smoking. I've never even tried smoking once. They were talking about Dr. King's visit, about all the preparations and who was invited to which part. There was so much to plan. I knew there would be a speech, but then there was a meeting beforehand, and a dinner, and who was going to pick him up at the airport, and who was going to get to talk with him before and after. Then they switched to what they wanted to do afterward. They wanted to make a protest against segregation. Sure, good, and I wanted to tell them about how in school I didn't get to take the classes that would help me get into college, and neither did most of the other Black kids, especially the boys. I wanted to tell them that, but they got busy talking about barbershops and New Jersey laws, and I don't know what else. There were some college girls there, Black and white, and nobody would let them get a word in; the boys kept talking over them and at each other. I was trying to think in my head how I was going to say what I wanted to say. Then I felt Mrs. Ransom touch my shoulder, and I didn't know why. Someone asked me something, and I didn't know what. I was embarrassed. I didn't say anything. I looked like a fool, and I felt like one. I still don't know who it was who asked me and what it was. They moved on, I mean who would wait for their dumb little sister to figure out what was up? I wanted to say something, but I couldn't figure out how, and I needed help and nobody gave it to me, and I had to figure it out myself, and there wasn't time. It all moved fast and nobody waited for me to get on board. If this is what college is like, I don't know if I can do it.

As she entered the post office, she saw Mrs. Ransom inside buying some stamps. *Why is this woman everywhere?* Fleur wondered.

"Hello, Fleur. My, you have a lot of packages today!"

"They are mostly watch repairs going back to their owners. Mr. Tanzer just finished a lot of them."

The postal clerk busied Fleur with all the return-receipt and insurance forms. Helen moved off to the side and pretended to be writing out a greeting card to post while she was there. She stuffed an envelope in the slot just as Fleur finished at the counter. "I'll walk out with you."

Fleur was shy and did not look directly into Mrs. Ransom's eyes. "Fleur, I want to say I'm sorry I put you in a difficult position the other night at the meeting."

"Oh no, ma'am, it was my fault. I should have listened closely. I let my mind wander."

"I could have explained better what the meeting would be like."

"No, ma'am, you did me the kindness to invite me. I guess I see more what college would be like."

"That's what I want to explain to you. That meeting you went to, they can be an intimidating group. Many are older and have been involved in campus politics for several years. And, I can say this to you, some of them are a little full of themselves, self-important. And they often speak over the women in the group. The dynamic isn't very welcoming to a young woman like yourself."

"It's like that in some of my classes at high school. The boys are clowns or show-offs, just trying to get all the attention."

"And how do you react to those boys?"

"I don't. I'm kind of quiet at school. Maybe college isn't for someone like me."

"College should be for everyone—man or woman, white or Negro, quiet or loud."

"I got the three that are harder."

"And what of it? There are plenty of quiet, thoughtful students who do their best work in written scholarship, not debate. And as for race, you've seen the progress during this last year. And Hamel is not like the South, we've had Negro and Puerto Rican students for a long time."

"I don't know . . . I just didn't know what to say."

"That was my fault. I should have told you that you could be very helpful to them. They don't know that; they think they know everything, but there isn't one of them in that group who knows Jamestown the way you do. You could help be a bridge between the campus and the community."

Fleur was truly puzzled. "I should get back to work."

"Wait just one moment, Fleur. The point is that you will face lots of discouraging situations as you move through life. And the question you must ask yourself is, will you let that stop you?"

Fleur now looked at Mrs. Ransom directly and hesitated for a moment. "Thank you, ma'am. I'll think on it." She folded all the receipts and change she held in her hand. She took a deep breath after she got outside and thought maybe she would ask Mrs. Tanzer to wait on Mrs. Ransom the next time she comes in the store.

I just want to forget about going to college, she said to herself.

Jamestown
November 22, 1964

The life of the town ambled on, passing through autumn leaves raked into gullies where street sweepers vacuumed them up. There were football pep rallies and that great trio of candy-fueled celebrations: mischief night, Halloween, and All Saint's Day. November in its topaz splendor descended upon the town, a moment of seriousness before the Santa gaiety would take hold. Winter was coming.

There was more coming that November than anyone could see. Desegregation was coming, violence was coming, Vietnam was coming. Even the Beatles were coming. The year's earlier spasms of violence were brushed over by American exceptionalism, confidence, and vigor. Then November 22 came for President Kennedy and the American dream.

The town and its people mourned for their young president, cut down by an assassin's bullet. No one would ever forget where they were, what quotidian task they were in the middle of, when the news reached them.

Fleur Williams was in the middle of a relay race in gym class when the bullet tore through Kennedy's neck. The first word came when she departed the locker room on her way to sign out for work release. She saw the school office staff and the deans and principal huddled around a radio. By the time she arrived at Tanzer's store, Kennedy's death was confirmed.

Elma Tanzer was cleaning the diamonds rings in the ultrasonic tank when her husband alerted her. They stopped their work to listen to the radio, but a few customers arrived, unaware, and Elma waited on them quickly and returned to the back room at intervals for updates. Her heart sank, reminded of the violence, war, and death she and her husband escaped decades earlier. Could it happen here too in America, some fanatical grasp for power? She gathered all the help together after Fleur Williams arrived and told them they'd be closing the store early and they could go home now.

Mario Sposeto heard the breaking news almost as soon as it happened. He was alone, his quiet lunch hour, and cried in his privacy. He kept his shop open, he knew there would be a stream of men who needed to be together, to talk, to dissect this horrible event as another example of how the world was going to hell in a handbasket. And they came. Mario turned up the radio and a dozen men sat and listened and talked. Communists? Cubans? Russians? Mario offered each man a trim or a shave, gratis, saying they were all going to be in church soon.

Father Halligan was taking a short nap after his lunch. He was awakened by Father Stanoch, who briefed him on the horrible, tragic events of the last fifteen minutes. Together they watched Walter Cronkite confirm the news that President Kennedy had succumbed to his injuries. He sent one of his priests over to the convent to pray with the nuns, another over to the school, and gathered the rest and the rectory staff into the chapel, where he led them in fervent prayer to guide the president's soul into heaven. He prayed for them and for the parish, the town, the country. When he opened his eyes, he focused on the stained-glass window of the Sacred Heart of Jesus. The Savior pointed to his gaping wound, the drops of blood, while staring back at him. "We must make our plan for services now," he said solemnly, and beckoned the others to his study.

Helen Ransom was at home reviewing some schedules and menus for the faculty Christmas party. Earl called to alert her and asked her to stand by, there were vigils to be planned. Helen called Celia and both held their telephone receivers away from their faces, moist with tears. Earl prepared a statement on behalf of the Hamel community; Helen helped him edit it. He was asked to speak at a few of the vigils, and Helen accompanied him. Together they mourned in public, an example of intellectual grief and rectitude. In private, their lamentations were more raw, surprising them both. Such beautiful promise cut down. What if it had been one of them? It was not the first time Earl and Helen Ransom compared themselves to the golden American couple who were Jacquie and John. Hamel was their own city on a hill, and it was an outpost of Camelot. Helen understood why the First Lady remained in her bloodied clothes. If it had been her, she said, she too would have cupped a piece of her husband's skull in her hands to show the world what was done on that November afternoon in Dallas. Together they watched Lyndon Baines Johnson sworn in as president, cursed that Texan they didn't trust, and cursed the hidden forces of history.

Russell Williams was riding his garbage truck with two hours left on his route. As he hoisted a can into the well, one of the borough's cops stopped his cruiser and asked if they'd heard the news. He learned about the gun shots, that Kennedy was rushed to the hospital. Two blocks later, a Department of Public Works truck flagged them down and said Kennedy had died.

"You have to finish your route, but finish up early if you can. Then you can go home," Russell was told.

His truck crew muscled on, muttering 'God damn" and slamming lids back on cans. They trimmed a half hour off their route and Russell hurried home. He heard Mathilde crying loudly and found her in her bedroom kneeling before a statue of the Blessed Virgin, clasping and wringing her hands, bowing in supplication. He gathered her into his arms and they both sat on the floor. They were soon joined by their children. Russell's face was grim and ashen, and he had no answer to Charlie's incessant questions of "Why?" He tenderly stroked his wife's shoulders.

"Fleur," he said, "take your brother and sister downstairs. I'll be down in a while." He closed the bedroom door behind them and gave Mathilde his full attention and love. He let her cry in his arms. He took a washcloth, wet it in warm water, and washed her face. He removed her stockings and dress and laid her on the bed, curled up on her side like a newborn animal. And he curled himself around her while stroking her arms, giving her everything he could, though he was wounded too.

Time stopped into before and after. People turned inward into themselves and their families, and outward to gather at vigils, Masses, and novenas.

The enormity of the president's assassination coalesced overnight, and by the next morning the nation had a full schedule of memorials. Holy Trinity Church held a vigil overnight to guide President Kennedy's soul to heaven, and had Masses, rosaries, confessions, and a novena scheduled for the next several days. Fleur and her mother were up early and knew there would be some cooking that had to be done. They left the house for the Acme store early, returned with heavy bags of groceries, put on aprons, and commandeered the kitchen in the name of the Father, the Son, and the Holy Spirit. They brought casseroles, bread, pickles, and potatoes to the rectory and the convent. The whole town was mourning. The shops and schools were closed.

But the news circulated. The newspaper still arrived at their door. The TV was on, and they watched Jack Ruby kill Oswald. Fleur and her father took everything in, trying to find the answer to why this happened.

"Who do you think did it, Daddy?"

"Could be a lot of different somebodies, and each one of them has their own 'Why.'"

"What do you think?"

"I don't think it was the President's Physical Fitness Council that got him killed."

The rest of autumn was cold and crisp. The Kennedy assassination was like a wind that chiseled the country's innocence. Thanksgiving followed in the wake of the national funeral, but the people did not rejoice in gratitude.

The Macy's parade went on as scheduled, but for many it was a pageant of tears. The national mourning lingered. Shock waves still rippled across the land.

Fleur buried herself in school and the daily news, asking "Why?" more times than she ever had. She and Russell were like twins every night after dinner, reading the newspaper, exchanging sections when they were done.

Eventually the commercial Christmas season poked through the grief, though it was more subdued than in other years. Fleur worked all the extra hours at Tanzer's she was asked, but it was less exciting this time. With each crystal goblet, charm bracelet, or porcelain nut dish she wrapped, she asked herself, *Why?* Still it was a successful season for Tanzer's, and Fleur received thirty dollars in a bonus envelope. The New Year arrived on the wings of the magical thinking people use to convince themselves the bad times were over. Surely the sorrows of this year will not be repeated, all their debts had been paid, all bad luck and worse motives spent out. Surely this next year will be better. It must be better.

WINTER 1964

Helen Ransom

She could put it off no longer. Helen Ransom must return to Tanzer's store and claim all her completed repair jobs. She was a little embarrassed about how many there were and the amount she owed. She would take care of it today, now that Celia's winter break was over and she had returned to Brown. It had been lovely having her daughter home, hearing about all her classes, her new friends, her opinions. Celia was ripe for everything college had to offer. Helen wondered if she'd even return home for summer break.

It had been awhile since Helen seen Fleur. She thought maybe she had scared her off after her little speech at the post office. Helen didn't want to think that Fleur was that easily scared off or intimidated. Could she be wrong about her suitability for college? Well, she was about to find out. Helen entered the store and found Fleur working at the front counter.

"Happy New Year, Fleur."

"Oh, the same to you, Mrs. Ransom." Fleur seemed surprised to see her.

"I'm afraid I've neglected to pick up all my repairs. I hope you weren't worried that I'd leave them here and not settle up my bill."

"Oh, no, Mrs. Ransom, not at all. We assumed you were very busy. It was a busy, and surprising, end to the year," Fleur offered.

"Indeed. How have you and your family weathered the loss of our young president?"

"It is still such a shock. My mother was devastated, him being Catholic and all. I just don't know what to think. Why would someone kill him?"

"I fear it will take a long time to uncover who and why, if we ever find out. Do they talk about it in your high school classes?"

"Not so much anymore. Certainly not in Business Machines," Fleur said with a sly smile. Helen smiled back; the ice was broken.

"I'll get your repairs." Fleur left for the back room and a minute later returned with seven envelopes containing different repair jobs.

"Oh my, I have been delinquent. I'm not sure I remember all these," said Helen. "I must rein in my job as custodian of the family jewels." Fleur laughed.

"You'll be happy you did these. Look at how well they came out." Fleur removed each one, and, besides the repairs, each bracelet, locket, charm, chain, and ring had been cleaned and polished.

"They look lovely. How much do I owe you?" Helen asked.

"With the sales tax, they all come to $58.64." Fleur showed her the itemization. Helen wondered if Earl would admonish her for this spending. She opened her purse and removed six ten-dollar bills.

"Thank you, Fleur. And please tell Mr. Tanzer thank you from me too. He does wonderful work."

"Yes, I'll tell him," Fleur said.

What next? Both women were silent and unsure who should speak next. And about what? Fleur broke the ice once again.

"I was wondering, Mrs. Ransom, if it would be alright if I came to one of the campus meetings again. The group that's planning the Dr. King visit."

Helen inwardly let out a sigh of relief. "Of course you may!" she exclaimed. "There's a meeting tomorrow night. Shall I bring you to the campus as before?" *How wonderful!* Helen thought. *She is ready to try again!*

"No, I think I can get myself there," Fleur replied. "What time should I get there?"

"Seven o'clock. This will be wonderful. At just the right time, too. Dr. King's visit will be very important for the campus. The town too, I think."

"Yes, I'm anxious to hear him speak." Fleur smiled, and Helen Ransom was relieved she hadn't misjudged her instincts. The girl was coming around. And just in time. She couldn't wait to tell Earl.

"Will I see you there tomorrow night?" Fleur asked Helen.

"Yes. Yes, I'll be there." *Of course* I'll be there, Helen said to herself. *With bells on.*

Russell William

It was another stiffed-back meeting in the living room of the Williams's home. Russell banished his younger children to the upstairs again, while he, his wife, and Fleur sat in their same positions relative to their guest—Mrs. Helen Ransom. How could he be both irritated and receptive to her intrusion into their lives? He shifted uncomfortably in his chair. Mrs. Ransom dispensed with her sports small talk this time and launched right in.

"I gather Fleur has told you the reason for my visit," she said.

"She has," Russell replied for them all.

"The college would like to offer Fleur a full scholarship to attend Hamel next fall."

"How was this decided?" asked Russell. "Fleur has not applied."

"The college has special funds donated by benefactors to aid in the recruitment of students from untraditional backgrounds."

"Is that what we are? An untraditional background?" Russell caught himself before saying more.

"Pardon me," Helen replied. "I should have said families for whom college has not usually been within their reach."

"And why Fleur? Surely there are many young folk you could choose from."

"I recommended her. I have come to know your daughter over the past year, and I believe she has shown remarkable initiative and growth during this time. Her grades from last semester are well within what is required for acceptance."

"So you know about her grades," Russell replied and allowed some silence to take up the uncomfortable pause. He continued, "We have discussed this before when we allowed Fleur to go to the orientation last summer. We do not know what the details and conditions are of this scholarship. Would you please tell us?"

Mrs. Ransom spoke at length about the usual cost of tuition, fees, and books and how the scholarship would cover those.

"It does not cover room and board—living on the campus—Fleur would be a day student. But she would be able to participate in all student and campus activities of her choosing."

"And what if she is not the student you hope her to be?" Russell asked, noting Fleur's expectant, hopeful face from the corner of his eye.

"The scholarship is renewable each year for up to four years depending upon a minimum grade level. If she falters, which is rare, there are academic advisors to help, and she is given a semester to improve her grades."

Russell saw that Helen Ransom was trying very hard. "And at the end of four years?" he asked. Russell was looking for some catch, something to justify his distrust.

"Fleur would graduate with a bachelor's degree in her major, which she would have to declare in her second year."

"Does Fleur have to apply for this scholarship?" It was almost like they were fencing.

"My recommendation will be accepted, but, yes, Fleur does have to fill out some forms and formally register."

"Does the scholarship have to be paid back?"

"No, not under any circumstances."

Some more silence. Finally, Russell asked his daughter, "Fleur, what is your interest in this offer?"

"I want to learn more. I think college would help me."

"Didn't high school teach you enough?"

"No, sir."

"Many high schools have a dismal record of steering only some of their students toward higher education," Mrs. Ransom interjected.

"Is it your view that everyone should go to college? High school was enough for me and Fleur's mother."

"I believe everyone should have the chance to go. Each must earn their own place in the classroom, of course, but . . ."

"But what?"

"Many public schools set the pathway for their students based on factors other than their capacity to learn."

This last remark chipped away at Russell's innate distrust. *That's the most sensible thing she's said yet,* thought Russell to himself.

"You mean they track students based on their color," he replied to her. A statement, not a question.

"Yes. That's what I mean," Helen replied.

Some more silence. Mathilde spoke up. "Fleur can continue to worship at Holy Trinity?"

"Of course. There are many Catholic students on campus who go to services at Holy Trinity," Helen replied. "She could join them."

Russell saw that his wife's politeness barely covered up her fear.

"The campus interfaith council works with Father Halligan to make sure Catholic students continue their worship at Holy Trinity. Fleur could actually be helpful in that regard," Helen offered.

Russell felt the fight in him ebbing. This was an excellent opportunity for his daughter, how could he not support it? But his distrust of white people lingered. What they gave could be taken away. And why must it come from their hands and not his?

"This is an important decision, and there is a great deal to discuss," Russell said. "We thank you very much for your time."

"One more thing," Helen Ransom added. "Dr. Ransom and I would like very much for Fleur to accompany us to the Rev. Dr. Martin Luther King Jr. speech on campus. She has been a helpful voice of the community to the student committee that is planning it."

Russell bristled inwardly. *Damn this woman!* he thought. *I want to appreciate her but then she goes and does something like that! There is no way I'm going to let that woman take the place of her mother and father. If Fleur goes, she goes with her family.*

"We will discuss it," promised Russell, and their meeting was over.

After Helen Ransom departed, Russell turned on Fleur and demanded, "What's this about you being helpful to the student committee on campus? You don't go there yet!"

"Daddy, I . . ."

"I guess you haven't been going to the library to do your homework, have you?"

Fleur blushed and shook her head.

"What is that student group doing besides inviting Reverend King to speak? What are you telling them as a 'young voice of the community?' How to shop for china?"

A few tears silently fell down Fleur's cheeks. Russell's stare had the full authority of a displeased parent, but he surprised her.

"I guess we better talk about what it is you want to learn. But not tonight. I'm tired." Russell turned away and went upstairs.

FEBRUARY 5, 1964

Mario Sposeto

A winter storm dumped six inches of wet, slushy stuff on the town two days ago, but today was balmy and breezy. Blue sky and sunshine melted the snow and rivulets ran down the gullies in front of Mario Sposeto's barbershop. He shoveled the last of the icy residue off his sidewalk and sprinkled sand for good measure. He didn't want any of his peanut gallery slipping and falling, the dear old knuckleheads. As if on cue, the first one—Salvador Guiliati—rounded the corner and teetered his way to Mario's outstretched arm. He helped him in, sat him down in one of the chairs, and asked "Cheeks or pecker?" They roared, and the day began.

The buzz about the Rev. Dr. Martin Luther King Jr. visit had been building, and tonight was the night. *This is like any other ordinary day,* Mario told himself, but he couldn't shake the vein of irritation that showed up as a headache. He finally raised it with his regulars.

"You going to hear that guy speak tonight?" Mario asked anyone.

"What guy? That moolie?" Tootie Manzone answered.

"Yeah, the moulinyan."

"What does he have to say to an old fart like me? Like I don't know discrimination? The nerve of some of them. Let them get real jobs and work for what they need like everyone else. Nobody here got a free ride. Why should they?" Tootie pointed out the worst examples he could think of, then added, "I don't hear the priests telling us we should be doing something different, only that pretty-boy president of the college."

It went on like this, each man alternating his story of hardship when he first arrived with how Black people should conduct themselves. It was unanimous—they had struggled mightily to overcome WASP disdain of Italians, now Black people had to do the same. Don't expect anybody to give you anything. Don't ask for favors. All agreed that the ambitions of Reverend King, of Hamel, of its president, Earl Ransom, would come to naught. Not to worry, it's all going to blow over. They began to leave for lunch.

"The wife's making me melanzane for dinner. Anybody want some? We'll eat those eggplants," said Salvator as he left, and everyone guffawed.

Mario assumed only outsiders would answer Earl Ransom's invitation, but his afternoon crowd was different. The businessmen, the mothers with their children, the high school and college boys—they were interested in Rev. King's visit. One was going. One said he regarded it as an historic occasion. One said it would be alright, but thank God they didn't invite Malcolm X.

Mario tended to his sidewalk again before closing up for the day. He noticed increased foot traffic in the town, coming from the train station and the bus stops. It was too early for workers from the city to be getting home. *Here come the outsiders*, he said to himself as they turned on Main and headed up Ridgewood on foot to the campus. He congratulated himself on his prediction, that it would be mainly outsiders flocking to hear the Dr. Rev. Martin Whatever come to tell them what to do, how to be. So secure was he in his opinion, he put out of his mind the other worry that had been gnawing within. There had been some talk, just whiffs, of attempts to integrate barbershops in northern Jersey and Camden. He felt sure the law was on his side, but he wasn't looking for this sort of fight.

He sprinkled one last dusting of sand on the sidewalk in case there was a freeze overnight. As he did so, he saw one of Roy Cassert's car service sedans go by. It was full. And it wasn't one of his usual drivers, it was Roy himself at the wheel. As they turned the corner, Mario got a better look. It was Rev. King and two of his lieutenants in the back seat. "What the hell?!" said Mario to the empty air, as the car turned in the direction of Hamel campus.

Fleur Williams

It was dark and cold when they left the house. Fleur asked to drive the family to the campus, claiming she knew the roads better, but her father would not allow it. She was annoyed at his stubbornness.

"You think I don't know my way in and out of that place?" Russell Williams barked at his daughter.

"No, Daddy, I don't think . . ."

"You aren't the only one in this family to step foot on a college campus."

"I know, Daddy . . ."

"Then it's settled."

He was making such a big deal out of this family excursion, insisting it was all his idea to begin with. Fleur didn't care if anybody else in her family came to the King speech tonight, but her father was taking his role as the head of the family a little too far. Why should he make LuLu and Charlie go? They're just stupid kids and won't pay attention. And why make her mother go? She doesn't need another late night, or the two cranky kids to keep in line.

Why didn't they all stay home and just let her go by herself and sit with Mrs. Ransom and the others? She thought that was exactly why her father insisted it be just their family together.

"I can find myself to a gymnasium," he told Fleur.

So could hundreds of other first-time visitors to the campus. When Fleur left work that day, she saw several Black families from out of town leaving the train station and walking the mile to the campus. More people walking around, more cars on the streets. More Black people walking through town.

"I bet they get a seat," muttered Fleur to herself.

At home, her father had barked his orders at everyone. He insisted they all have dinner just regular as always, and then clean up the kitchen too. Fleur said they should get there early, they should skip the dishes, or better yet, just skip dinner—were any of them starving? Russell admonished Fleur and advised no back talk or she'd find herself the only member of the Williams family not at the King speech that night. He was really worked up about making this a family thing and his idea and all. She put on her impassive face, like she'd seen her mother do many times, and just let him have his way. She just made sure the kitchen was cleaned up as fast as possible after an unbelievably slow eating of hamburger stew.

"Why we gotta go out?" Charlie whined.

"We're going to see a king," Russell chided, trying to lighten the mood. "He's all the royalty we Black folks got, so we better go see him."

"Will he wear a crown?"

"No."

"Then how do we know he's a king?"

They pulled into the back entrance of the campus. Fleur directed him toward the visitor parking lots, only to see barricades and men with flashlights directing traffic to the other side of the main hall. It was seven forty. Russell rolled down his window, and the cold night air came inside.

"Can't we pass through?"

"The parking lots are all full," said a volunteer directing traffic. "You'll have to park on the field over there. Follow that line of cars."

"On the practice field? That can't be good, it'll get all rutted up."

"There's no more parking up here, sir."

"Daddy, please!!"

"Now you hush, Fleur!" He turned the car around and steered it behind a line of red tail lights bumping their way down a small rise and onto the practice field.

"This is very bad for the turf. All those boys going to be tripping over these ruts we put into here. Gonna take a couple of wet springs to smooth these out. Hope they pay the doctor bills for those players who going to break their legs."

"Daddy, please hurry!"

"I'm not going to rip up this practice turf, king or no king." Russell slowly drove onto the field, and, with the greatest consideration for football players and track athletes he would never know, parked the lumbering Buick in line along with several dozen others.

Fleur was out of the car and gathering LuLu and Charlie into her anxious outstretched arms to save precious seconds. "Please let there be seats left," she said under her breath. She took charge of their defile and held onto LuLu and Charlie by their hands and marched up from the practice field, her mother and father following. Once up on the road again, she quicken their pace even more. She wanted nothing more than to get to the gymnasium in time.

When they arrived it was seven minutes before eight o'clock. There was a crowd outside the gym doors and some confusion as people jostled. There was no formal line that she could see. In a way she had never done before with her parents, she took charge, handed the two younger children over to her mother, and told her father to wait. She made her way toward

189

the door and saw several of the CRAC students acting as hosts at the door. Fleur recognized them and asked, "Are we too late for seats?"

"I'm afraid so," said a young woman. "It was full almost a half hour ago."

"Oh! Nothing inside? I'm here with my family; we just got here."

"We're sending people to the student center and the science auditorium. They've got an intercom set up."

"It's full over there now too," the other student corrected.

"Oh!" cried Fleur again, disappointed and vexed.

"How many of you together?"

"There's five of us."

"Are you willing to stand?"

"Anything!" Fleur thought of the endless hours on her knees or standing in the warm stuffy church during Mass—they could surely stand.

"We're putting some people in the locker rooms," said the first student. "You should be able to hear pretty well, but you have to stand."

"Wait, I'll go get them!"

Fleur wheeled around and made her way back to her family, who had taken a turn for the crabbier. She grabbed Charlie's and LuLu's hands and beckoned her parents with her eyes to follow her. They were brought around to one of the side doors, then through the gym. As they hurriedly walked down a path between the folded chairs set up on the basketball court, Fleur, Russell, and Mathilde all noticed the packed bleachers, the stage set up with the American and New Jersey flags, the filled seats everywhere. The hall was buzzing with people's conversation; there must have been a couple thousand people there. Fleur had no idea Rev. King's speech would be greeted with this much curiosity or enthusiasm.

Fleur and her family arrived at the boy's locker room, the girl's already full with another fifty people crowded near the doors that opened to the gym. LuLu pointed at the urinals and laughed, but her mother gave LuLu and Charlie her evil eye and commanded their better behavior. Soon the locker room was full with fifty more people crowded in. Charlie and LuLu and several others sat on the benches, while everyone else stood near the doors so they could listen.

From there Fleur looked out into the gym. It was more full than at any other time in its history. She saw some families from school, some customers from work, some of her teachers, but mostly people she didn't know. At the other end of the gym she could see the raised stage set up with several chairs and a podium. There was a roped-off area on the left side in the front with about six rows of seats. *That's where I could have been*, thought Fleur. It was full now with other people. She could see Mrs. Ransom sitting in the front row talking with others beside her.

In the next moment, she saw Dr. Ransom enter from the left and ascend to the stage. Several others came out and joined Mrs. Ransom in the front row. Fleur was just happy they had made it in time.

Now the gymnasium was quiet, and Dr. Ransom was at the podium. Squeals and squeaks and pops pierced the dead air as Dr. Ransom and the sound engineer tested the microphone. Everyone waited patiently. And then—

"Good evening, everyone . . ."

Dr. Ransom thanked all involved, greeted special guests, described how the evening would proceed, and then began his introduction of Rev. King. Then a man strode out from the side and arrived at the podium to great applause, everyone on their feet. Russell and Mathilde applauded too.

He's short, thought Fleur, amazed that this big-hearted, big-profile famous person came up only to the shoulder of Dr. Ransom. *So short*.

And he began, his sonorous voice immediately recognizable, immediately wending its way into all those in the room. Although he was short, it seemed as though his entire body was a megaphone that amplified every word he spoke. There was more sound, more vibration, more meaning and resonance to every word and gesture. She could see—no, feel—that he was a powerful speaker. No priest or principal or politician could compare.

He spoke. And for the next fifty minutes, the people listened.

The sound of his voice captured Fleur's imagination, so much that she found herself lost among his phrases, not grasping everything he said. Rev. King spoke of philosophy, religion, history. He spoke in poetic cadence that delighted her. He used words she didn't understand— *filibuster, agape, creative maladjustment*. But full round sounds emanated from his chest and poured like honey through his lips and into the air! She looked around to see if he was having the same effect on others. It appeared so. Her father looked alert and pensive. Her mother concentrated and nodded her head every so often. All the grown-ups around seemed caught up in Rev. King's talk—the sound or the words themselves, she could not tell, but all—even Charlie and LuLu—gave their focus and respect to this short man with the powerful voice. The rhythm of his sentences, the way he modulated his voice, his arm flung out in pointed gestures. It was a remarkable and complicated performance.

"The American Dream," he said, "is an unfulfilled dream." So, thought Fleur, she's not alone in having an unfulfilled dream, everyone has dreams, and there is potential within everyone everywhere. She thought her social studies class should consider this speech.

"The clock of destiny is ticking out."

Thrilling, but she wasn't sure what it really meant. And a world perspective? She wondered, *What is that? How does it work?* The speech was an English, history, philosophy, and science lesson. Eros, Friendship, Agape. Plato's yearning of the soul for the realm of the divine. Fleur saw her mother begin to nod at "agape" and "death of the spirit."

There was lots of religion talk, and she wondered how her father was faring with it. The heat of the crowded room began to get to her, she grew sleepy, and just as she found herself doubting, asking herself how making a speech helps, the words "an action program" rang out. She saw her father getting interested, saw him shift his weight back and forth like he does when watching a ballgame or a horse race.

Rev. King talked about men, "all men," and "brothers," and "brotherhood." It wasn't until he was close to the end when he said, "Men of goodwill, women of goodwill," that Fleur realized it was the first time she saw herself in his words, that they might include her in their promise. But what can she possibly do? About fair housing? About poverty in other lands? And she didn't really understand the role of legislation; she was never given a civics class.

"Things are still happening . . ." he intoned, ". . . students by the thousands . . . employment discrimination . . . register Negro voters . . . the philosophy of nonviolence."

Fleur was embarrassed to not understand everything he said and was now glad she was not seated in the reserved section with Mrs. Ransom and the others. All of a sudden everyone was clapping. What did she miss? It was not the end, but a pause because he had said something so wonderful that people began to applaud. It was urging passage of the Civil Rights Bill.

Aristotle. Plato. More philosophers. She didn't understand how the philosophy of nonviolence worked. What did her parents think? She imagined her mother must admire it, for she saw Mathilde slowly nodding with her eyes closed. It was sort of a Catholic idea. She imagined her father favors it less so.

Fleur stood between her parents as Rev. King explained the love ethic at the center of a nonviolent movement. She didn't understand this, and saw that her parents, and others, were perplexed or had their doubts. Fighting violence with love. How could that work? But it is the proximity of these three, the position of Fleur, confused, between her two parents, that is the promise of progress. None of them understood yet how they were going to get to that fulfilled American Dream Rev. King spoke of. None of them knew what they would be called upon to do.

The speech was over, and Rev. King answered some questions. Then Dr. Ransom concluded the evening with more remarks. There was more picture-taking and handshakes. People began to filter out of the locker rooms, only to run into the larger crowd in the gym making their way out through the two side doors. Mathilde jostled LuLu and Charlie to attention, and sleepy with crabbiness, they made their way out of the locker room to wait their turn at the exit doors.

Once outside, the cold air refreshed them all and they walked quickly to their old Buick, each quiet and in their own thoughts. LuLu and Charlie were sleepwalking mostly, still in their dreams of wild horses and trucks. They complained of the time, the cold, the walk, the hour and were quietly ignored.

Fleur saw that her father was lost in his own thoughts, but he surfaced just in time to guide her mother around a pothole in the drive. "Watch it, Tilly," he said, and he grabbed the sleeve of her coat and pulled her toward him. In a playful nature Fleur rarely saw, he drew his wife close with his right arm while his left encircled her waist and lifted her sailing over the pothole. Her mother uttered a surprised sound—part surprise, part delight—and then they both bent their heads in and laughed softly.

Fleur watched her parents ahead, saw her brother in her peripheral vision, and felt her sister's presence by her side. They walked this way, not knowing what would happen next, to themselves, to the world, to all the Black and white people in the land and in their town. The old Buick woke up like a large sleepy animal and crawled off the practice field. It felt like a magic carpet ride. They soon pulled into their driveway, and her father turned off the ignition. Fleur and Charlie opened their doors when Russell called, "Wait!"

The strength of his voice, without harshness, without criticism, alerted them that something was new. They gave their father their full attention. Russell turned to face his three children in the back seat. Only his door remained ajar to allow the little ceiling light to cast its small glow.

"We heard a good speech tonight."

"Yes, sir, we did," murmured Charlie, with no prompting or nudging from anyone. "He's a king alright."

"Amen," concurred Mathilde.

Fleur registered this moment as an important one, though the time demanded that they all now tumble out of the car, go into their home and to bed. Fleur fell asleep thinking of Rev. King's speech.

"An action program."

"Moral ends through moral means."

"The hour is late and the clock of destiny is ticking out."

She fell asleep, wondering when the alarm clock would beckon her awake.

Father Halligan

Father Halligan shifted in his seat in the confessional. Saturday afternoon, the time his flock confessed their litany of sins before the sacrament of the Holy Eucharist at Sunday Mass. There was never a lull during his two-hour shift; they came one after another, with the same sins, the same remorse. Theft, infidelity, cursing, disobedience. "Bless me Father for I have sinned. It has been one week, one month, one year since my last confession . . ." He gave them a penance. He absolved them all.

"Dominus noster Jesus Christus te absolvat; et ego auctoritate ipsius te absolvo ab omni vinculo excommunicationis et interdicti in quantum possum et tu indiges. Deinde ego te abslovo a peccatis tuis in nomine Patris, et Filii, et Spiritus Sancti. Amen."

He knew his flock, each individual sheep, their wayward steps. His divine duty was to shepherd them through their dark valleys, instruct them to be better sheep. He preserved the anonymity of the confessional box, but he knew who they were and what they did. He closed the window on one sinner and opened it on the next. *A young girl, that Williams girl. Well, let's see what she has to say.*

"Bless me Father for I have sinned. Please hear my confession and absolve me."

"Tell me your sin." A pause. "Speak, child, you are with God."

"I don't know if I have sinned," came the small voice.

"If you think you may have sinned and you are here to seek absolution, then it is a sin. God sees all, so speak your sin and be redeemed."

"I want to know why some things are sins and some aren't."

"This is a question more for the classroom, not the confessional," Father Halligan impatiently intoned.

"If I tell you something I thought of, will you tell me if it was a sin?"

"Go ahead," and he let out a big sigh.

"Is it a sin to think about other churches?"

"It depends. In what way do you think about them? Do you want to join another church? Tell me specifically your own thoughts and actions in this."

"I've been thinking how some things feel more church-like to me than actually going to church."

"Go on."

"Like hearing someone tell his thoughts and beliefs."

"Are they against the Church's beliefs?"

"I don't think so, he is a preacher too, but a lot of people in our church don't like this person."

"The Holy Mother Church of Rome has had many detractors. What does this preacher say about Our Lord?"

"Oh, he's a believer, alright. He praises the Lord and asks for His mercy and blessing. But he is not Catholic. His church is not ours. It's not even in a building. I think it's bigger."

Father Halligan shifted his weight again, and this time it was like gravity moving. He straightened, pulled his shoulders back, readied himself. Too bad his opponent, the Devil, chose a young foolish girl who likely didn't know what she was talking about and had no idea who was really behind her questions. But he knew—he'd jousted with this demon before. And here was another practice round. *All right then*, he thought, *I'm ready for you.*

He peppered the Williams girl with questions and didn't wait for her answers. He told her, lectured her, declaimed, and argued. He raised his voice, and the girl, trapped by the etiquette of the confessional, knelt there and listened and replied in one-word answers to his demands to know of her particular engagement with the devils of other churches. Did she attend services elsewhere? Did her parents know of her wandering thoughts? Did she attend the catechism classes? Well, she better start again and lay bare her soul and her confusion to good Sister Emily, who will set her straight. Did she take communion elsewhere? Confess all now and she would be forgiven, absolved, snatched back from the Devil himself, for certainly that is who's behind these dangerous thoughts. Did she know that? Well, you know it now, little missy, and for your penance you are to recite five complete rosaries and perform five stations of the cross. Contemplate the crucifixion of Our Lord and understand He withstood His own murder so foolish girls could have foolish thoughts and yet still be redeemed in time.

"Go in peace." Father Halligan abruptly shut the mesh window on her side. But before he turned and opened the window to the next confessor, he took a moment to dab his forehead. He'd been louder than he ought. But he hoped he scared some sense into her and whomever else out there waiting their turn.

That's their third mistake, he said to himself, thinking of the Williams family. It was imperative that he get her back into catechism classes. He didn't like the way this was headed.

Fleur Williams

The night of Rev. King's speech and several more nights thereafter, Fleur sought the library of her bed, the encyclopedia of her pillow. The sonorous tone and cadence of Rev. King's voice played over and over in her head as she tried to understand. It would help if she could read a transcript of the speech—maybe the school would have one. Maybe it would be published in the newspaper; she would look for it. She wasn't troubled, more restless. She knew there was more than she had taken in. She felt like she was already in college, ready to discover whatever there was for her in this famous man's words. Had she been able to go out with the CRAC students after the speech, she would have heard them dissect his speech and what they thought it meant. Maybe at their next meeting, just a few days away.

Fleur knew she had had some sort of experience that she could not put into words. It felt like what she was supposed to feel like in church. She decided to ask her mother.

"What church is the Rev. King from?" she asked her mother.

"The Ebenezer Baptist Church in Atlanta, Georgia."

"Is there one of those here?"

"No."

"But he's a religious man?"

"Oh yes. But not of our church."

"Does it matter?"

"Does going to heaven matter?"

"Mom."

"What do you want to know, ma 'tite," asked Mathilde, not without affection.

"Do we believe in the same things?"

"Mostly. But the details matter. They matter to a lot of people. People fight wars over details."

"This isn't a war."

"Not yet."

"I just . . . it sounded like a prayer when he talked, Mom."

"I thought it sounded like a sermon."

"That too. But Mom . . . you listened. I watched you and Dad."

"There's a difference between a prayer and a sermon. Prayer seldom rouses public passions."

"What did Rev. King's speech mean to you?"

"The Rev. King's speech was a fine speech, and it was a sermon, and a lot of people are going to talk and do things about it, and some will get into trouble. I am more interested in prayer and grace."

"You and Dad are different that way."

"Like night and day, child."

A few days later, Fleur made her monthly confession. She took out the black lace doily she kept in her purse and pinned it to her hair, opened the heavy side door, and went to the side pews by the confessionals. The light was on—a priest was there—and one man before her. Usually she was anxious about making confession, but this time she was curious and sought a dialog, if not answers. Her turn arrived and she entered the confessional. The mesh screen slid open; she felt the heavy presence of God.

"Bless me Father for I have sinned. It has been four weeks since my last confession," Fleur began.

"Tell me your sin." It was Father Halligan.

She paused, then he impatiently urged, "Speak, child, you are with God."

It went sideways from the very start. She may not have sought forgiveness for something she wasn't even sure was a sin, but she hadn't sought an argument. God fought her in the confessional, turned her questions against her, upbraided her thought that Rev. King had a kingdom too. The only interpretation for what Fleur felt was that Satan had many forms. She knew the harshness of the Catholic faith, its beautiful edges, even some of its decency and piety. But she never experienced such an excoriation, not even by the most severe nuns when she was in grade school.

"Go in peace," Father Halligan said and abruptly shut the mesh window on her side and opened the one on the other side.

Peace? Flushed, confused, regretful, and a little angry, Fleur exited the confessional and was mortified to see eight people waiting in the pews who had no doubt heard the priest's harangue. She sidled off to a side altar and knelt to say one Hail Mary and one Our Father—nowhere close to the full penance she was given. And she never would.

Maybe she would find someone she could talk to at school. She had seen a few of her classmates and teachers there. She decided to approach Mlle. Richert, her French teacher, who was so young many thought she was one of the senior students. After French class, Fleur lingered and tried to ask her question in French.

"*Etes-vous allé au discours* Dr. King?" she asked in halting French.

"*Mais oui,*" replied Mlle. Richert.

"*Que-c'est se pense vous?*"

"*Etait magnifique. Et vous, Fleur, que-c'est se pense vous?*"

"*Je suis en train de le comprendre.*"

"*Bravo.*"

"Can I ask you something in English?" Fleur asked.

"Go ahead."

"What do you think we are supposed to do?"

"A lot of people in this school, in your town, don't want you to do anything," was her teacher's matter-of-fact reply.

"What do you think, ma'am?"

"We are overdue for a new American Dream. I think that's what he meant."

"How do we do this?"

"'An action plan.' I think you should think about what you want to do, Fleur."

"Nobody's ever asked me that," replied Fleur, knowing that wasn't quite true. Mrs. Ransom had.

"No kidding. Not this school. Not the Catholic Church. Sorry Fleur, I don't mean to disrespect your church, but there is a great deal of Catholic history you don't know yet."

"Like what?"

"How far back do you want to go?"

"I don't know. I just know the lives of the saints."

"I have an idea. Here, take this. It's a book of poetry by Carbet, a Martinique writer. You won't understand all of it, it's for advanced classes, but work your way through it slowly, a word at a time if you need to."

Fleur looked over the slim volume, *Point d'Orgue,* "I don't think I can understand most… ."

"Don't worry. Just take the book. Keep it. Take it one sentence at a time. Just start."

And Fleur did. She started.

SPRING 1964

Mario Sposeto

Mario Sposeto shouldn't have been surprised that his barbershop was targeted for the first demonstration. Picketers could easily be noticed from Main Street whether people were driving through or walking. But he was surprised. Even though there had been murmurs about a demonstration here in Jamestown, Mario ignored them. Here in Jamestown, where everybody knew how to get along. It just didn't square.

No one was denying anybody a haircut. They had their barbers and we had ours, thought Mario, enough business for everybody. Why was some Black kid who wasn't even from around here trying to get a haircut in his shop when there was a Black shop not three blocks away? Of course it was outsiders behind this, had to be from the college campus, he bet, those pointy-headed troublemakers who only knew how to talk and tell other people how to live. What sort of work did they do? He lay it squarely at the feet of that college president who invited more and more outsiders to talk to anyone who would listen about how the Black people were so oppressed.

Oppressed! What a joke. The Black people he saw either had jobs and worked hard or they were lazy good-for-nothings who drank and dropped babies everywhere. Oppression had nothing to do with it. The way he saw it, you worked hard and paid your own way like anybody else—white, Black or blue—and if you didn't, well, sorry brother that wasn't his fault and it certainly wasn't oppression. Black people didn't want to mix with whites any more than whites wanted to mix with them. It was one thing to nod hello to someone on the street. But they had their own businesses, just like they had their own churches and music and way of life. They were a different people and weren't meant to mix; he was sure Jesus Christ would back him up on that.

Mario smirked a little thinking how the Black barbershop in the area must be losing business to him. It was one thing to have Negroes come to the white shops and expect to be served, but if they thought whites would reciprocate and patronize the Negro shops, they were very mistaken. He figured he was doing them a favor by refusing service to this young Black man standing so insolently before him.

"I told you, I can't cut your hair," said Mario firmly.

"But I made an appointment. This is the time and day of my appointment."

"I don't care if you have twenty appointments, I ain't gonna cut your hair."

"Why not?"

Mario looked him over. About twenty years old, tall, clean-shaven. Not from around here.

"I don't have the right tools." Mario's group of regulars who had remained dumbfounded until now rippled with stifled laughter.

"What sort of tools do you need to cut my hair?" asked the determined would-be customer.

Mario wanted to be rude right back at this troublemaker. Maybe a lawnmower, he thought to himself. Or hedge shears. Or wire cutters.

"Don't know. Why don't you see if Roy Atkins has the right equipment to cut your type of hair."

"You aren't going to give me a haircut?"

"No, I am not."

Silence for a few moments, all the men sizing each other up. Mario noticed that the Black man had not come alone; there were several others outside on the sidewalk, and there were white people with them too. He didn't recognize any of them—students, and maybe one of their professors.

The young Black man turned to those outside the door and called out to them. "Did you hear him? He's not going to give me a haircut." They nodded but kept quiet. "Well sir, I'm sorry you feel that way. But I made an appointment with you and I came for my haircut. It's within my rights to have a haircut in your shop."

Mario inwardly fumed. "Listen, I don't want any trouble here. Your friends, my friends—none of us want any trouble. Why don't you just go over to Roy's and get your haircut there?"

"Because I'm here for my appointment now."

"An appointment's got nothing to do with it. I'm not going to cut your hair."

"Why not?"

"Look, I'm asking you to leave. You and your friends, please leave now."

"Not until I have my haircut."

What should he do now? Mario could feel the eyes of his regulars staring at him from behind, waiting to see how he'd react. He looked outside and saw a small group of people—most likely from the college—standing on the sidewalk. He didn't recognize anyone. Outsiders. He decided to be cool about this.

"I'm asking you one more time to please leave."

The young man stayed put.

"OK, wise guy," Mario stated, "you leave me no choice."

Mario walked over to his telephone, picked up the receiver, and dialed the number of the Jamestown police station. He spoke softly then paused and nodded while listening to the response from the other end. The others heard and knew he had called the police and asked them to come by. Mario returned and folded his arms across his chest and addressed the young man.

"Police will be here soon. Do you still want to stay?"

The young man didn't reply but looked over to his companions nearby, made eye contact, then crossed his arms and stood his ground. It was quiet like that for several minutes, nobody moving, nobody saying anything, just waiting. Mario saw that the group outside had grown a little bigger, passersby stopped to see what was going on. He recognized a few, including that Black girl the Kraut jewelers had hired. "That's when all this started," he reasoned to himself. "Thinking they belong everywhere on Main Street."

Two Jamestown police officers arrived in their deep-blue shirts and badges, cuffs, black holster. Mario spoke to them, explained the dilemma and reiterated several times that the young man, who stood silent in the shop, refused to leave. The policemen asked the young Black man to leave, and again he refused. The police took Mario aside and they talked among themselves for a while, then parted again. When they returned to where the young man stood, the police calmly informed him that he would have to leave with them. By now a larger crowd was out on the sidewalk looking in the windows

"Am I being arrested?" the young man asked.

Nobody really wanted to arrest this guy. They just wanted to get him to leave Mario's shop and go back to wherever he came from. They wanted to shoo the gawkers along and divert attention away from this sorry little episode of defiance. *For what?* they wondered. *What did this have to do with equality?*

"Listen," said one of the policemen, "we don't have to book you with anything if you just go of your own accord, but soon as we put our arms on you, you'll be charged."

"Go ahead, take me in."

Mario wondered; the police wondered; Mario's regulars wondered: *What's with this guy? What's he trying to prove, that he can get arrested?* They had no idea what was ahead for all of them.

The police put cuffs on the young man and led him outside. Some among the crowd outside immediately cried out their objections.

"What are you charging him with?"

"The boy just wants a haircut."

"End discrimination now!"

They followed the police as they placed the young man in the squad car for the three-block ride to the station. The police did not turn on lights or their siren. Others in the crowd wandered about seeking answers to their questions.

"Who was that?"

"Where's he from?"

"Was there a robbery?"

"Did they catch him with the money?"

Oh brother, thought Mario, now this is going to get all over town. As if by prophesy, a man emerged from the lingering crowd and came into the store to speak with Mario. "Can I ask you a few questions?" he asked, and that's when Mario saw the man's notebook and realized this had all been set up. And he'd been set up to take the fall for all the white shop owners in his decent little town.

"Get out of here," Mario growled, unleashing his pent-up anger at this reporter called into service, no doubt, by those pinheads on the campus. He regretted he did not hold onto his cool for a few minutes more, but this was too much. He'd done nothing wrong, nothing any other businessman in this town would have done, but for all the bad luck around, he was the one at the center of their target. He hadn't figured it out until after he tripped their snare. He yelled at the crowd outside. "Everybody from Hamel out! Go back to your campus! Learn something useful."

Mario tried to buck himself up and hold his own among his regulars. The knuckleheads animatedly replayed the whole episode among themselves and for the curious who gathered outside, amplifying Mario's and their own bravado with the "should've said" and "could've said" that never came out of their mouths. Mario felt sick in the pit of his stomach but didn't let this show. For his friends and regular customers, Mario was the hero of the hour, the man who stood strong in the face of that Black kid who wanted a haircut at the white shop instead of going to the one of his own kind. The conversation took a raw and ugly turn with suggestions of an extreme sort of haircut. Mario said little, allowing the others to vent for him. It had been a trap, and he didn't see it. What was next? What was going to happen next in this decent, miserable, stupid little town?

Elma Tanzer

Elma Tanzer reviewed her order for the china and silver distributor. Wedding season was coming up, and she wanted to carry more stock in the patterns chosen by the soon-to-be brides. Lenox "Rose" was always popular. "Eternal" was the budget-minded choice. "Buchanan," with its cobalt and gold rims, was as opulent as the society family that chose it for their debutant daughter. That young lady was probably going to get a full set for eight, maybe even twelve, so Elma doubled up on that pattern.

Although pleased that their business did well since their move to Jamestown, Elma and her husband were not immune to the tensions building in their town. The college campus was taking the brunt of it—"outside agitators" railed some of the other business owners. There was a regular picket line in front of Sposeto's barbershop, and people lined up their allegiances. Most Main Street merchants supported the credo that any business should be able to deny service based solely on their good judgment. The Tanzers mostly agreed with this, because how else are you going to deal with a drunk or a vagrant? But they knew the abuse of this sacred tenet of shopkeepers. They saw the subtle choreography of the town that would shun their own employee Fleur from patronizing their stores. An unwelcoming stare. Too abrupt service. Fleur gained entry only because she was on an errand for them.

"It is the same monkey business we had back home," her husband said. "Someone always trying to be bigger than the other, or grab more than they deserve."

Every town and city in Germany had their own "nobody's people," Blacks from the African colonies, who came for trade and opportunity, who became Germans. Their civil status deteriorated, especially between the wars. By the time the Tanzers left for America, Blacks were lumped in with Roma and Sinti. Then the Nuremberg Race Laws came for them too. Shame for her home country's treatment of Jews and racial minorities put the Tanzers at odds with some merchants on Main Street. When Fleur Williams walked into their store for the first time almost two years ago, she and her husband saw one of the "nobody's people," not one of the many derogatory names they heard for Blacks. So wrapped up in his repair work and engraving, her husband did not appreciate the sensitivity of Fleur working in their store. But Elma saw, and she wondered if they had contributed to the tension now building in their adopted town.

When Helen Ransom next came in, she lamented that whatever enthusiasm there was for Rev. King's visit was matched by disinterest or worse.

"I try so hard to bridge town and gown," whined Mrs. Ransom.

So irritating and meddlesome, thought Elma with an impassive face. *It's not a bridge, it's more like blowing up a bridge.* Then she wondered, *Could violence erupt here in Jamestown?* Would she and others be called to defend their 'nobody's people?'

Later that evening, Elma asked her husband what they would do if their store was picketed.

"Why would we be picketed? We don't deny service to anyone," he replied, a bit puzzled.

"No Negro people come to shop in our store now. But if they do?"

"We treat them as any other customer. Why wouldn't we? If they want to buy from us or get their watch repaired, that is fine."

"But they don't seem to want to buy from us or get their watches fixed," Elma ventured, getting at her real question. "They go elsewhere."

"Well, when they do come to us, we will welcome them."

Welcome them, thought Elma. That is the answer. To this and so many other problems. *What is gracious living for if not to welcome everyone?*

Fleur Williams

Fleur arranged to take the afternoon off of work; she told the Tanzers she had a dentist appointment. Instead she had an appointment at two thirty that afternoon at Renee's Beauty Spot for a haircut and styling. But Fleur wasn't after a new hairstyle, she didn't expect to get one. She was after a whole new Fleur.

Fleur chose this business because of its location—she had learned about the importance of location from the campus CRAC group. If they had planned this, this would be the one they'd have chosen. But they hadn't planned it, she did, impatient that her suggestions were always ignored and passed over.

She had looked through the telephone directory with a keen eye for their advertising distinctions and settled on Renee's Beauty Spot. She had a pretty good idea what sort of place it would be—a small neighborhood salon with two chairs for cutting, a sink for washing, and three dryer chairs. She thought a young person like her would not arouse anyone's suspicion.

When she called to make her appointment, she adjusted her voice slightly and said her name was Flora William.

She was acting alone. No one at the college, her parents, or anyone else knew what she was up too. She knew they would scold her, but maybe now they would take her seriously. Fleur thought herself heroic, and if she waited around for any of the others to include her in their plans, she might wait forever. "An action program," she remembered Rev. King saying during his speech. "A philosophy of nonviolence."

She was almost there. This was a white neighborhood, but it wasn't unusual to see Black women here—the cleaning ladies, housekeepers, and babysitters for some of the families on these blocks. Fleur walked up the stairs, opened the door, and entered the salon. A little bell rang. She stood in front of the reception stand. She was about to commit an act of civil disobedience and didn't know what the outcome would be. She might be getting herself into a lot of trouble: Surely she was going to make her parents upset; she might lose her job. She didn't know how people at school or church would react, but she thought it would not be a positive reaction. But the chance to break out of the background, to be somebody, made this worth this risk. She didn't want to hurt the people she loved, but she believed they would still love her. She didn't want to let down the people she respected, but if they did not return her respect for what she was about to do, that would mean something important between them must change. "No one knows what we will be called to do," Rev. King had said.

She stood there, and a young woman not much older than her came over. The young woman was heavily made-up and had a large bouffant hairstyle. She wore a pink work smock with her name embroidered on it—"Angela." Fleur had seen her at church but didn't know her.

Angela asked, "What can I do for you, girl?"

"I'm here for my appointment." It was two thirty sharp.

"What appointment would that be?" Angela asked with genuine puzzlement.

"For my haircut and styling."

Angela opened her mouth in surprise, then her face flushed and she began to narrow her eyes.

"Who are you?" she demanded.

"I'm Fleur Williams and I have a two thirty appointment."

Angela, flustered, quickly paged through the appointment book, taking more time than necessary to locate the afternoon's schedule. She looked around Fleur to see if there were any others outside, then to the back of the salon where her boss, Renee Phillips, was rolling a customer's hair and chatting amiably. Fleur saw that there were two other customers under the dryers. None of them had noticed her yet.

"Look," Angela trumpeted and rapped the counter with her ring to get Fleur's attention, "there's no appointment for a Fleur Williams."

"Flora William, I mean. That's my name, Flora William. Please check again."

Angela stared at her, and Fleur, nervous but resolved, stared back and smiled weakly.

"Listen, Flora or Fleur or whatever your real name is, you may have an appointment here, but we can't cut your hair," declared Angela.

"Why not?"

"You know exactly why not. Don't pull your little act on me. You can turn around right now and leave and nothing else has to happen."

"What if I stay to get my haircut?" Fleur asked.

"You aren't getting a haircut, not here anyway."

"Are you refusing me service?"

Angela colored and fumed. She turned without a word and went to tell Renee what was happening. Fleur saw Angela whisper something to Renee, who suddenly become alert. Without turning, Renee looked over her right shoulder at Fleur. Fleur watched Renee and Angela watch her and thought, *There's no turning back now.*

Now she saw two more pairs of eyes dart over to look at her—the ladies under the dryers. The woman whose hair Renee was rolling up stopped talking when she finally saw Fleur in the mirror. The two women turned off their dryers and lifted the hoods. Everything became silent. Everyone stared at her. Fleur watched Renee as she put down her scissors and comb and walked over.

"I understand you want a haircut," said Renee Philipps, the salon owner.

"Yes, ma'am. I have an appointment."

"Well, I can't serve you here, and I won't be honoring your appointment. I'm sorry for your inconvenience."

Fleur saw one of the dryer ladies, Mrs. O'Connor, also from church, nodding in silent agreement.

"Would you please leave now?" Renee thought to add.

Fleur countered, "I'm sorry, ma'am, but I came for my haircut and styling, and I'd like to have it."

Renee shook her head in disbelief, and she too looked out the front window, even opened the front door to look outside. She then returned to face her square on.

"Look, Fleur Williams, I'll give you just one minute to leave. Otherwise I'll call your mother and Father Halligan. I bet they won't be very happy to hear about what you're up to."

"It won't change anything," Fleur replied.

"Alright, Miss Know-It-All who doesn't know her place. What will it take to change this?"

"If you give me my haircut and styling."

"That is not going to happen."

"Then I'll just wait here until it does." Fleur walked over to an empty chair near the dryers and sat down and picked up a magazine. Renee stood in front of her with her hands on her hips, and Fleur buried herself in an article on "Family Friday Casseroles." She could smell the chemical nature of the beauty salon—dyes, bleaches, relaxers, perfumes all mixed together. She could feel Renee's stare burning into her. She was perspiring and her skirt was sticking to the leatherette chair. She heard Angela repeatedly dial the telephone in frustration. Busy signals no matter where she called. Finally, a call connected and Angela turned away to murmur low into the receiver, then she conferenced with Renee after the call finished.

"They said we should just handle it ourselves," Angela told Renee.

"Who said that?! Father Halligan?" Renee asked in disbelief.

"No, he was busy. It was one of the acolytes."

Fleur pretended to read but listened carefully to all the sounds. She heard the customers begin to gather their things. She heard Renee and Angela talk to them.

"I'll finish rolling you up and you can dry at home."

"So sorry for this, of course no charge."

"You can return the rollers next time."

"Who would have thought here in Jamestown?"

Fleur heard the door open and shut, and the little bell rang three times. All the customers would be gone now. There was a radio on in the background. Mary Wells was singing "My Guy." Finally she heard Renee's and Angela's heels on the floor coming closer. They stopped in front of her, and Fleur raised her eyes to see both of them towering over her with folded arms and scowls on their faces.

"Have you changed you mind yet, Fleur?" asked Renee.

Fleur looked them in the eyes and shook her head.

"Alright then, Fleur Williams, if this is the way you want it. But you're a disgrace to your family and the Church."

Renee turned to Angela and said, "Dial the police station please." Both women turned away and left her. Fleur heard Angela dial the phone, heard her ask for a police officer, for two. She sat there waiting, for what she didn't know. Sitting in that sticky chair, she heard Mary Wells sing confidently about how nothing could make her untrue. Fleur wished for that sort of confidence. "The clock of destiny is ticking out," she remembered from Rev. King's speech. "Time for a new American Dream." Whatever was going to happen, would happen soon. She sat and waited.

Helen Ransom

Helen Ransom looked around the room she was in. Pale-green paint, peeling at the ceiling, a radiator collecting dust in the corner, fluorescent lights casting their sickly pall. She hadn't expected to spend the afternoon in the Jamestown police station. Helen reflected on this surprising turn that happened no more than two hours ago. She didn't want to forget any part of it. She couldn't say who was more surprised—herself or Fleur.

A police officer stepped in with a cup of water. He pushed it across the table to her.

"We'd like to ask just a couple of questions, then you are free to go," he said.

"Go?" replied Helen. "I'm not going anywhere until you release that young girl."

"I'm sorry ma'am, but as you are not her parent, we can't speak to you about that."

"Well, I certainly don't have to speak with you either!" she retorted. "I'll stay here until I see that she is unharmed." She crossed her arms and turned her gaze elsewhere.

"As you wish, ma'am. But you are free to go." The officer left.

Helen replayed the sequence of unusual events from these past two hours, but really, it began much earlier. She'd had a feeling that Fleur was up to something. She knew Fleur was impatient with how the campus CRAC group ignored her input. It took a lot for the girl to speak up among them. She thought the CRAC would be more receptive to a local's point of view, but they weren't. The last time she saw Fleur, just a few days ago on campus, she seemed aloof and noncommittal about her work with CRAC. Helen never saw her on one of the picket lines, not unusual because she was still a minor, but she regularly came to their meetings. There was something a little evasive about Fleur's demeanor that day she last saw her. Evasive, but also dropping a little breadcrumb of a clue. She mentioned she was going to miss work one afternoon coming up because she had a dental appointment. Helen thought it an odd mention. When she looked at Fleur's face, she saw the telltale creases of a lie, familiar to her from her own children's dissembling. *What was the girl planning?* She made a mental note of the dental appointment date.

Helen wasn't proud of her suspicions, nor that she decided to follow Fleur discreetly from school on that appointed day. She drove around Jamestown that afternoon at the time she knew Fleur departed to go to her job. She saw her walking her usual route to downtown, but then she detoured into one of the north end neighborhoods. She saw Fleur stop and check an address on a piece of paper then continue. Fleur finally arrived at her destination—not a dental office, but a small beauty salon operated out of the front rooms of the owner's home—Renee's Beauty Spot. Helen parked her car half a block away and waited. Maybe it was nothing at all, but her instinct told her it was. It was two thirty in the afternoon.

After a few minutes, she saw a young woman poke her head outside the door of the beauty salon and look up and down the street, then retreat. Several minutes after that, an older woman did the same. A short time passed and then a succession of three older women left the salon in various stages of hair styling completion, some still in rollers. They were very animated, talking and gesticulating, angry. One walked by her parked car with a grim face, tying a kerchief over the hair rollers. But no sign of Fleur.

Helen began to put a scenario together. Why would Fleur go to a beauty salon in a white neighborhood? Now it began to make sense. *Brava*, Helen said to herself. *Well done. Why didn't I think of that?* Minutes ticked by with no sign of Fleur or anyone else. She began to worry, fueled by her protective maternal instinct as well as an insatiable curiosity about what was going on inside the Beauty Spot. *If I don't see her in five minutes, I'm going in.*

Helen peered into the small front door window. She could see nothing. She opened the door and heard a little electric jangle. She walked in and saw the owner and her employee standing over someone sitting in a chair, glowering with their hands on their hips. She heard the older woman say, "You're a disgrace to your family and the Church." The two women parted when Helen walked in and revealed a resolute Fleur Williams sitting defiantly, eyes straight ahead.

Renee Phillips turned to Helen and said, "I'm sorry but we've just had to close the salon. We aren't serving anyone at the moment."

"Is there some problem here?" asked Helen. Fleur looked up and her eyes widened when she saw Helen. Helen signaled approval to Fleur and repeated her question.

"I'm sorry, ma'am, maybe I can help you. Do you have an appointment? We'll have to reschedule it," asked the young woman with "Angela" embroidered on her smock.

"No, I've come to make an appointment. But I see you have a lot of empty chairs. Could you fit me in right now?"

"No, I'm afraid we can't. We've had to close unexpectedly."

"Whatever for?" said Helen looking around the salon in faux puzzlement.

Angela tried to draw Helen Ransom away from where Fleur sat. "Please step over here and I'll write you into our schedule."

"Are you sure you can't give me an appointment now? I just need a trim."

"Please, ma'am, come over here and I'll take care of you."

"Why, what's wrong with here?" Helen challenged.

Renee Phillips rose to Helen's bait. "What's wrong is that we're having an incident right now, and we've called the police to remove a customer who doesn't have an appointment at our establishment." She gestured to Fleur.

"You don't look terribly busy here. Why don't you give both of us our haircuts?"

"As I've explained, we're closed right now. Maybe I can help you with something else?"

"You can help me by giving this girl what she came in and asked for," Helen retorted. She glanced over at Fleur, who looked mortified.

Helen and Renee argued, raised their voices, while Angela stood helplessly off to the side.

"The police will be here soon. I suggest you leave now."

"If the police are going to take Fleur away, they are going to have to take me too." Helen sat in the chair next to Fleur, and they both stared ahead.

The police arrived in two squad cars. They asked what the problem was and tried to get both Fleur and Helen to leave on their own. Fleur refused, and Helen took her cue from her.

"Young lady," one policeman said to Fleur, "if you don't leave, we'll have to take you to the police station. You too, ma'am."

"I'm not going until I get my haircut," stated Fleur.

"Will you get up then and come with us?"

"You'll have to take me."

Helen watched as the two policemen positioned themselves on either side of Fleur. They hoisted her to her feet, and when Fleur refused to walk, they lifted her up under her arms and advanced to the door.

"Is that really necessary?" Helen raised her voice.

"Apparently it is, ma'am. Are we going to have to carry you too?"

"No, I'll walk. But you're taking me to the same place you're taking her."

Helen got up and intercepted Angela, who had gloves, a towel, and some disinfectant spray. She sprayed and wiped down the chair Fleur sat in.

"Don't forget to do mine," Helen said as she passed Angela. "Forget about that appointment," she tossed off to Renee.

"Gladly."

Outside, the police put Fleur in the first squad car, and as Helen tried to follow, they shut the door and led her to the next car. While the first car drove off, Helen protested.

"Where are you taking her?"

"Ma'am, I'll be happy to drop you off at home," said the remaining cop.

"Why would I want to do that?" Helen surprised herself with how quickly that came out of her mouth. "You're going to take me to the same place you are taking her!"

"Ma'am, I think it would be best if you just went home."

"I insist, you tin hat wop!" Helen meant her deliberate insult to antagonize the policeman so he would take her in. It worked.

There were no sirens, no handcuffs. Both cars arrived at the municipal building and went around to the back, where Fleur and Helen were escorted through the employee entrance. Fleur walked this time. Once inside, the police separated them and took Fleur down a hallway.

"Don't tell them anything!" Helen yelled after her. "Ask for your parents! You are a minor, they're not supposed to do anything to you! I'll be here, I'll stay!"

Helen was escorted to this dingy interview room and left alone. She was breathing shallowly and began to collect her thoughts. Her hunch had been right. *But what was going to happen to Fleur now?* Helen was free to go, but how could she go, not knowing what would happen to Fleur? And her next thought was, *Earl is going to kill me.*

After an hour of sitting alone in that dreary interview room with no sight of Fleur or anyone else, Helen wondered if indeed anyone else would know about this incident. Surely one of Fleur's parents should have been here by now. In the next minute, a policeman escorted in a familiar face—Earl.

"Darling, are you alright?" he asked with a worried expression.

"Of course I'm alright," Helen replied. "Why wouldn't I be?"

"The police told me you might need a ride home."

"Is that what they said? As if I had car trouble?"

"No. They told me about the incident with Fleur," Earl said.

"The incident—that's a nice, vague word."

"Well, can you fill me in?" he asked.

Helen recounted all she had seen, professed her own innocence at showing up at the right moment.

"But you never get your hair done there," said Earl.

"I was going to try a new place."

"Did you plan this with her?"

"I did not."

"Because if you did, that would put both you and I into a difficult situation," scolded Earl.

"Us in a difficult situation? What about Fleur? Who knows what's happened to her! Aren't you concerned about that?!"

"Of course I am. The girl shouldn't have acted alone, but you shouldn't have helped her."

"What about now? Shouldn't we help her now? Nobody is here for her." implored Helen.

"They've called her family."

"I'm going to wait right here until I know Fleur is alright."

"Let's go to the car."

"No! I said I'm waiting here until someone comes for her."

Helen knew her husband of twenty-five years could be a little aloof, but she'd never seen him heartless. This was such a surprising day.

"Then let's wait in the car," replied Earl, "I don't want us sitting here in the police station."

"Because someone might see us?"

"Please, Helen, I'm parked right in front. We can see anyone coming in or out. We'll wait for Fleur to come out there."

Earl and Helen Ransom walked through police reception without a word to any of the several policemen watching their exit.

Russell Williams

It was Charlie that answered the phone.

"Is this the Williams home?"

"Yes, sir."

"Can I speak to your mother or father?"

"Dad!" Charlie yelled. "Telephone!" as he ran back to his place in front of the television set.

"Hello," Russell said into the receiver, like a statement, not a question.

"Russell? This is Ken Burroughs down at the municipal building, at the police station."

Russell froze. No good ever came from phone calls from police stations.

"What can I do for you, Ken?"

It seemed like an eon before the reply during which Russell imagined nineteen different types of hell.

"It's Fleur. You need to come get her. We have her here."

Fleur? Now he imagined a twentieth. "What's the problem, Ken?"

"I'll fill you in when you get here, Russell."

He hung up the phone and went upstairs, rummaged through the second drawer of his bureau, and cupped his hand around an old tennis ball can. He removed five twenty-dollar bills and put them in his wallet.

Russell drove down to the municipal building and parked right in front of the police station where he would never otherwise park, but this was police business. With damp hands he set the emergency brake, pocketed his key, walked to the door, and stepped into police reception. He took it all in, the various men at their desks and on telephones, the noise, the smoky air, all stale and used up. Everyone stopped what they were doing and looked at him. Their noise wound down to silence.

Russell didn't know anything, didn't know why Fleur was there or in what condition he'd find her. He didn't know what he'd be asked, but he expected some sort of interrogation that had no shape or sound or purpose yet. That's what always happened when a Black man walks into a police station—they get to ask the questions first. He knew nothing, and everyone on the other side of the counter knew more. He planted his feet firmly to accept whatever came next, and in the plainest voice he could summon, Russell said, "I'm here for Fleur Williams."

The desk sergeant rose. Silence in the once-clattering office. Russell saw Ken Burroughs just beyond and nodded polite recognition, then returned his attention to the man before him.

"Is Fleur Williams your girl?"

"She's my daughter, yes."

"You Russell Williams that works in sanitation?"

"I am."

"Your girl caused a disturbance this afternoon. You know anything about it?"

"I do not. This will be the first I hear about it."

Russell remained guarded and focused, his eyes on the wall calendar behind the desk sergeant so as to avoid a direct stare by either party. April 28—no particular day except this was the day he was in the Jamestown police station about to find out what befell his daughter. Where was she? How can he possibly protect his children from all this? He tried to see himself as the other men saw him and adjusted his posture to convey nothing more than that he was a man and a father. He let his shoulders drop. He would ask now.

"What has Fleur done?"

He heard the retelling of Fleur's visit to Renee's Beauty Spot, how she asked for a haircut and style and refused to leave when told her appointment would not be honored. They did not have the right equipment, the right lotions or scissors, that this was not the right place for her. He noted from the corner of his eye the interest all the others took in the retelling of this tale of disobedience, even after half a dozen barbershop demonstrations this spring. This was different—a girl, a local girl, not an outsider, not someone from the college, but a Catholic daughter of one of the local garbagemen. Russell knew how to keep his face grave and impassive, he knew how to control the corners of his mouth and eyes. He listened intently with what looked to the desk sergeant as respect, but deep within Russell's soul, he smiled.

He heard how Fleur wouldn't budge when the owner asked her to leave, how the owner called and demanded—yes, demanded!—that they bodily remove her from the premises. He heard how the customers complained about the smell and how the owner had to disinfect the chair Fleur sat in after she was lifted up by two policemen who carried her into a squad car. How the police of this town had more important things to do than to discipline a foolish girl who ought to know better. How Father Halligan would probably have plenty to say about this too, but not just him, maybe the police chief too.

Russell drew in his breath and prepared himself for whatever would be revealed next. Everyone was quiet; everyone was looking at him. Whatever precious little trust among men that accrued over years of employment as a garbageman, and Russell doubted there had been any, evaporated in that stifling room.

"May I see Fleur now?" he asked.

The desk sergeant motioned to one of the officers who then went down the hall. More silence. How would he find Fleur? Ever since the phone call, he awaited and dreaded this moment. He kept looking at the wall calendar while everyone else looked at him. The officer finally brought Fleur in, and Russell anxiously sought her eyes. He could see she was unharmed but thoroughly scared. He relaxed a little and turned his attention to the sergeant.

"What have you charged her with?" he asked.

There was an uncomfortable pause.

"We haven't charged her with anything," he finally said, but clearly rued the fact. The rest of the men shifted their gaze between Russell, Fleur, the desk sergeant, and each other. Russell saw where this might lead. He might have to sacrifice his job. He might have to give up the house and move his family away. But he would if he had to. He was almost pleased about it.

"Then I will take her home now." Russell gestured to Fleur to come to him and he quietly conferred with his daughter.

"Do you have all your things?"

"Yes."

"Did they send a matron to you?"

"Yes."

"Then let's go now, Fleur. Let's go home."

The defiance that had gotten her this far suddenly drained from her and she fell into her father's arms. He took her by the elbow and straightened her around. They walked to the door while a dozen sets of eyes followed them. The desk sergeant's voice halted their progress.

"Williams. You keep that girl under your control, understand?"

Russell stopped and his mind was filled with all the possibilities of the moment. The mayhem and violence that could ensue. The sacrifice of dignity and pride. The twenty-eighth of April—one child on his arm, and scores more lost to whatever protection a Black man in this world has. And this fool wants control?

"You understand me, Williams?"

He did not face the sergeant, only half turned his head around and down. He said, "My children were raised in the Church. They know their Commandments. 'Honor thy father and thy mother.' I'll be happy to tell Father Halligan that Fleur Williams honors me."

Then they walked through the door and into the night.

Russell was walking his daughter down the steps and toward their car when they were quickly approached by two people—Dr. and Mrs. Ransom. She spoke first.

"Mr. Williams, this is my husband Earl. We want to make sure Fleur is alright."

"Happy to meet you, Russell, I'm glad to meet Fleur's father." Earl offered his hand to a surprised Russell. *What are they doing here?* he wondered.

"Are you alright, Fleur?" Helen Ransom anxiously asked.

"She's alright, ma'am. Thank you for asking," replied Russell while Fleur kept silent.

"Are you sure? Did anything happen to you in there? Did they charge you with anything?" Helen asked.

"Helen, please," said Earl, trying to restrain his wife's questioning. "It's not for us to ask."

"Oh, but it is. I was there when the police came and carried her into the squad car. If anything happened, I can be a witness. I followed her to the station, and I waited, didn't I, Earl? I wanted to make sure Fleur was alright."

"Thank you, ma'am," Russell responded. "I appreciate your concern."

"Are you alright?" Helen implored, looking into Fleur's surprised face. Fleur nodded a shy "yes."

"Did they charge her with anything?" Helen asked Russell.

"No they did not," he replied.

"I don't know if that's good or bad," mused Helen.

"I think we can all agree that it is good," said Earl Ransom, trying to steer his wife into leaving. "Come, let's go now."

"I was so worried about you," Helen declaimed to Fleur, who was looking more frightened by the moment. "I followed you here to make sure you were alright."

Earl intervened again. "Come, Helen, her father is here, your job is done."

"Please let me know if I can help," Helen said to Russell, as they left. "I can be a witness."

Russell opened the passenger side door for Fleur and helped her in. He got into his own side and started the car. He drove a couple of blocks in no particular direction. Fleur still didn't say a word. He pulled over into a parking space and turned off the car.

"You want to tell me what happened?" he finally said.

Fleur burst into tears and cried loudly, big heaving sobs of tension and release; she hadn't cried like that since she was a little girl. She buried her face in her hands, wiped her cheeks with them, then wiped her hands on her skirt, and over and over again until she drained herself of enough of the electricity jangling around inside her so she could squeak out a few words. Russell pulled his tender girl closer to him and rested her soggy face on his shoulder. He wasn't good at this, was completely inept when Mathilde cried, all he could do was leave the room. But he sat there in the growing darkness, not caring what passersby might think, not giving what part of town he was parked in any further thought. He let his daughter cry herself out with her head on his right shoulder. He spoke to her gently.

"Fleur, did anybody hurt you? Did anybody touch you? Why were you there?" He waited for her story.

She told him, in halting stops, between sobs and gasps for breath. No one had hurt her, no one had touched her except for the two policemen who picked her up from the beauty salon chair and carried her into the squad car. She had walked from the squad car into the police station, no handcuffs, but firmly flanked by those two large men. They wrote her name into their ledger; fingerprinted her; took her purse, sweater, and belt; and led her back to a holding cell.

"Did anyone touch you where they shouldn't?"

"No, Daddy, I told you. They sent a matron to sit by me."

She told of the scary drunks and others in the nearby cells who watched her being led in and called out to her with filthy words. This is what upset her the most, not the police, not her arrest, but being in the jail itself. Men, white and Black, who leered at her, who made noises and said what they would like to do to her. The matron told them to shut up, but she returned to her magazines and ignored Fleur and the others in their cells. The men just lowered their voices and talked among each other, but she knew they were talking about her. She was in the holding cell for two hours before they called her father.

"What was Mrs. Ransom doing there?"

"I don't know! She just showed up."

"Did she talk you into doing this?" Russell accused.

"No, Daddy! I did this by myself. I didn't tell her anything. I wanted this to be my own plan."

"You sure?"

"Yes!" she protested.

"That woman has a habit of showing up in your life."

"I did this all my own. I wish she hadn't been there."

"She's really annoying, isn't she," Russell stated. They both laughed.

Russell started the car up again, and they drove around. He showed Fleur some of the other houses they had looked at when they were trying to move out of their apartment; it seemed like so many years ago, but it was only nine.

"You hungry?" asked Russell. Fleur nodded. They stopped at the submarine sandwich shop near the Acme store and Russell drew out one of the twenty-dollar bills he had slipped into his wallet. He was quite pleased that he was buying sandwiches for himself and his daughter with that money and not something else. They sat in a back booth and ate—roast beef for Fleur, Italian combo for Russell. They talked for a long time—about the rabbits in the garden, Fleur's job, his work before he came to Jamestown, and the people in town.

"Fleur, this won't be the end of it. They didn't charge you, but something will happen. I just want you to be prepared."

"Daddy, I did this so something would happen."

"It won't turn out like you thought. These things get mixed up."

"It will be good, you'll see, Daddy."

They wrapped up the parts of their sandwiches they couldn't finish and drove back home. It was late. Mathilde would be worried.

Father Halligan

Before Fleur even arrived at the police station, Father Halligan was on the telephone summoning Mayor Garrity and Police Chief Rosario to the rectory. By the time Fleur was brought in, they had conferred and decided how they wanted this episode handled. They agreed there was no reason to make a fuss over Fleur's demand to be served in a beauty salon where she wasn't wanted. After all, this was a young high school girl, this demonstration didn't carry the weight or importance like the barbershop events. The town was already seeing a boycott of two of the shops. No, this one should just fade away without much notice, and that's exactly what they intended to have happen. The girl appeared to have acted alone; she didn't seem to have the support of the college or others, and so far no reporters had shown up asking questions. Police Chief Rosario was more worried than the other two and pointed out the potential damage.

"This may seem like an insignificant demonstration, but it was a local girl, from this parish."

Mayor Garrity offered a reassurance. "There weren't any of the usual protesters involved. She acted on her own."

"But Earl Ransom's wife showed up in the middle of all this," the police chief informed the others. "She's at the police station now."

"What was her role in this?" asked the mayor.

"Unclear. Claims she went to the Beauty Spot to make an appointment, our squad arrived, she insisted on coming in to make sure the girl was OK. She's there now."

"I think that can be managed," said Father Halligan.

"And there are townspeople honoring the boycotts. It's not all outsiders anymore," warned Rosario.

The others considered this and agreed they didn't want these racial protests growing into any sort of local movement. They still didn't understand why this was happening in their town. They knew how to treat their Blacks; people weren't unhappy; everybody knew how to get along, because everyone kept to their own kind. What was wrong with that? But a young girl, one of the town's own, threatened that view. Father Halligan held back, let the other two men hash and debate each other, then he spoke up.

"First and foremost, Chief Rosario, make sure to treat this girl with kid gloves; no mishandling, no rough treatment, and no charges. Is that understood? Yes? Good. Next. No press seems to be involved, so let's keep it that way."

They prepared a unified response for anyone who asked questions, just enough to sweep this under the rug and keep anyone from focusing on it and making it more than what it was. Something like a local teenage girl, high-spirited and good-intentioned no doubt, wanted to see what it would be like to get arrested—laugh, laugh—not as much fun as she thought—more benign chuckles—but no matter, she wasn't charged, it was all a youthful experiment, and she was released to her father, who no doubt had some stern words for his child. No harm done, end of story. Yes, that would work best for all of them to respond in kind.

And finally, how to keep this from happening again. That must be handled even more delicately than Fleur Williams's arrest. How to send a subtle, indirect message, not just to the Williams family to keep their girl in line, but to everyone who might use this moment in Jamestown history to grandstand and disrupt a peaceful way of life. The three men did not discuss this. These sorts of things are best left to silence and one's own machinery. But each man—the mayor, the pastor, the police chief— independently arrived at the same conclusion that life should become just a little harder for the Williams family and in ways that appeared to be from their own doing, which of course it was.

Father Halligan thanked the men for coming by. "Oremus," he said— Let us pray. They said the Lord's Prayer in Latin together, and the Pastor of Holy Trinity blessed their work.

"*Gloria Patri, et Filio, et Spiritui Sancto*. Amen." Then he placed a discreet phone call to Earl Ransom.

Elma Tanzer

"Thank you for stopping by," Elma Tanzer said to the Jamestown police officer standing before her in the store.

"A professional courtesy, ma'am," he replied. "We thought you should know."

She couldn't tell if his bland expression hid a slight smirk or not. It probably did, she decided. "Good day," she replied, and he left the store. Fleur would not be in for several hours. It gave Elma time to think about how to respond. But respond to what? They said Fleur caused a disturbance and was brought to the police station. But she wasn't charged with anything and they released her to her parents. So far there was no gossip on Main Street, but it was early. It was easy to explain a police officer's visit to a jewelry store, should any of the more nosy shopkeepers inquire. But how to explain what Fleur did? Elma spoke with her husband. They agreed they must do something—but what? They conferred; their response to Fleur did not come easy, but they felt it was fair.

When Fleur arrived in the afternoon, she started her work in the back room washing some of the china; a new bridal registry display would go up in time for Saturday. Elma Tanzer came back and asked the others to leave her with Fleur.

"I guess you did not have a dentist appointment yesterday."

"No, ma'am," Fleur replied sheepishly.

"The police came by this morning to talk to me 'as a professional courtesy.' Do you know what that means?"

Fleur shook her head.

"It means they want to stick their nose into my business."

She told Fleur about when they first came to this town, about the discrimination they went through because they were German and the memories of the war so fresh. How they keep their own counsel, make some effort to get along, be part of the downtown business community, but mostly concentrate on making their business successful. She told Fleur that she still had her job, but they were going to keep her in the back cleaning for a few days. After that, people's curiosity will move on to the next thing.

"But . . . " said Fleur.

"It's not a punishment," Elma cut her off.

She took some time to explain the nuance of her decision, that giving people more opportunity to talk about Fleur and her actions was not in her best interest, nor the store's.

"I didn't do anything wrong," protested Fleur. "I did it so people would wake up to the discrimination in this town and start talking about it."

"I don't disagree, Fleur," Elma Tanzer said. "But I have a business to run, and for all my years and experience, I think this is the best course of action. If you don't like it, well, Mr. Tanzer and I would be sorry to lose you."

Fleur looked disappointed. *Would she stay?* Elma Tanzer wondered. She hoped she would, but the nature of youth is to be impetuous. She watched Fleur eat her disappointment that day and each day thereafter. She remembered her own hard lessons, that little good came from righteously standing on principle. She wanted Fleur to learn that there were always paths forward and that living well was the best revenge. Fleur stayed in the back washing china, quiet and sullen, through the weekend. Fleur washed, dusted, polished, wrapped packages, and set them out for someone else to take to the post office. This continued for the following week—nine days, a sort of novena.

Just when Fleur had to be wondering if she would be banished to the back room forever, Elma Tanzer came in and said, "Fleur, we need you out front now."

Fleur smiled and took off her apron. "Thank you," she said. And she stayed. Elma Tanzer was very glad.

Helen Ransom

Helen Ransom strode through the Hamel Woods, tugging her sweater close for warmth on this cool, cloudy spring day. She left home in a hurry without a jacket. She and Earl were having an argument—a really heated one—and suddenly she asked herself what she was doing there. No good answer came to her, so she advanced upon these woods to see if she could find a reason to go back. The day started hopeful, even their argument was bracing, but then this ultimatum. What had happened? How could her innocent gesture of concern for Fleur have led to this? Well, maybe not so innocent, but still. She replayed the last twenty-four hours in her mind while tromping along trails, trying to parse out a future for herself.

After they left the police station yesterday, Earl dropped her off at her car near the beauty salon. With little conversation he told her he had to go to a meeting on campus and that he'd skip dinner tonight. "We'll talk about this tomorrow," he said. Helen noticed the "Closed" sign in the beauty salon window as she drove off, thinking now of all the meanings of that word. Back home she fixed herself some tea and cheese and crackers. Trying to make sense of her experience with Fleur, the beauty parlor, and the police, she hurriedly jotted down notes so she wouldn't forget anything. *What did this episode mean and will it amount to anything?* she wondered. She was glad she got involved—who knows what would have happened to Fleur if she hadn't. She crossed a line, but not the line she thought. She imagined she saved Fleur from something bad, but maybe she just butted in where she wasn't wanted or needed. Or did she cross a line with herself? Yes, she did that. And she didn't care what Earl or anyone else on campus or in the town thought. She took a stand for fairness and equality, no matter how blundering and ridiculous she might have been. Nothing to apologize for.

She crossed out some notes, added others, circled sections, and moved them around. Something was beginning to take shape here. Could she see herself doing more of this? Yes, she could. Not being served in barbershops was one thing, but wasn't tracking high school students by class and race a greater wrong? Wouldn't this be a better use of her time? Exhausted, she fell asleep before Earl came home.

The next morning Helen told Earl everything she had thought about since yesterday afternoon. How she wanted to join the campus work on civil rights. How she had been in a funk since Celia went away to school. How this was a better use of her time and would serve to keep him well informed. Earnest and energized, she had lots of ideas and was ready to start right away. She wanted to write a letter to the editor of the town paper about this experience. She wanted to work with the CRA committee, they clearly weren't listening to Fleur's local perspective. She wanted . . . she wanted . . .

"Wait," said Earl.

"For what?"

"Until things settle down," he continued, avoiding her eyes.

"Things aren't supposed to settle down," she answered, "This is just the right moment to stir things up."

"I can't have you active in the CRAC."

"Why not?" Helen asked, thoroughly dumbstruck.

"You are my wife. Your actions represent me as well as yourself, and I have to walk a careful line. There is enough faculty involvement. Your active presence will inhibit the others. Be my eyes and ears in town."

"Isn't what I did yesterday representative of what you believe in?"

"Of course, I believe . . ."

"I'm already your eyes and ears in the community," she interrupted. "I've been with you every step of the way. I've done everything you've asked me to do. I can do more; be more. I won't be over-involved, I'll take their direction, I'll be another foot soldier."

"Please, Helen, support me on this. It will make it hard for me to have you involved."

"How?"

"With the trustees, the faculty council, and others." Again Earl avoided her eyes. "Please, Helen, don't ask me for this. I can't give it to you."

"I wasn't asking you to give me anything. I was telling you what I thought I could do, should do. I'm not asking for permission."

"Good, because I can't give it to you."

She paused, not quite believing this was her husband before her. "What wrong with you? I know you believe in the civil rights cause. And I thought you believed in me."

"Both are true. But sometimes we have to stand back. We're seen as leaders in this community, and that means we must balance our actions and be careful."

"Careful about what? Not offending ladies who would use disinfectant to wipe away the cooties of a Negro girl?" Helen had never seen Earl so ridiculously cautious. "I have done everything to help us get where we are today. We can afford to be less cautious now, and the times demand it. Please, support me in this."

"No, I can't."

"Why?" she demanded.

"Because I can't have you interfering in areas of campus or community politics."

"Interfering? Am I not an asset to you in these areas too?"

"No. Just the opposite."

"I don't believe you. Would you deny me this?"

"Yes."

"At least allow me to send a letter to the Editor of the *Jamestown Gazette*. I've already started it. It's about how Fleur was . . ."

"No, you can't do that. You mustn't."

Another pause while Helen weighed her words. "Well then, perhaps we've reached the limit of our partnership."

"What is that supposed to mean?"

"I have helped you, worked for you, raised our children, been by your side all our years together. Can't you be by my side this time?" Helen pleaded.

"Not this time."

"Why?"

"It won't be good for us."

"Us? I think you mean *you*. And shouldn't what's good for us take a back seat? What about Fleur? What's good for her, her family, all those Negro students being prepared for manual labor? What's good for them?"

After a long silence. Earl said quietly, "Please don't ask me for this. I can't. I don't expect you to understand."

"Well, thank you for that endorsement."

"It's more complicated than you think. My position here could be jeopardized. I have to walk a fine line in this community."

"But isn't this what Hamel stands for? What you stand for?"

"I don't like being put in this position any more than you do."

"Oh, you're wrong," Helen retorted. Where did she find this within her? "I do like this position, this difficult stand. It's much better than my downtown whisper diplomacy and tea with the deans' wives. And it would be good for us too."

Earl pleaded, "Please, Helen, forgive me for this, but I can't allow it."

"And what if I go ahead anyway?"

"You leave me no choice. I will have to rescind Fleur's scholarship offer."

Did her world just crack open and fall apart? Yes. She must remember this. Stunned, she asked, "You would do that?"

"I don't want to, but I must have your cooperation in this matter."

Who was this man standing before her? She didn't recognize him. Or maybe she didn't recognize herself? She walked out of the room, out of their home, walked into Hamel's dark woods, walked to find her way.

Helen was gone for several hours. She walked every loop in the woods, parsing every part of their argument. It was outrageous that Earl would punish Fleur to get her agreement. How dare he! She wished she had brought her gloves and car coat. She grew cold and hungry. Clouds arrived and it looked like rain. It was cold in the woods, but also at home. She returned to the president's house, stood outside the door and asked herself if she really belonged there. She found an answer and went in. Earl was still in the house, working in his study but clearly waiting for her. He looked up at her and stood. His eyes asked, "What will it be?"

Helen took a piece of paper and handed it to him. "Here is the letter to the editor I began to write last night. I will give it to you to do what you want under these conditions: One—Fleur gets her scholarship, and it's a four-year scholarship. Guaranteed. Two—this scholarship will be a new endowment at Hamel, given each year to a promising Jamestown senior for whom college has not been part of their family's life. And three—you and I will seek out a new role for me on this campus and all others in our future. One of substance and action. I can no longer remain by your side the way I have been. Do you agree to this?"

Earl issued a sigh of relief, then wiped a tear from his eye. "Yes. I thought I had lost you."

"You did. The old me. Now you have to make room for the new me."

"Shall I name the scholarship after you in gratitude?"

"Absolutely not, save that for the donors, you know that's how that works. I already have several people in mind."

Earl reached to embrace her, but she sidestepped and went to the kitchen. She was so hungry. They survived this crisis. And she was just getting started.

Fleur Williams

The day after her beauty salon protest, Fleur Williams went to school expecting some notice for her action. Usually she attracted very little attention from her classmates and teachers, so it had to mean something that a few students looked and pointed at her in the hallways and lunchroom. Her algebra teacher called on her for the solution to a moderately easy problem and praised her for her answer. Some sophomore twerp bumped into her between classes and snickered, "Nice haircut, Fleur!" before careening down the hallway with his scrum of joking friends. When she signed out at the office to leave for work release, Mrs. Jenkins, the Black secretary, was particularly friendly and wished her a very good afternoon.

She walked downtown to her job at Tanzer's Jewelry Store. Did she imagine that people stared at her and whispered? She held her breath as she walked by a parking enforcement officer issuing a ticket, then quickly entered the jewelry store. Mrs. Tanzer was waiting for her. She spoke her piece, and if Fleur wanted to keep her job, she had to stay in the back room for several days and do her work there. Fleur angrily washed dishes and silver and wiped a few tears from her eyes. "Is this it," she wondered, "nothing else?" In defiance of other's indifference, she straightened her shoulders and set her chin. Her posture was perfect and she walked with purpose.

The next day at school, Patty Atkins invited Fleur to sit at her lunch table with her friends, the cool Black kids who never had time for her before. They peppered her with questions about her arrest, and Fleur was gracious, forthcoming, but reserved. She enjoyed the attention but resented that it came with only six weeks left before graduation. She acted a little aloof with them, pretended that she was so beyond high school already, lied about how she practically lived on the Hamel campus now.

Fleur scanned the Newark newspaper each day for any news about her arrest—there was none. The *Jamestown Gazette* was also silent, not even a mention of a juvenile on the police blotter. Her action earned a one-sentence mention in the Hamel campus weekly paper, but only in the context of the other barbershop demonstrations, and it did not mention her name.

Fleur went to the next CRAC meeting the week after her arrest. Emory Richardson, the student leader of the group, was already talking, going through the evening's agenda. Everyone stopped talking when Fleur arrived—an uncomfortable silence. Fleur hadn't known what to expect. Emory spoke first.

"Welcome, Fleur. We are glad you're here. Your action of last week, it's one of the things we want to talk about."

Fleur intuited that there had already been a meeting to discuss her action and arrest. Emory explained that they weren't pleased that Fleur had acted on her own, without the knowledge of the group or the support of their organization. Some thought it was selfish and wasteful. Others thought they should take advantage of her unexpected action and expand the barbershop protests with women going to the beauty salons. Most thought that would dilute what they already put into motion, and they had voted it down.

Fleur thought she had more support than what was on display now. Melanie Roberts in particular was keen to expand their protests. She was tired of being the group's scribe, which didn't even let her become its press secretary. She and Rosie Alberts championed Fleur within their group but did not prevail, and because Fleur was still a high school student, they too felt the sting of embarrassment that she had shown them up. This was not Fleur's group, nor her time, they reasoned, and dropped their advocacy for her. Still, they needed to show some concern. And respect. Melanie and Rosie were as dissatisfied with their own lack of traction within the structure and agenda of the CRAC. They were always being told in one way or another that the women would have to wait. Melanie interrupted to make a play for her own relevance.

"First of all, Fleur, we want to know if you are alright. Did anything happen to you?"

"Not really," Fleur answered.

"Did the policemen touch you?"

"Stop, you're embarrassing her," said one of the men.

"This is appropriate. If she doesn't know now, she should learn what happens to some sisters when the police take them. And I mean take them."

Fleur looked from face to face trying to see if anyone of them actually cared about her. Emory looked pained, Melanie defiant.

Fleur said, "The police did not touch me other than to carry me out of the beauty parlor and put me in the squad car. You seem disappointed."

"Fleur, we're just checking."

"For what? To see if I'm OK? You could have done that last week."

"You've put us in a difficult position . . ."

"Unexpected, Emory" interjected Melanie. "Be real. This isn't difficult. You were just surprised by a young girl."

"We had a plan," Emory replied. "And we still have one. This is diverting our resources."

"Yeah, and you sure don't want some girl changing plans on you."

Rosie asked, "Fleur, did anything happen in the jail?"

"No. No one touched me. A matron sat outside the cell."

Rosie pressed on. "Were you in one by yourself?"

"Yes."

"Anything else happen?"

"The men there, they said lots of bad things to me."

"Do you have any bruises? Did they yank you around?"

"No."

"I don't think we have anything here to work with."

The group feel silent, and it was left to Emory to tell Fleur that while they all admired her conviction, she was wrong to act alone. It was dangerous too. She was to never do it again. Did she understand? Yes, she did, all too well. Fleur didn't go back to the campus meetings the rest of the school year.

Jamestown High School had one more surprise for Fleur. Her guidance counselor, Mrs. Simpson, called Fleur to her office. Perhaps she had finally found her a typing class?

"It's come to my attention, Fleur, that you helped another student with his algebra homework. By giving him yours to copy."

Fleur was mortified and felt heat rise from her chest to her face. She didn't even try to lie.

"How did you find out?" Fleur asked shyly.

"That's not important. Did you do it?" Mrs. Simpson asked sternly.

"Yes, but it was last year," cried Fleur. "I haven't done anything like that since."

"I'm afraid that doesn't matter, Fleur. You helped someone cheat his way through a class. That is against the student code of conduct."

"Lots of kids do it. People are passing their homework around all the time."

"That doesn't make it right."

"I'm sorry, I really am. He wasn't worth it."

"Men rarely are."

"I never did it again. And I swear I won't. Why can't you punish him?"

"Both of you will be reprimanded."

"What's going to happen?"

"That's up to the dean of students. I'll be speaking with him this morning, Fleur. Come by my office before you leave for your job."

In fear and anger, Fleur rushed from the office into a girl's lavatory, where she had a good cry. She should have known the guidance office would offer her nothing useful, but why this roadblock now? Later that day Mrs. Simpson delivered the corrective to both Fleur and Johnnie—they could not have the credits for that algebra class, and both would have to take it over. And until they did, they could not graduate.

The worst part was telling her parents. Fleur told them at the end of dinner when all of them were together. She wasn't going to hide or pretend she was wronged, but she wanted to say it just once, and then move right into her penance. She was ashamed of herself and felt terrible about the example she was to LuLu and Charlie. This was as bad as all the confessions she made of her Catholic sins.

"I did something wrong at school, and they caught me," announced Fleur.

Everybody stopped eating. Charlie and LuLu looked at each other, then slowly began to push their forks around their detested vegetables.

"Please go on," said her father.

She took a deep breath and spoke to her plate. "I helped a boy with his homework; I helped him cheat. I gave him my homework to copy."

Mathilde began to clear the table; Russell gently bade her to stop.

"The school found out . . . " she continued.

"How?"

"I don't know, but they did and now we are both to be punished. I know it was wrong."

"Who's the boy?" asked her father.

"Johnnie Abercrombie."

"From last year?"

"Yes." The shame for all of it flushed her cheeks.

"Did he rat on you?" asked Charlie.

"I suppose. I don't know how they came to ask about it. It's not like he'd volunteer the information."

"Was that the boy you were sweet on?" Mathilde asked.

"Mom! Stop!"

"What's going to happen now?" Mathilde asked.

"We both have to take the class over. It doesn't count toward graduation."

"Oh. When will that happen?"

"I don't know. We didn't get that far."

"Not much time left," said her father.

And the obvious, whether Fleur could graduate or not, was now out in the open.

"I'll come over to the school on my break tomorrow," said Mathilde.

"No, Mom, don't . . ."

"I will and I am, so that's that. Just want to learn what they're gonna have you do so you can graduate. You did wrong and you are going to make amends. Your parents need to understand what is expected of you. I'll call the school and tell them to expect me. Now, apologize to your sister and brother."

"I'm sorry," said Fleur softly.

"Continue," commanded Russell.

"This is not the example you should follow."

"Thank you, Fleur. You are excused from the dishes, you have other things to do tonight. Charlie—to the kitchen."

"That's not fair. Why are we punished? She did the wrong thing!" Charlie protested.

"Like you never did something wrong?" Russell admonished. "Like you never tried to get something for nothing? This is not a punishment, this is your chore tonight. Fleur is gonna feel the sting of this beyond her hands in hot water. You mind your own business, Charlie."

Fleur felt the sting. What was she going to do now?

Father Halligan

Father Halligan's thoughts wandered during the Mass. It was the early one at eight thirty, not his usual rotation, but he had ceded his place at nine thirty Mass to one of his junior priests this week. He struggled to become fully awake in this earlier hour and thought, while good for him, it was an inconvenience he'd avoid in the future. He had wanted to say the earlier Mass, his reasons were private. He'd thought a lot about it, prayed over it, and decided today was the day before too much time had passed.

He looked out from the altar at his flock. A smaller part of the congregation than the nine thirty Mass, but plenty of people were here. He began.

"*Oremus.*"

The Prayers Before the Altar. The Introit. The Credo then the Gospel. He kept the sermon short and only hinted at what was about to happen. Plenty of introspective parishioners would put it together later. It was important to not be obvious. He prayed over this too. *Union with Christ in*

Holy Communion is the bond of charity that makes us one with our neighbor, he reminded himself. And now he was about to sever that bond with two of them. He gave himself the consecrated host and taste of wine, the same to the altar boys, then proceeded to the altar rail. Sanctifying grace was his to bestow or withhold. In the name of God, of course.

But wasn't the purpose of the Holy Eucharist to increase sanctifying grace, to promote spiritual growth and strengthen the bond with Christ? Was what Fleur Williams did a mortal sin? Certainly it was a venial sin, but mortal? He felt sure it was close, and to receive the Holy Eucharist in a state of mortal sin would add the sin of sacrilege. He reasoned that withholding Communion from Fleur and Mathilde Williams left them in a greater state of grace. And would teach them a lesson.

The Williams family was lined up at the altar rail, the two youngest children first, the mother, then Fleur. He gave Holy Communion to the two youngest children. They were innocent of their older sister's sin. He will not give Holy Communion to Mathilde, who as an adult and responsible for her daughter, sinned as well. That was the family's fourth mistake, and it was time for them to learn a lesson.

He placed a host on the extended tongues of Charlie and LuLu who bowed their heads in prayer and made their way back to their seats. They placed their heads in their hands to pray their thanks for this greatest of Church blessings. They did not initially notice that their sister and mother were still at the altar rail awaiting their sacrament and blessing.

Mathilde was next in line. She closed her eyes, raised her chin and laid bare her tongue to receive her Lord. Father Halligan walked on, and passed Fleur Williams too in the same posture as her mother. The altar boy was confused, but Father Halligan encouraged him on. They stopped in front of the next parishioner, Mrs. Stella Bruni, then the next, her daughter Mary, and onward. He could feel the confusion emanate from the two Williams women; he went on. "Corpus Christi. Amen. Corpus Christi. Amen."

The Body and Blood. It was here he glanced back. It was a very quick gesture, one would miss it if they were in their post-Communion prayer. He only needed two people, well, maybe a few others, to see it, and the quick glance back did not fail. He made eye contact with Mathilde and Fleur and allowed his disapproval to burrow its way into their chests where they would feel it most. He heard a slight gasp and turned away as his peripheral vision caught Mathilde reaching out to him and her daughter restraining her. *Good,* he thought, and proceeded down the rail. There were many seeking Communion that morning, and he needed to make two more passes down the rail. Each time Mathilde and Fleur were still there. Each time he passed them by. He intuited Mathilde's questioning tears and Fleur's glare in defense of her mother. *Good,* he thought, *let her bear the responsibility for their fall from grace.*

He finished Communion, the washing of the vessels, post-Communion prayers. "*Oremus,*" he said when he turned back to face his congregation. He saw a dozen or more surprised faces, their eyes and mouths in exaggerated ovals. *Good,* he thought, *let them learn too.* And he turned his back and finished the Mass.

Fleur Williams
Friday Evening, June 5, 1964

Fleur scowled at herself in the mirror. "A light-colored dress and white shoes," the instructions said. She didn't want to go, but her parents were making her. Stupid, stupid, stupid—the whole thing was stupid. They weren't letting her graduate yet, someone in the school took care of that with the eleventh hour discovery of her indiscretion last year. Yes, she did a wrong thing, but difficult kids at school got away with a lot worse. She was being made an example of—for her beauty shop protest? Or something else?

"I don't want to go!" Fleur cried dramatically.

"You're going," replied her father.

"Why?"

"Because we said so!" Russell shouted back in a voice that meant she was really going, no more discussion.

It was Friday night, June 5, 1964—Graduation for the Jamestown High School class of 1964. The greatest class, the best class, the most fun, talented, successful, and kind class their town had ever seen. That was the message from every teacher who spoke, every parent who beamed their pride, and every excited senior who would soon be ceremoniously released to the world as a full-fledged high school graduate. The school gave her the option of joining her class for the ceremony, even being listed among all the graduates in the program but with an asterisk by her name. Everybody knew what that meant. It meant you weren't smart enough, or you were a screw-off, and you had some finishing up to do. Fleur wanted no part of it, but her parents insisted.

"You're going to walk up to that stage with your head held high and let everyone know that you are Fleur Williams and you deserve to graduate," her father explained. But now he was getting exasperated with her protests.

"We leave in ten minutes," he said.

Fleur went to work as usual that day, even wrapped several presents for the graduation parties that would commence in a few hours and continue all weekend. The town was full of jubilation, like a home football game, and the Great Class of 1964 was their winning team, bringing honor to them all. But she felt no part of it. This was a sham graduation. Fleur didn't care anymore. So what if Patty Atkins invited her to sit at her lunch table? So what if the Hamel CRAC asked about her? So what if she still didn't know how to type? They were hypocrites—all of them. The only place where she felt like the grown-up she was becoming was at Tanzer's Jewelry Store. She was going to have to start summer school next Monday. Tonight's graduation ceremony seemed like a rebuke.

Her mother hustled all of them into the car, sitting in the back seat squished between her two youngest. Fleur sat in the front with her father. She was wearing her white gown and held her mortarboard in her lap, eyes straight ahead. Well, if she had to go through with it for her family's sake, she would make sure she wouldn't enjoy it. They drove to the high school in silence. Once there, her father said, "Show them who you are."

"We love you and are so proud of you," her mother added.

Her brother and sister made stupid faces at her. Fleur rolled her eyes and headed for the auditorium.

The auditorium was hot and sticky. People were fanning themselves with their programs. Fleur had already looked hers over. Sure enough, there was that offensive asterisk next to her name and several others on the list of graduates. The legend explained, "* pending completion of requirements." She was the only girl among half a dozen known screw-offs. The school band played the national anthem, then the school song, then they recited the Pledge of Allegiance. This could not end soon enough, but first everyone had to listen to the speakers.

Fleur was surprised Dr. Earl Ransom was giving the address, usually it was a minister or coach or mayor. She saw Mrs. Ransom sitting next to him on the stage that she would soon have to walk across. Fleur had seen less of her since the arrest six weeks ago. She didn't know how Mrs. Ransom walked into the same beauty salon she was trying to integrate, and she didn't want to know. It was all so awkward. Fleur had wanted to do something on her own, and then Mrs. Ransom barged in and fluttered around her as if she were in mortal danger. She knew she should think of it as a show of concern, but really, she wished she hadn't been there. Fleur was embarrassed to tell her about her algebra class cheating infraction and assumed the offer of a scholarship would be withdrawn. Well, Mrs. Ransom could read the asterisk now and know that she really wasn't graduating.

Dr. Ransom spoke about the changing world they were graduating into—the challenges and opportunities ahead, the new roles they must take on. He quoted from the speech Rev. Martin Luther King Jr. gave at the campus earlier in the year, and President Johnson's "Great Society" speech. His address was more somber than ebullient, and the graduates shifted uneasily in their seats. But then he changed the mood. "To help prepare our youth to accept the responsibilities this new world demands, I'm pleased to announce that . . ."

It was a new endowed scholarship, for a promising Jamestown High School graduate, for all four years of college. Murmurs of surprise and approval rippled through the auditorium. "Through generous contributions from Hamel trustees, alumnae, and local donors . . ." He explained this was a permanent endowment and that each year another graduating senior with promise and need would be selected. "Hamel is indebted to Jamestown, our host community, and happily offers the promise of higher education to someone for whom this may be out of reach. And now I'd like to introduce my wife, Helen Ransom, to announce the first recipient."

Fleur began to get nervous. Hamel must already know about her algebra homework cheating. Were they about to give her scholarship to someone else? Her mortification was complete. But then she heard Mrs. Ransom describe someone who came from examples of hard work, who then took on that mantle herself with a job she did well. Someone whose intellectual gifts may have been overlooked. Someone not content to stand by when others said "no" or "not now." Someone of the name of . . .

"The first recipient of this new endowed scholarship is Fleur Williams!"

The audience erupted into applause, and Fleur, stunned, froze in her seat, hands covering her face. Someone motioned her to ascend to the stage, someone cleared out the row so she could, someone nearby cheered her name. Fleur walked down the aisle and climbed the few steps to the stage where Dr. and Mrs. Ransom beamed at her, shook her hand, posed for a photograph, and handed her an envelope with congratulations and the terms of her scholarship. Helen Ransom turned Fleur to face the audience and vigorously applauded, stirring the audience to follow suit. Her parents were the first on their feet, then others, not all, but many joined them.

They passed Fleur on to the principal and the board of education president for more handshakes, then she returned to her seat. She made her way back to her row with classmates cheering all the way. Girls she didn't know well hugged her. Boys cleared out her row again so she could return to her seat and met her shy eyes with grinned approval.

"And now," the principal intoned, "I present to you the great class of 1964. All rise!" Everyone rose and cheered.

"Annette Andolino."

"Richard Andrews."

"Bernadette Arrignalla."

So it went for about two hundred more names before Fleur Williams was called to the stage again. She walked across proudly and accepted the empty diploma holder with a broad smile. Another round of applause went up from the audience. She saw her beaming parents and returned an equally dazzling smile to them.

When she found them later after the ceremony, she ran joyously into their arms, crying and laughing at the same time.

"That's why you made me come! How did you know?"

"Mrs. Ransom told us. It would have been embarrassing if you weren't there."

"I'll say! Oh, I'm so happy!" Fleur opened up her empty holder, laughed again, then placed the scholarship letter where her diploma was supposed to be. "There!" She grinned broadly and someone came up and took a photo of her and her parents.

Father Halligan

Jamestown Gazette – June 11, 1964
Hamel University Announces New Endowed Scholarship for
JHS Students
Fleur Williams Is First Recipient

Father Halligan picked up the *Jamestown Gazette*, though he already knew the news behind the smiling photo of the Williams family. *A clever feint,* he thought. *Was it Earl or Helen who had this idea?* It wasn't so much the scholarship that bothered him, it was the way it was presented. No, not a word about Fleur's action, nor Helen Ransom's involvement. Just as he insisted. The Ransoms acceded to his request to the letter, if not the intent. But they put Fleur on a pedestal, even if they did not say why, and let the town applaud her. Well, this was too bad. They may have hurt the Williams family instead. What bothered him most was the triumphant smile of Helen Ransom, as if she had gotten one over him. Yes, it must have been she who came up with this idea. He must remember this in the future.

As soon as this month's weddings were over, Father Halligan would take a short vacation to visit his mother. He'd use that time to think through his next step.

SUMMER 1964

July 2, 1964 – Civil Rights Act of 1964 signed, banning discrimination based on race, color, religion, sex, or national origin in employment practices and public accommodations.

Elma Tanzer

Spring had been difficult, and Elma Tanzer was glad to see things calm down. Wedding and graduation season was over, and the town settled into its summer lull. Normally Fleur would have started full-time hours, but she had to go to summer school to retake a course and didn't start her days until noon. She was glad Fleur stuck it out. The girl had learned some hard lessons this year, yet she remained a very good employee, though Elma needed her for those morning hours too. Hamel University was on summer recess now, so the barbershop protests stopped. It had gotten disagreeable with some townspeople boycotting one or another of the shops. Now the dispute was up to the state courts and the town had some peace again.

It was Fleur's last week of summer school, and Elma Tanzer planned a little surprise for her. She gathered the others in the store and explained they would soon have a party.

"A graduation party for Fleur—*shhh*, don't say a word. It will be a surprise. We will close the store and have a celebration for her."

Betty and Joyce, even Mr. Tanzer, were delighted. They rarely closed the store for anything.

Elma Tanzer took a long, thin bracelet box from the safe and opened it. Inside was a silver charm bracelet made of many interlocking links, naked of the charms that would tell a story of her life.

"We are making a present from the store for Fleur," Mrs. Tanzer explained. "We will give her this bracelet from everyone here. I want each of you to choose a silver charm to put on it. Mr. Tanzer will fix it all up with soldering, a safety catch, everything. No charge. You just need to pick out the charm that comes from you."

Betty immediately brought the trays of silver charms over so they could begin their selection. She and Joyce pored over the trays and began eliminating the obvious—not the pair of ice skates, not the sewing machine, not the bowling pin or pair of hockey sticks. Just as their eyes alighted on the best, first choice, Mr. Tanzer reached through from where he was standing on the side and picked his charm—a silver rose in full bloom.

"I pick this one, a flower for Fleur."

"Can there be engraving?" asked Betty.

"I don't see why not," said Mr. Tanzer.

Joyce retrieved the graduation charms from the safe where the other seasonal charms remained until their time approached.

"There. Here is mine," Joyce said, retrieving a mortarboard and diploma.

They talked about what Fleur liked, about any hobbies she had. They thought this should be a charm bracelet that displayed the essence of this young girl, not a jumble of jangly charms that expressed travel souvenirs or random fancies. Each made a pick, and Mr. Tanzer set them all on his workbench to put together.

On Tuesday the following week, Fleur left Tanzer's store at lunchtime and walked to the high school to pick up her diploma. With Fleur out of the store, Mrs. Tanzer, Betty, and Joyce made their preparations and welcomed the other guests. They hung a sign on the front door that they were "Closed for a private party." Fleur's parents came with LuLu and Charlie. Mr. and Mrs. Tanzer, Betty and her husband, and Joyce with her son and daughter were there. Even Russell's mother and sister from Newark came. When Fleur arrived, the guest of honor, she was momentarily confused by the sign on the locked door. Then Betty opened the door and they all congratulated the most recent graduate of Jamestown High School, Class of 1964. There in the room with all the displays of china and silver and crystal, with a flower arrangement and candles, they began their graduation party for Fleur. They drank soft drinks from the crystal stemware, ate hors d'oeuvres from the china using silver forks, munched on nuts and candies placed in beautiful little bowls. There was a cake from Schuler's bakery and cups of coffee served from one of the display tea sets. LuLu and Charlie were on their best behavior with gracious manners never seen before.

Then Mr. Tanzer presented Fleur with the graduation present from the entire store: a silver charm bracelet with charms picked out by each member of the staff. Fleur, grinning in teary joy, unwrapped the slender box with a bow in her school colors. Her hands trembled as she opened the box.

"Oh, my," she exclaimed. Fleur removed the completed charm bracelet from its cotton cushions and held it up at each end with thumb and forefinger—the silver shine and brilliance of a chain of links with five charms spaced evenly along its length. At one end, Joyce's mortarboard and diploma; at the other end a brushed silver banner with "Class of 1964" in shiny relief. Flanking them was Mr. Tanzer's simple rose charm and Mrs. Tanzer's choice—a bordered lozenge with Fleur's birthstone, a pearl, set in the middle. And centered among them all was Betty's charm, a classic representation of Fleur simply being who she was—a filigreed heart engraved with her monogram in script, **FWS**.

Such a party! Elma Tanzer thought to herself, beaming at all the guests. *Such a change to enjoy all the things we wash and wrap.*

After their celebration, Mrs. Tanzer bade Fleur to leave early with her family.

"You are our guest, we will clean up. Work will come soon enough tomorrow."

The Williamses left, thanking the Tanzers for a lovely party. Betty and Joyce helped Mrs. Tanzer clean up and put the store away for the night. The Essex "Minton," the Towle "Regale," the Oneida "Baroque," and the Lenox serving bowls were washed and put back on their shelves. No one would know that these were now "used" goods. Full from the hors d'oeuvres and cake and salted nuts, no one bothered with dinner that night. And no one remarked that the Williams family had just become the first Black customers at Tanzer's store. Russell had bought a delicate wristwatch from the store for his daughter's gift from the family, and his mother had purchased Fleur a simple pearl ring—the Tanzers offered both at a generous employee discount.

Elma Tanzer slept especially well that night. It was easy to think of the store only as work, as the careful calculations she and her husband made all the time to keep their business going. But today she remembered why they got into this business in the first place. The joy they created, the beauty and craftsmanship that surrounded them, the love they got to witness. She went to sleep thinking about how happy Fleur must be with the charm bracelet on one wrist, her new watch on the other, and the pearl ring on the ring finger of her right hand.

Fleur Williams

The one person who might have expected to be invited to Fleur's graduation party and wasn't stopped in the store the next day. Fleur greeted Mrs. Ransom, who had yet another long lost charm for the perpetual bracelet. She admired Fleur's new wrist adornment.

"What a lovely bracelet, Fleur," exclaimed Mrs. Ransom. "It's new isn't it?"

"Yes, ma'am," Fleur replied, letting on nothing about the party. "Everyone here at the store gave it to me. And the watch is from my parents and the ring from my Nana. I officially graduated yesterday!"

"Congratulations! What lovely gestures!" Mrs. Ransom said. "Then you have cleared the final hurdle. Well, then. About college: There are registration materials you need to fill out, and you'll need an appointment with your academic advisor. He can get you set up with your course schedule. It's mostly required introduction classes the first year. Then there are some orientation sessions at the end of August that you should get on your calendar."

"Oh, my. There are a lot of steps to do!" Fleur said with equal amounts of apprehension and excitement.

"And there are people to help you."

"Will my classes be scheduled like in high school?"

"No, dear, they are scheduled differently, and they will be in different buildings throughout the campus. Can you take a work break for a few minutes? We could talk about this in much more detail."

Fleur took her lunch break a little early and went with Mrs. Ransom to the soda fountain at the five-and-dime store. Mrs. Ransom explained that Fleur would not have to declare her major right away, and she'd take classes like Introduction to Sociology, Psychology 101, Survey of American Literature.

"Most of these classes will take place in a large lecture hall. You'll get a syllabus, reading list, and exam schedule on the first day of class. These classes usually meet three times a week for a little over an hour. You are expected to do quite a bit of reading between classes and write essays and papers. You'll be graded on the written assignments and exam scores."

Fleur did not know what a syllabus was. After Helen explained it to her, she said, "It sounds like a lot of homework."

"It is. It's more demanding than your high school classes, but also more engaging and relevant to the world we live in. I think you'll welcome the challenge."

"Will I be able to continue with French?"

"Yes. Hamel has a foreign language requirement, and you'll have to take two years."

"Do I get all the books from the school?"

"You have to purchase them from the campus bookstore. Some of them can be quite expensive. But don't worry, your scholarship comes with a very generous credit at the bookstore."

"What else do I have to know about the scholarship and money?" Fleur asked.

Mrs. Ransom outlined the scholarship terms. Fleur would get a full tuition waiver and a stipend each semester for books, supplies, and student activities fees. All Fleur needed to do was participate in the work-study program on the campus.

"What's that?" Fleur wanted to know.

"It's a part-time job on campus. Most scholarship students have these jobs, and it helps the college too."

"What kind of job?"

"Most likely in the cafeteria or housekeeping department."

"You mean like washing dishes or doing laundry?"

"Well, yes. The students get tuition and job experience and the college gets reliable workers. The scholarship students seem to like the arrangement."

Fleur blinked at the word *arrangement*. She lowered her eyes and said softly, "I already have job experience washing dishes and working in a laundry. How do I do this and stay on at my current job?"

"Well, I thought you'd be leaving the Tanzers' employ," stammered Mrs. Ransom, clearly not anticipating this road bump. "Your job with the Tanzers might not accommodate a college schedule, and it takes you away from the life of the campus. It's about being part of the campus community. It's a fresh start for you, Fleur."

"Can't I keep the job I have now? How is washing dishes or doing laundry a fresh start?" Fleur countered.

"Because it's college," Mrs. Ransom declaimed, a little exasperated.

Fleur felt something shift inside her. She had thought "work-study" had something to do with study groups and was surprised she would have to hold down a ten-hour-a-week job at minimum wage as a condition of her scholarship. She had thought the young workers she had seen on campus were employees. Now she knew they were financial aid students—largely foreign students, African Americans, and children of immigrant families—working in the cafeteria, laundry, and cleaning department. She saw hundreds of other students *not* doing this work, and they were mostly white kids. Fleur wasn't against working, far from it, she thought it would be good to still have a part-time job while a student. She assumed she'd stay with the Tanzers on some sort of part-time basis, maybe work all day on Saturday and again on Wednesday night for shopping night, so that the ladies could still have that time off.

Fleur asked if there were other work-study jobs, perhaps in the library or the admissions office giving campus tours.

"Not for the first-year students," replied Mrs. Ransom.

Hamel had its own blind spots. The day students, the foreign students, the poorer white students were a group unto themselves, and their work-study jobs were just one way they were kept from a more privileged participation in campus life. This seemed like going to a more grown-up high school.

"I think I better get back to work now, Mrs. Ransom," Fleur said and rose from the counter.

"I'll bring the registration forms to you tomorrow. Dr. Ransom and Celia will be so pleased to know you'll be joining Hamel this fall."

"Yes, thank you, Mrs. Ransom," Fleur said without passion as she left.

Mario Sposeto
Early August 1964

Mario Sposeto turned the dial on the radio while he gave his customer a mirror to check the length in the back. He had wanted it left a little longer. The new music coming from Britain irritated him, so in love was he with the teen ballads of his youth. "So in love, so in love . . ." in harmonizing chords—now that was a song, not this yeah-yeah stuff. He wanted his oldies.

"That will be two dollars," he said as he shook the minimal hair off the drape. Longer hair meant fewer haircuts. *What's next?* he thought to himself. *Beards?*

The man gave him three dollars and said, "Keep the extra buck for your defense fund. Can't let those people tell you what you have to do."

Mario thanked him and put the extra dollar bill in a jar labeled "NJ Barbers Defense Fund" clearly visible to the customers and peanut gallery. It was getting full. He should send it over to the law firm in Elizabeth who was working on their case. It wasn't just him; there were other barbers in Jamestown and dozens more throughout north Jersey.

Early August and business was a little slow. People on vacation going to the shore aren't thinking about haircuts. It was hot and humid, and he kept his door to the street open and the fans whirling. No picketers in over a month. All that nonsense slowed down after those nutty kids went back to Mom and Dad for the summer. He'd lost some customers; gained some too. Would this all start up again in another month when college was back in session? He hoped not, he was weary of the stupid dance he had to play—let the picketers do their thing, keep the entrance clear for customers, keep cutting hair, keep his cool. But if it did start up again, the barbers would soon have the courts on their side, he was sure of it. The lawyers cost money and every barber in town had a jar like this, even had special days for the defense fund when the brotherhood of barbers worked for free.

But it was almost normal now, and Mario looked forward to closing up shop for his own week at the shore. He was tired, and things were changing too much, too fast. What would his father have done? He was pretty sure his grandfather would have cut the hair of any man or dog, no matter what color, so desperate was he to escape his Sicilian poverty. "Money has no color!" he'd say. But not his old man, God bless his soul, he'd have stood his ground just like Mario did.

Mario glanced over at the St. Martin prayer card he had taped up on his mirror. It was getting a little worn around the edges and yellowish from age and sunlight. He should replace it. There had always been a prayer card of St. Martin de Porres in the shop since he could remember, and in every other barbershop. Barbers prayed to him to intercede on personal and business matters with God. No plea was too minor for St. Martin— health, family, girlfriends, sports teams, and race horses. The Pope had just canonized him two years ago, and what a celebration there had been in his shop—food, drink, and free haircuts. The way Mario figured, St. Martin must have been a stand-up guy, looking out for poor people and pretty much debasing himself as he did. But where was he this year during all the troubles with the Blacks? For months he had prayed to St. Martin to put an end to the nonsense, but the saint was silent on this matter. Mario knew Martin of Porres was Peruvian and a half-breed, but he assumed his parentage was Indian and Spanish. All the prayer cards he'd ever seen showed a Martin with dark-olive skin and European features, even the one taped on the mirror in his shop. During the long road between beatification and canonization, Martin of Porres's life was dissected, his miracles challenged, his rejection of the material world scrutinized. He emerged as holy as any other saint, worthy of a place in the pantheon of Catholic holy beings. And it was certified that his mother was a former Black slave from Panama. Maybe that was why St. Martin was silent.

St. Martin's prayer card nagged at him since the protests began. He almost took it down. He even went to confession and told the priest, one of the young ones, of his ambivalence. The holy father asked him, "What do you think St. Martin would have done if he worked in your shop?" Mario knew he would have cut the hair of any man, Black or white. And his grandfather would have too.

This did not help him. He did not change. He soldiered on in his battle against the state and anyone else who told him whom he must serve in the castle of his own shop. But St. Martin's eyes were always there to rebuke him, wide and round, staring forth from his holy perch. He sent away for a new prayer card, and the new one arrived with a more African visage than before. Mario decided to keep the old one and retaped it to the mirror. Still, he blessed himself before it each day. He gave free haircuts to his dear old uncles in the peanut gallery. He did his penance after confession.

Later that year, on November 3, the feast day of St. Martin of Porres, Mario went to church before opening his store. He lit a candle, said a prayer, put some coins in the box before the altar, and thanked the saint for all his barber profession gave him. Would he have cut St. Martin's hair? Then he went to vote, because it was also Election Day, and he voted for Barry Goldwater for president of the United States of America.

Russell Williams
End of August 1964

The summer was long and hot. The barbershop boycotts in New Jersey dwindled after campuses emptied out. If Jamestown was in a placid stupor, the South was surely on fire. Voter registration drives in Mississippi became violent, and Freedom Summer took the lives of Black and white voter registration workers. Russell Williams and his daughter Fleur read the newspaper every night and listened to the news.

"Will it be like that here too, Daddy?"

"It's different up here, the problems for Black folks are more hidden. I don't think it will come to Jamestown, but the big cities . . ." Russell didn't say any more.

On July 2, the US Congress had passed the Civil Rights Act of 1964, outlawing all segregation. Later in the summer riots broke out in the northern cities of Chicago; Rochester, New York; and Harlem.

Monday was as fine a day as there could ever be in Jamestown. The summer heat over the weekend had broken, and a dry breeze blew down from the north. Soon people would stop being summer people with their barbeques and maggoty trash and get back to work and school. Russell would be on summer schedule two more weeks, until the days tipped the garbage collection crew back to their usual schedule. The cooler morning energized Russell and his truck mate Floyd. They swung into their rig like schoolboys and began their daily haul of everything the town had coughed up over the weekend. This was the best time to be a garbageman. He'd be done by two thirty in the afternoon, and there would still be enough daylight for something else. Maybe some fishing on the Passaic. A nice river fish for dinner sounded grand.

As he and Floyd pulled back into the base yard at two twenty-five that afternoon, their crew boss was waiting for them.

"The city manager released the new budget this morning. There will be some layoffs."

"How many?"

"Who?"

"Each department got some letters. Go inside and see if there's one for you."

Russell knew the town was doing some belt-tightening, but garbage collection usually survived intact—one reason, despite the lower wages and distasteful work, the jobs were attractive. Steady work, everybody always had garbage.

Russell went in. The closed-mouth clerk didn't look at him, just handed him a white envelope with the seal of the Borough of Jamestown and the State of New Jersey and his name typed on the front.

Dear Mr. Russell Williams:

Effective immediately you are furloughed from your duties as Sanitation Worker II. We regret this change in your employment with the Borough but due to budgetary restraints, we found it necessary to reduce our workforce. We serve the tax-payers of our town, and I ask you to respect the decision of the city manager who approved this budgetary correction in response to the directives of the City Council. Should the Borough need your work, you will be notified at the address we have for you on file. Please let the office know if you change your address.

Signed, Mr. Harold Harriman, City Services Supervisor

"Other people here get these letters?" Russell asked her. She shrugged and still did not lift her eyes. He went to his locker, removed his few belongings, kicked the door shut, and left, swearing to no one in particular.

Russell stood on the bridge and dropped his line in. A couple of worms he dug up on the bank would have to do for bait. He needed this time to sort things out on his own before telling Mathilde. He wouldn't put it off long. Maybe tomorrow. *Effective immediately,* he muttered to himself. It was all an insult, but that stung the worst. No warning, no two weeks' notice. He had no doubt this was connected to Fleur's action at the beauty salon. Her algebra class. That damn priest who refused Mathilde her Communion. Now him. Everybody has garbage; collection men rarely get laid off. In a way he had been expecting this. His good fortune in finding this job, this town, this house was more than a Black man from Newark usually got. Almost a miracle that it had lasted this long. Now the town was jittery, and it seemed everybody had to learn some sort of lesson from this—but the Williams family had to learn it first.

He could cobble together a variety of odd jobs day-laboring around, but he'd be working a trapline that had its own costs. It wasn't a great solution, but it could be managed for a short time. Less likely was a permanent position like he had had with the borough, the steady paycheck, the five paid holidays, the one week of vacation.

He did not catch any fish. It was the wrong time of day.

The next evening, the Williams family sat down to a fried-fish dinner of sunnies that Russell plucked out of the ponds outside of town. He had talked it through with Mathilde, and together they told their children. They were quiet and crestfallen, disbelieving, then angry.

Fleur said, "I bet you get called back real soon. The people won't want their garbage not picked up."

"It's still going to get picked up, just won't be me doing it."

"Who's gonna do it?"

"All the others who didn't get that letter."

"You said the town was going to takes its revenge. Is this it?" Fleur asked.

Russell replied, "Can't say for sure, but I hope you all like fish."

"You got some fish, Daddy," piped up Charlie. "We'll be OK."

They ate in a quieter fashion than usual, Mathilde looking worried, Russell trying to be stronger than he felt.

"What's going to happen?" asked Fleur.

LuLu took a turn. "We're gonna be poor, right?"

"Gonna be?" Russell answered.

"Are we going to stay here?" Fleur asked.

Mathilde tried to be optimistic for the children. "We're gonna try to. Daddy will be looking for other work here."

Russell knew where that would go. The more prosperous Black families were the ones who had their own businesses—the barbershop, the funeral home, the body shop—and they hired other Black men, but the wages were not great. The white businesses hired some too but mostly for heavy labor hauling, the best was inventory at the grocery store. Russell knew he would be looking beyond Jamestown too.

"Do you think there's a chance the borough will call you back?" Fleur asked.

"Always a chance, but it wouldn't be smart to count on it. Our neighbors getting upset about their taxes. Other cutbacks too. I'm just one. The last in, first out."

Making the monthly rent for their house was always hard, but it was the number one priority and Russell was never late with his check to Frank Henderson. He had a deal worked out with Frank, who was alright for a white man, but there was nothing but cold, hard business between them. Besides the monthly rent for the house, Russell had been paying a little extra on a contract for deed to eventually buy it. They reviewed the accounts of it each year, and all was square, but there wasn't enough yet for the down payment. Not that this meant he could get a loan or that any of this was even possible anymore. Still, there might be some money there that they could work with.

Russell went to have a talk with Frank, who seemed to know what this would be about. He was ready to deal when Russell came by his small, dingy office where he worked making tiny, exquisite implements that dentists would install in peoples' jaws. They got down to business right away. Frank had already reviewed the books and done the accounting. Russell could use the extra he had already paid in the contract for deed account beyond the monthly rent. There was enough to last several months. He'd have to start over saving for a down payment.

The house they lived in belonged to Frank's mother. She was in a nursing home now, and the rent was used for her nursing care. Frank said he'd just as soon sell the place to him as anyone else, no problem there, but he couldn't afford to not rent it out in the meantime. And who knows, if his mother's care got much more expensive, he might have to sell the place sooner.

A three-month reprieve was on the table. The Williams family could continue to live in their house for three more months before the down payment fund was depleted. If Russell found more work beforehand, this might stretch out a little. Between what Mathilde and Fleur made they wouldn't starve and they could pay the utilities, but that was about it. Would the town call him back? Could he find another job nearby? Could they find somewhere cheaper to live? He'd been happy to pick up people's stinking garbage for the respectability he thought he was buying. Had it been worth it?

Russell left Frank's office with a new month-to-month lease in hand, rent drawn from the down payment account. He had three months to find a new job or move.

Elma Tanzer

After all the jewelry was removed from the safe and set out in the windows and display cases, Elma enjoyed the morning hours at the store. It was a chore to move everything this way, but it couldn't be helped, they had to protect themselves from burglaries, the professional kind mostly, but these were good habits to guard against the casual opportunistic thieves too. They had suffered losses over the years, but nothing big. The worst she had to worry about was an aging husband who worked too hard, and a college president's wife who didn't know when to leave well enough alone.

As if on cue, Helen Ransom entered the store. Unusual, thought Elma, she usually comes when Fleur is around; she always had things to discuss with the girl.

"Good morning, Mrs. Ransom," she greeted.

"I do wish you'd call me Helen."

"Ah, but this way, I have to remember only one name not two, surely an advantage for the older brain," she parried.

"You have a point; I might use your idea."

"Here to pick up your charm bracelet?" Elma guessed.

"I'm dropping off these forms for Fleur," Lorraine responded cautiously. "They are registration forms for the college next term. Fleur is interested in coming to Hamel. Has she talked with you about this?"

"I understand the college has awarded her a scholarship. Very generous," she replied. Elma knew Fleur's quiet ways. And she knew Helen Ransom's incessant interest and plans.

"I'm afraid she may be having second thoughts," said Helen.

"But young people change their minds a lot, don't they? Of course, you would know better than I."

"Yes, they change their minds about who they like, the major they will study, whether they will attend this talk or go to that party. College is all about change, really. But this is different."

"How is it different?" Elma asked politely.

"There is so much at stake for Fleur. This is such an opportunity for her, for her family, for her . . ." At this, Helen restrained herself with only dim awareness she might be overreaching.

"Have you spoken with Fleur?" asked Elma.

"Just yesterday, and I told her I would drop off the forms she has to fill out. She needs to do this soon. I got the impression that . . ."

"Yes?"

"That she may be having second thoughts."

"She must have her reasons."

"That's just it, she didn't. I wonder, did she mention anything to you?"

"No, nothing in particular."

Elma watched Helen think through her next move. She finally asked, "If Fleur decides not to go to college, what would that mean for her work here?"

That is not for you to know or influence, Elma thought with a hot flush fanning over her face. But instead she said, "Nothing has been discussed." True enough. But thought of? That was a different story.

"Mrs. Ransom," Elma said, "Mr. Tanzer and I do not get involved in our employee's lives." A small lie. "We run a business. They work for us. We pay them fairly. It's best to leave it at that."

"Do you really think so?"

"Yes. With all due respect, I think that is how you and Dr. Ransom treat the people who work for the college. The college is a good employer."

"But Fleur . . ." Helen left the girl's name hanging in the air like a question mark. She didn't understand at all. "Would you please make sure that Fleur gets these forms?"

"Of course."

"And I'd like to purchase a charm for Fleur's new bracelet. Such a lovely present to give her for her graduation. Could I see some of those?" She pointed to a nearby tray with silver trinkets like a thimble, a tennis racket, a horse. What to choose? Which charm would convey the hope she had for Fleur's future?

"Perhaps," Helen said, "I should get her a watch."

"Ah," said Mrs. Tanzer, "a lovely thought. But her parents have just given her a watch for graduation."

Helen sighed. She looked over the tray of charms and decided to get one of a book. She paid for it, and Mrs. Tanzer wrapped it up with a small pink bow.

"Thank you," said Helen Ransom, and she left the store without any mention of her own bracelet.

Fleur arrived at the store to work the afternoon and evening for shopping night. Not that it would be terribly busy, shopping night in the summer was rarely was, but the Tanzers thought it important to keep to the regular schedule. Elma and her husband would catch up on accounts and repair jobs while Fleur waited on the few customers. This would be a good time to bring up the question she'd been wanting to ask Fleur. She brought over the large envelope Helen Ransom had dropped off.

"Mrs. Ransom stopped by and asked that I give these to you." Fleur accepted the envelope with thanks but did not look inside or offer any acknowledgment of its contents. "She expressed some urgency that you fill out these forms." Elma looked into Fleur's eyes and saw hesitation. "Fleur, you are bothered by something. It won't go away on its own. Is it about your scholarship?"

"Yes, Ma'am," Fleur whispered. "Mrs. Ransom says I must take a work-study job on the campus. And that I probably shouldn't work here too."

Hmpft, so that's it! Elma thought to herself. But to Fleur she said, "And what is it you wish to do?"

"I would have to work in the cafeteria or laundry. I don't want to do that, I'd rather work for you," Fleur said softly.

"Is this a condition of your scholarship?"

"I'm not sure. I just learned about it yesterday. I thought I could continue to work for you, that is if you want me to."

"Of course we want you to, Mr. Tanzer and I were just saying so. But we need to know how many hours you can work here and still go to college. I think you should plan that your school work will be a little harder than in high school."

"Yes, ma'am, I know. I want to do both—go to college and work for you and Mr. Tanzer. Is that wrong?"

"Of course not," Elma exclaimed.

"Mrs. Ransom seems to think so."

"She may be married to the president of a college, but that does not mean she knows everything. May I see those forms?"

Fleur gladly shared them. Elma Tanzer read them through, muttering and going back and forth between the papers. Then she said to Fleur, "It is not clear whether you must take a campus job for your scholarship. It could be that campus jobs are there to help scholarship students make some extra money—in other words, optional. You won't be living on campus, so this may not apply to you. Mrs. Ransom may have assumed too much." *That was it exactly*, Elma thought, but held herself in check.

"Mr. Tanzer and I hope that you can continue to work for us on some sort of part-time basis, but we need to be able to plan a schedule that is good for you and us."

"Of course. I thought I could work at least on Saturdays and shopping nights. And in the summer too. I don't know when my classes are yet."

"First you must learn whether a campus job is necessary for you, or optional. Have your parents help you with this. If you need more help, I'll talk to Mrs. Ransom too." *Will I ever*, she thought to herself. She began to care little for the Retirement Fund.

Elma Tanzer thought this was all being sorted out without her, and that was fine with her. Summer in the Great Swamp of New Jersey may be drawing to a close, but it still had days of searing heat and dense humidity. The air-conditioning in the store ran constantly, laboring and wheezing, until it finally quit one day. Mrs. Tanzer told the staff to take it a little easier until a new air-conditioning unit was delivered. It was a slow day, not so many customers, but still plenty of cleaning and repair work to do. They sweated in the airless back room until Mrs. Tanzer could take it no longer. She stopped at the cash register, took out some money, went out, then came back with a box of strawberry ice cream. She dished some up for everyone.

They stood around the break room, keeping an eye out for any customers, and they ended up finishing all the ice cream. It smoothed out and lost its shape so fast, it was better to just stay ahead of it by scooping out more spoonfuls for everyone. The usual chit-chat prevailed—talk of upcoming weddings, the heat and humidity, the desire to go to the community pool. They wondered about the country club life of some of their customers, where green lawns wreathed a trio of pools—one for children, one for swimming, and one for diving—all nestled up to a golf course. They imagined the dinners served in the clubhouse and thought it might be nice, but how could a club, even a fine restaurant, offer what they had right now in their hands—a soft mound of strawberry ice cream in a stemmed cut-crystal goblet—Waterford "Essex,"—eaten with a silver teaspoon—Towle "Renaissance." They might as well have been wearing tiaras.

"Fleur, are you looking forward to starting at the college next month?" Joyce asked.

"I am not going to go," Fleur said softly.

"Not go? But it was all set up."

"I decided not to go." And she took up the empty sherbet goblets and the sticky spoons and filled the sink with hot water. She silently washed the dishes; Mrs. Tanzer motioned for the others to leave them.

"Fleur. You have changed your plans about school, it seems."

"Yes, ma'am."

"Was something wrong about the scholarship?"

"It wasn't that. My father lost his job with the borough. There are some layoffs and he is one of them. We just found out a few days ago."

"Oh, my dear, I am so sorry!" Elma Tanzer knew about the proposed belt-tightening in the town. She and her husband supported it in principle, taxes were high enough, but to know Fleur's father was one of the casualties stunned her. "What will your family do? Is there another position for your father with the town?"

"My dad doesn't think so. He thinks he's being made an example of."

"Of what?"

"Because of what I did." And Fleur began to cry.

Elma Tanzer embraced her and let Fleur have a good cry, all the while thinking about how this could be repaired. But she knew the town, and while the people were able to accept—barely—a young Black girl on Main Street, fixing her father's employment was a different matter.

"Listen to me," Elma Tanzer said to the sniffling Fleur as she raised her chin up to look in those paler-than-expected eyes. "Mr. Tanzer and I will try to help. We'll ask around to see if there is work for him. Is it so certain that you can't still go to college?"

"This isn't the right time for me to go to college. I want to do whatever I can to help. I can't spend my days studying while we are like this. And who knows if we can stay here in Jamestown." She began crying again.

"You have decided this for yourself? Or has someone else?"

"It's my decision."

"And do you think this is a good decision?"

"I don't know. How do you ever know what is a good or not so good decision until later on, after it all plays out?"

Elma Tanzer stifled a small smile. This was a serious matter, but the girl unexpectedly delighted her sometimes.

"No, it not always clear. It's not even usually clear. Come, let us talk to Mr. Tanzer."

Elma Tanzer did not tell Fleur that she and her husband had already discussed her future at the store. Of all their employees, Fleur was the one with the energy, imagination, and ambition most aligned with Elma's. Whether she remained a part-time worker or not, they had thought about how to offer her a pathway to something bigger. Of course this was dependent on Fleur being able to stay in Jamestown, or its proximity. And now that was in doubt.

They told Fleur they were prepared to bring her on as a full-time employee and increase her hourly wage. There was more, too, but that would wait until later. Elma admired how the young girl knew her own mind on this, was willing to be clear-eyed about the limits placed on her family, and the limits of Hamel's vision for a girl like Fleur.

"You should speak to your parents. We could start the new arrangement right away. We don't want to lose you," Elma said. She looked intently at Fleur once more and saw her pull back her shoulders, straighten her back, and set her jaw. "Come now, I want to show you how to open the safe and lock it. There's so much more to learn."

FALL 1964

Russell Williams

The belt-tightening of the town was intensely debated for about two days, then everyone moved on except the families of the laid-off workers who had to contend with real belt-tightening. Even though Jamestown was growing more prosperous each year, the almost imperceptible social gain achieved by the Williamses and a few other families was lost. Jamestown, always a town with tradesmen doing the bidding for New York wealth that escaped to the country, remained true to its blue-blood past. In another decade, Russell would look back and berate himself for his foolish idyll of growing some corn on his own scrappy plot of land. The town was overrun by rabbits, increasing with each year. But at the start of this three-month reprieve, he was still full of anxious hope that it would work out, that he'd have his corn and his wife and children, and they'd have their home here away from meddling family, away from the cities that couldn't afford to pick up its own garbage. Russell came home, took his usual bath, and smoked his half cigar, then he took a deep breath and went back out there to find some work.

Russell and Mathilde prepared as best they could. They could hold out for a few months, but even with Fleur working full-time after the summer, they knew they'd have to find a new home soon. Russell went over to Sam Goodman's to pick up a few hours of loading and unloading refrigerators, but he couldn't keep up with the high school boys. Sam was sympathetic—it was his idea that Russell come over for some extra work—but he couldn't replace the Williams' lost income. He gave Russell leads of other work, always temporary and a few towns over. A few worked out, but none was steady or high paying enough to replace what he'd lost from the borough.

Mathilde stopped bringing food over to the convent; now she was on the receiving end. It shamed her to accept a casserole to bring home after the Saturday morning cleaning. Their children knew it wasn't her cooking, even after she scraped the au gratin potatoes out of some woman's pan and into her own, adding green onions and a sliced tomato on top from their garden. It didn't hide anything.

There was some unexpected support. Dr. Gorman, the dentist, gave Charlie and LuLu free dental cleanings and filled a few cavities. He supervised a dental student's pokings, then stepped in and took over the main affair. Cranky Mr. Florida, their reclusive neighbor with the scary garage, came over with arms dripping in honey, holding a block of beeswax he cleared out from a bee's nest.

The end came quicker than any of them thought. Frank Henderson, their landlord, didn't make it any worse, but he told them they would have to leave by the end of the year if they couldn't pay the full rent. Henderson had been more than decent, but the home equity balance would be used up by then. If they couldn't make the full monthly payment for January, they would have to leave. Russell went out drinking for a few nights to avoid the conversation he would have to have with himself. He drank more Johnny Walker that week than in the previous year. But this ran its short course, and Russell didn't think this was so bad for a period of mourning.

He and Mathilde talked quietly in their bedroom, discussed whether to leave, where to go, the effect it would have on the children, where the work was going to come from. Russell didn't talk about corn or lettuce and tomatoes. He didn't say he would be relieved to get away from the rabbits. Mathilde reminded him that it was he who wanted this suburban dream and if he didn't want it anymore, it was fine with her, she never felt part of this place.

"You only feel at home in a church, Tilly."

"True enough, but I'm at home with us too, wherever we are. Churches are everywhere."

"Newark or Queens?" he asked.

"Find the job first. Then we'll tell the children."

"What if it's near my family?" Russell knew it was likely to be.

"Plenty of churches around there."

But there was one bright spot during this autumn of reckoning for the Williams family. On October 14 the world learned that Rev. Dr. Martin Luther King Jr. would receive the Nobel Peace Prize. Their memory of his visit to their town, their witness to his powerful message, resurrected pride in being there for that moment. Maybe that was the best Jamestown had to offer them. Russell's dream of homegrown corn and pickles shrank next to King's dream for all of them. That was when Russell decided to look for work in Newark, the city he tried to escape. Not that it held hope or promise for him now. Instead he found more strength and resiliency in himself. He could try again.

Helen Ransom

Helen Ransom put down her purse and gloves and sat in her car. She tossed the envelope of enrollment forms into the back seat. *What just happened?* she wondered. She went into Tanzer's Jewelry Store for the express purpose of retrieving Fleur's presumably filled-out paperwork. Classes were going to start in just a few weeks, and orientation even sooner. And now Fleur was not going to be among the new incoming students. After all that work getting her a guaranteed four-year scholarship! No matter what the circumstances, Helen thought Fleur ungrateful and that she should make a bigger effort to accommodate herself to this unique opportunity. She was less aware of the impact of the town's cutbacks than she should have been. As a tax-exempt institution, Hamel had little stake in the town's politics to shrink property taxes.

Fleur was there in the store, and Mrs. Tanzer excused her for a few minutes so Mrs. Ransom could speak with her. So, Elma knew of Fleur's change in circumstance. "Nothing has been discussed," Helen remembered bitterly. Well, it looks like they've discussed it now.

Fleur told her she wouldn't be going to Hamel after all. She said "wouldn't," not "couldn't." Helen's face flushed with embarrassment and—yes, go on, say it—betrayal. She expressed sorrow and concern over Fleur's father losing his job with the town. She hoped he could easily find another. She said she'd be on the lookout for him. But she did not understand why that had to stand in the way of Fleur going to Hamel. Lots of students experienced family setbacks that interfered with college; advisors and deans helped with that, sometimes she and Earl did too. Didn't Fleur understand that Hamel was like a big family ready to accept her and help her on her way?

Helen offered a deferment, one semester, maybe two, before she would have to start her classes. Maybe her father would find a new job by then. Fleur asked if she could perhaps attend classes at night.

"Hamel is not that sort of school," Helen answered.

"We may have to move away from Jamestown," Fleur revealed.

"You could take the bus to campus."

"How do I work and commute and go to college all at once?"

Helen did not have an answer to that. Instead she asked, "Is it so hopeless?"

"I'm sorry, Mrs. Ransom. I appreciate everything you've done for me. But I can't. I can't go to college while my family struggles this way, when I can be of help to them. I just can't."

Helen moistened her lips and looked around the store, trying to think if there was something she could buy or repair that would set things right. There wasn't, of course, so she excused herself, saying how disappointed Hamel would be to not welcome her to the campus this fall, how she and Earl and Celia would be especially sad about this development. She left the store with the envelope of blank enrollment forms dangling from her hand like a lifeless appendage.

How was she going to tell Earl? And worse, what was he going to tell her? That she got over involved? She knew that. She fought for that scholarship for Fleur, and now it was going to go begging. Let Earl explain that to the trustees. This was personal for her in the same way that Celia leaving for college was—all her children leaving her and now she was alone. How could she raise money now for a scholarship turned down by exactly the type of person it was designed for?

That didn't turn out to be such a problem, and Earl was good at his word to find her a more esteemed role on campus. He placed her on the Advancement Committee among the trustees. She hosted more meetings now for donors than deans' wives. She distracted herself with the work of the college and the growing confrontations within and between the political parties. A war that wasn't called a war began to take some of the young men away from college campuses. Race relations became flash points and angry encounters, not the genteel discussions of the interfaith groups she attended. There was plenty for her to get involved with, though part of her just gave up.

She stopped off at Tanzer's Jewelry Store less often, only enough to know that Fleur was still working there. She was now in the business of getting over it. She didn't know that there were groundskeeper jobs open at the college. How could she know everything? When she finally did know, it was too late—they were gone, though Fleur continued to work at Tanzer's.

But Helen did pay a visit to the Jamestown High School guidance counselors and informed them that she would be helping them in their Career Day selection. And that she'd be part of their committee to select the next recipient of the Reynolds Scholarship (it had a name now) for a Jamestown graduating senior. She was looking forward to their work together. In fact, she couldn't wait to get started.

Fleur Williams

All fall Fleur decorated the windows with pride. The sapphire, opal, topaz rotation marked the months and was the background for her window design. She still honored the four Birmingham schoolgirls murdered a year ago—Addie, Cynthia, Carole, and Carol Denise—by placing a jewelry grouping of four that she imagined might appeal to them. In her imagination, the four dead girls wore scarab bracelets, gold circle pins, pearl pendants, and birthstone rings. Years from now she'd pick out wedding patterns for them. Fleur didn't reveal the symbolism behind her window displays. It was always a grave meditation for her as she regarded how her life gained texture and meaning while theirs stopped.

Throughout those months, college students stopped by the store for gifts, watches, and repairs. It didn't bother Fleur when she had to wait on them. She was building confidence every day and doubted that would have happened at Hamel. Mrs. Ransom came by less frequently. It had been so hard to tell her that she couldn't—wouldn't—take the scholarship, but in a way she thought Mrs. Ransom took it even harder. They were cordial in the store; Fleur asked about Celia and Mrs. Ransom asked about her parents. Mrs. Ransom held out more hope than she did that something was going to work out for her father's employment that would allow Fleur to come to Hamel. She was a little relieved that she wasn't a student at Hamel. She did not have to live up to Mrs. Ransom's dreams for her. She could take a little time to find them out for herself.

Mrs. Tanzer had started teaching her more things, like how to prepare deposit slips and send out billing statements. Mr. Tanzer taught her how to size a ring. He was supervising her work on soldering links on charms and bracelet clasps. Fleur now had her own short stack of jewelry repairs. Her new responsibilities looked promising to her. She was content. She felt full of purpose and commitment—to her parents to help them, to her job, and to herself. This was where she wanted to be.

But Jamestown would not be home for long for the Williams family. While Fleur and her mother worked their jobs in Jamestown, her father had to go increasingly farther away to find his. It wasn't easy. He had to give up on the dreams that led them here—a better job, a house, schools—and the homegrown corn that never filled out the stunted cobs. Fleur knew hers and her mother's earnings weren't enough to keep them going in Jamestown. She knew leaving was more likely than not. Her father spent every day working a day-labor job, or looking for work. She hated to see her father like this. It culminated in the last week of October when Russell Williams came home drunk a few nights. But then, like a fever, his humiliation broke and he held his head up high and went to Newark, where he knew he'd find something. He did. And now the family was to move there after Thanksgiving, into an apartment building where Fleur would still have to share a bedroom with LuLu. But that was alright because she was still going to work at Tanzer's. She already figured out the bus schedule to get her there and back every day. It was all right, fine even. A fresh start for all of them.

They celebrated Thanksgiving in their Jamestown home, telling the Newark Williamses that they would see them soon enough. It was a smaller feast; Mathilde did not make extras for the convent or rectory. They sat down together at the table, and Russell asked to say grace this time.

"We thank you, the Lord Almighty, for the food on this table, for the hands that fixed it, and the strength You give us. Amen."

"Amen," the rest answered.

"Wait!" said Russell in a way that let everyone know they better not touch their forks yet. "We are moving on. We are not moving back. We each made our mark on this town. We shall have pride, not regrets. You got that? Every one of us."

"Yes Daddy," said Charlie. "Can we eat now?"

"Yes, we can. Dig in!"

It was a busy beginning to the holiday season at Tanzer's. Fleur went to work early and stayed late. While Fleur was at work on their final Saturday in Jamestown, her family boxed up all their housewares. She left their house at twenty to nine with it looking mostly normal with breakfast dishes in the sink and the frying pans hanging on the wall. By the time she came home, every fork and plate and glass was wrapped up in a box. Fleur had already packed up her clothes and things. The rooms looked bare—boxes set on furniture, nothing on the walls.

With all their kitchen items packed away for their move the next day, the Williams family enjoyed a rare treat. They went out to eat. All week long it had been the talk around their table—where should they go?

Chinese. Pizza. Italian subs. Each lobbied for their favorite, and Charlie made the final convincing argument for Chinese food at Long's. They sat in a crowded booth and performed badly with their chopsticks, laughed, and suffered the withering looks of the other customers. They did not care. It was their last night in Jamestown. One dish was full of blazing hot peppers, and although Russell picked them out, their searing heat remained. And so they wept too in this unexpected way.

Fleur, Mathilde, and the children went to their final Mass at Holy Trinity the next morning while Russell removed and packed all the bedclothes. It took him just an hour to make sure everything was in a box or suitcase, and finally the moving truck. Hymie Stinson provided the truck and himself as the driver. George Stancel and Charles Harrison from the neighborhood moved the furniture out with Russell. By the time Mathilde and the children returned from church, they were almost ready to go.

But before that, Sister Regina Savior had arranged for Fleur, her mother and the children to have breakfast in the convent after Mass. Sr. Regina had to remind Father Halligan that this was the last time the Williamses would worship in this parish, that they were off to Holy Redeemer in Newark. But he did not stop over to see them off.

At the convent, many of the church ladies and most of the nuns had gathered to wish them well. Not only did they feed them orange juice and scrambled eggs and toast with jam, they sent the Williams family off with a hamper basket of their lunch, dinner, and next morning's breakfast to get them started in their new home. Some fried chicken and pickles. A green bean casserole. A loaf cake. Some sliced ham and rolls. Mathilde protested, felt ashamed of falling into receiving what she usually doled out, but everyone pressed the food upon them in thanks for what she had contributed to the larger church family for all these years. No priest was there to bless the food, so they did it themselves.

They arrived back home laden with food, which they squeezed into the old Buick. Fleur was allowed to drive it while Russell rode with the men in the truck, leading the way to Newark. A cold and bright day with little traffic, they shed themselves of Jamestown like a snake its skin. Newark was now their refuge and their future—it would be what each made of it.

For LuLu and Charlie, it was new schools, new friends, and their cousins. For Mathilde, it was the sanctifying volunteer work at Holy Redeemer parish with a new convent to clean. For both she and Russell, the old family tensions with his sister and mother bloomed anew. For Russell, ever willing to lean his body into hard work, he would be last in and first out at a series of industrial jobs that evaporated over the decade. Next week, Fleur and Mathilde would join the league of African American women on bus, train, and foot commuting to their jobs. They would come to enjoy the sorority of all the ladies who cleaned something—babies' bottoms, clothes, sinks, silver, and china dishes.

They didn't know it yet, but they all would be tested. With Jamestown in the rearview mirror, Route 24 under their tires, and Newark straight ahead, the experiment was over and a new one about to begin. They arrived just as many people and jobs were leaving. They began again as others gave up. They kept beginning and beginning as long as they could.

Father Halligan
Sunday, November 29, 1964
The First Sunday of Advent

Father Halligan's irritation was obvious to all—he made no attempt to hide it. People assumed it was because this was the first Sunday Mass that was supposed to be said mostly in English. The Second Vatican Council had decided that the Mass should return to the people and be conducted largely in each parish's native tongue, not solely in Latin. That altars should be turned around to face the congregation. That the priests should simplify their vestments and allow for other musical expression of their faith. Like the Folk Mass. And just when he was meant to prepare the hearts of his flock to await the birth of Jesus Christ, this, the First Sunday of Advent, was when these changes must begin. He fumed while he prepared for the nine-thirty service. Reprimanded the altar boys. Was brusque with Sister Regina Savior when she reminded him that Mathilde Williams and her family were having breakfast in the convent and that it would be meaningful if he came over to bless them. It was their last Mass at Holy Trinity. He told her to handle it herself.

He knew they were leaving; didn't he practically arrange it? He believed he saved his parish and its larger community from trouble nobody wanted. He was proud of that and all the other levers he pulled in Jamestown. But that was not why he was mad. His ire sprang from a diocese letter from Paterson that informed him he could expect to be transferred from Holy Trinity sometime in the first half of the coming year. His next parish was still under consideration, but would be selected to take advantage of the many talents and accomplishments he had shown at Holy Trinity. That was shorthand for being farmed out to a small parish in a rural backwater town where he'd have to start out saying the six-thirty morning Mass again. He prided himself on his foresight, took such care to prevent cultural turbulence, but he never saw this coming. He would not be celebrating his twenty-fifth Jubilee in the style he thought he deserved. Maybe he would not celebrate it at all.

Growling at the altar boys to get going, he emerged from the sacristy in full regalia. He lit the first of the purple candles of the Advent wreath. "*Oremus,*" he bellowed. And he turned his back on his parishioners and faced the altar.

Afterword

On February 21, 1966, the New Jersey Supreme Court decided that a state-licensed barber "cannot discriminate against a prospective patron who seeks his service, be he Negro or any other race."

All persons shall have the opportunity to obtain all the accommodations, advantages, facilities, and privileges of any place of public accommodation without discrimination because of race, creed, color, national origin, ancestry or age, subject only to conditions and limitations applicable alike to all persons. This opportunity is recognized as and declared to be a civil right. (N.J.S.A. 18:25-4)

It shall be an unlawful discrimination: For any owner, or employee of any place of public accommodation directly or indirectly to refuse, withhold from or deny to any person any of the accommodations, advantages, facilities or privileges thereof, or to discriminate against any person in the furnishing thereof. (N.J.S.A. 18:25-12(f))

July 12–17, 1967 – Riots erupted in Newark, NJ. It was one of 159 race riots that broke out during the "Long, Hot Summer of 1967," mostly in northern cities. Among the most destructive, the Newark riots were rooted in unemployment, poverty, deindustrialization, abusive policing, redlining, poor housing, and white flight to the suburbs. Amidst looting, violence, fires, and property destruction, twenty-six people died and hundreds were injured.

Acknowledgments

Every small act of history is a drama of time, place and people.

All characters in this book, with the obvious exception of several historical figures, are fictional. I took a small act of history from my childhood that wasn't talked about much and created a story behind it. This story has been in my heart for decades. I did not plan that it should land now at a time of social reckoning over racism, but nor does it seem accidental.

If I have failed to translate the drama of this particular moment of time, place and people into a work of respectful resonance for today, it is my fault alone and not that of the wonderful people who helped me.

Much gratitude for all librarians and local historical societies everywhere—they preserve the stories of our lives, put them in context, and create imaginative programs that educate us all.

For early guidance and support I thank Anya Achtenberg, and The Loft Literary Center. Later on, Krisen Bakis and class cohort at the Hudson Valley Writing Center provided similar help. I am much indebted to Steve Eisner and the team at When Words Count, especially Barbara Newman, Colin Hosten, Ken Sherman and Steve Rohr. I thank David LeGere and the team at Woodhall Press for their unwavering support in bringing this book through its final phase. Early readers Charita Brown and Kortney Menikos, and developmental editor Sharyn Skeeter gave their advice, stories and encouragement. I thank everyone for conversations about the complexity of white authors writing about persons of color, and how to use a prior era's language today.

Closer to home, I thank my family members for our common connection, the tree in the middle of the road, and so much more. I thank my personal friends whose love and support followed me to Minnesota, Hawaii, California and New York. And my childhood friends, neighbors and teachers for all the lessons of growing up.

No words can convey the strength and grace I receive from Claire and Richard for their unfettered love.

—A.M.D.
June 2022
Croton-on-Hudson, New York

About the Author

Anne Dimock is the author of *Humble Pie: Musings on What Lies Beneath the Crust*, a finalist for a Minnesota Book Award and the reason Garrison Keillor called her "the Proust of pie." An eclectic writer of plays, short stories, and essays that cover topics like women's health, alternative sentencing, *Moby Dick*, Cyrano de Bergerac as a woman, and prize-winning ribald limericks, Dimock's work has appeared on stage and in print. She resides in Croton-on-Hudson, New York.